Biblioasis International Translation Series
General Editor: Stephen Henighan

1. *I Wrote Stone: The Selected Poetry of Ryszard Kapuściński* (Poland)
Translated by Diana Kuprel and Marek Kusiba

2. *Good Morning Comrades*
by Ondjaki (Angola)
Translated by Stephen Henighan

3. *Kahn & Engelmann*
by Hans Eichner (Austria-Canada)
Translated by Jean M. Snook

4. *Dance With Snakes*
by Horacio Castellanos Moya (El Salvador)
Translated by Lee Paula Springer

5. *Black Alley*
by Mauricio Segura (Quebec)
Translated by Dawn M. Cornelio

6. *The Accident*
by Mihail Sebastian (Romania)
Translated by Stephen Henighan

7. *Love Poems*
by Jaime Sabines (Mexico)
Translated by Colin Carberry

8. *The End of the Story*
by Liliana Heker (Argentina)
Translated by Andrea G. Labinger

9. *The Tuner of Silences*
by Mia Couto (Mozambique)
Translated by David Brookshaw

10. *For as Far as the Eye Can See*
by Robert Melançon (Quebec)
Translated by Judith Cowan

11. *Eucalyptus*
by Mauricio Segura (Quebec)
Translated by Donald Winkler

12. *Granma Nineteen and the Soviet's Secret*
by Ondjaki (Angola)
Translated by Stephen Henighan

13. *Montreal Before Spring*
by Robert Melançon (Quebec)
Translated by Donald McGrath

14. *Pensativities: Essays and Provocations*
by Mia Couto (Mozambique)
Translated by David Brookshaw

15. *Arvida*
by Samuel Archibald (Quebec)
Translated by Donald Winkler

16. *The Orange Grove*
by Larry Tremblay (Quebec)
Translated by Sheila Fischman

17. *The Party Wall*
by Catherine Leroux (Quebec)
Translated by Lazer Lederhendler

18. *Black Bread*
by Emili Teixidor (Catalonia)
Translated by Peter Bush

19. *Boundary*
by Andrée A. Michaud (Quebec)
Translated by Donald Winkler

20. *Red, Yellow, Green*
by Alejandro Saravia (Bolivia-Canada)
Translated by María José Giménez

21. *Bookshops: A Reader's History*
by Jorge Carrión (Spain)
Translated by Peter Bush

22. *Transparent City*
by Ondjaki (Angola)
Translated by Stephen Henighan

23. *Oscar*
by Mauricio Segura (Quebec)
Translated by Donald Winkler

24. *Madame Victoria*
by Catherine Leroux (Quebec)
Translated by Lazer Lederhendler

25. *Rain and Other Stories*
by Mia Couto (Mozambique)
Translated by Eric M. B. Becker

26. *The Dishwasher*
by Stéphane Larue (Quebec)
Translated by Pablo Strauss

27. *Mostarghia*
by Maya Ombasic (Quebec)
Translated by Donald Winkler

28. *Dead Heat*
by Benedek Totth (Hungary)
Translated by Ildikó Noémi Nagy

Dead Heat

DEAD HEAT

BENEDEK TOTTH

TRANSLATED FROM THE HUNGARIAN BY

ILDIKÓ NOÉMI NAGY

BIBLIOASIS
WINDSOR, ONTARIO

First published in Hungarian as *Holtverseny* by Magvető Kiadó, Budapest, Hungary, 2014.

FIRST EDITION

Library and Archives Canada Cataloguing in Publication

Title: Dead heat / Benedek Totth ; [translated by] Ildiko Noemi Nagy.
Other titles: Holtverseny. English
Names: Totth, Benedek, 1977- author. | Nagy, Ildiko Noemi, 1975- translator.
Series: Biblioasis international translation series ; 28.
Description: Series statement: Biblioasis international translation series ; 28 | Translation of:
Holtverseny.
Identifiers: Canadiana (print) 20190116293 | Canadiana (ebook) 2019011648X | ISBN 9781771963015
(softcover) | ISBN 9781771963022 (ebook)
Classification: LCC PH3382.3.O87 H6513 2018 | DDC 894/.51134—dc23

Edited by Stephen Henighan
Copy-edited by Emily Donaldson
Cover designed by Zoe Norvell

PRINTED AND BOUND IN THE USA

Let them think what they liked, but I didn't mean to drown myself. I meant to swim till I sank—but that's not the same thing.

—Joseph Conrad: *The Secret Sharer*

WILD BOAR

We're flying down the new bypass when Ducky turns to ask where the fuck we are, but no one says a damn word 'cause they're all clueless I guess, or they don't wanna say something dumb that'll just confuse him and get us even more lost. I don't know the neighbourhood, plus it's not like you can actually see anything in this shitty weather, but I'd be really happy if we figured out where we are, 'cause there's no way in hell we're gonna get home otherwise.

"Isn't that the slaughterhouse?" I say, pointing to a huge factory building that looks vaguely like a wild boar.

Ducky's like, *dafuq you talkin bout?* and even though he turns his head in the right direction, he misses it 'cause the view's suddenly blocked by sound barriers on either side and everything's all stretched out kinda like in *Star Wars* when they make the jump to light speed. There's something Harrison Fordish about Ducky actually, especially if you look at him from the back when it's dim. He's always the one driving, even though he doesn't have a licence, he just borrows Mishy's. Mishy is his cousin and they totally look alike on the ID picture. How the kid even landed his permit is beyond me, 'cause he won't be sixteen till next summer, but no one's gotten busted with it yet. I seriously doubt Ducky's ever gonna have his own licence. He flunked the driving test three times, even though his old man paid off the examiner.

Even now we're tearing down the road in one of his pop's whips. Of course the little shit's saying that Pop let him take it, but I know he didn't. Ducky's pop is cool but there's no way he'd just hand over a three-hundred-horsepower sedan worth eighty-five grand to his son. Ducky's gripping the wheel with one hand, his other hand fumbling around inside a McDonald's bag, till he yanks out a Big Mac and stuffs it in his face, whole. Wilted bits of lettuce drop into his lap. Zoli-boy leans forward, to ask something I guess, but as he tries to squeeze his head between the seats, he head-butts the backrest hella hard. He's always hyped as fuck no matter what he smokes or pops. I have no idea what booze does to him though, 'cause he never drinks. I lean forward super casual, trying to peek over Ducky's shoulder to read the speedometer, but then the jittery blue line of numbers detaches from the dash, floats off into space, and all I can piece together is that they start with a three or an eight. The car interior's swirling with dense, sticky smoke, like we were sitting inside a huge bag of cotton candy. Ducky glances down into his lap, trying to sweep the pieces of lettuce onto the floor, and he fumbles around long enough to smear the sauce all over his pants.

"Fucking hell! I'm gonna blow up that motherfucking Burger King!"

He's going batshit crazy.

"We were at McDonald's," Zoli-boy points out quietly, patting his forehead.

"I don't give a shit," Ducky growls.

"Chill, dude," Buoy grins, zen as fuck. "It'll come out of fake leather easy."

Buoy's a polo player and got his name from no one being able to drag him underwater. He's two hundred and thirty pounds of solid muscle. The math geeks named a unit of measurement after him. And he was the first one with hair on his balls.

"Whaddya mean fake leather, asshole?" Ducky barks, insulted.

"Fake leather," Buoy says. "Like train seats."

"Your dick is what's fake," Ducky tries to shoot back, but he's bursting with laughter.

Buoy rides shotgun and stretches out all comfy on the reclined seat, like on a deck chair, a fat joint glowing between his middle and ring fingers. He's hella faded too, not even breathing really, just grinning into space like a big yellow banana. I start counting to see how long he can go without air when he jerks awake from his stupor. He glances at the spliff and takes a sleepy drag, holding the smoke in as he extends it towards the back seat. His arm's all stretchy, like Inspector Gadget's.

"Thankyou, thankyou, thankyou," Zoli-boy chants. "I thought you were gonna bograt... bograt..."

He gets tongue tied and makes a few more attempts, but fails, so he just snatches the joint from Buoy's hand. I'm super grateful, 'cause now I don't have to move if I want to smoke. Zoli-boy inhales a couple of quick hits, and as he tugs the j from his mouth, the paper sticks to his lips and tears at the tip. It seems like an eternity by the time he passes the joint, but I'm in no hurry. I want to enjoy every second of it. I smooth the paper back carefully and roll the warm blunt between my fingers for a while. It scratches my throat a little as I inhale. They stuffed it with too much tobacco again, that's why it's so fat, not from the weed. Ducky's freaking out that his old man will smell the hash, but I doubt old Pops even knows what *weed* smells like, and it's not like he'll bust our balls just 'cause we're smoking. He's always got a cigarette dangling from his lips when he's driving.

"What was in that thing?" Buoy asks, wrinkling his forehead.

His words turn over slowly in his mouth, like that Bud Spencer-lookalike TV healer, who screws over cancer-ridden old folks.

"Hash, nigga," Ducky tells him. He's been crazy about some hick gangsta rappers for the last couple of months. That's what he's punishing us with on the amps now, and whenever he gets high it's all *nigga this* and *nigga that* and he starts talking in rhymes.

"I mean that Big Mac," Buoy says, squinting.

The smoke stings his eyes.

"The Big Mac?" Ducky asks.

"Yeah," Buoy says, then burps his words, "sm-ells fu-cking fo-ul."

He can burp even longer sentences than that. His stomach's as big as his lungs.

"You keep talking shit and you're out," Ducky says, trying to act tough.

Buoy swirls the ice cubes around in his cup, chilling, knowing it's an empty threat. Ducky's scared of even slowing down ever since he managed to get the car in drive. There's no way he's stopping now in the middle of nowhere just to kick Buoy out. *Fucking foul* reminds me of a joke, but I'm kinda hoarse and by the time I clear my throat, Buoy's got his nasal laugh cranked and I forget what I was gonna say.

"The chicks…" he screeches, slapping his knee. "The chicks…" he's choking, eyes welling up. "They dipped their…" he gasps for air, "…their… in the ketchup…"

He says something else, maybe about tampons, but I

can't really catch it, because he's wiping his eyes and snorting. Me and Zoli-boy are just staring at him, and he's looking at Ducky, and then back at us. He's a nice guy, but sometimes I worry about him.

"There's no *ketchup* in Big Macs," Zoli-boy pipes up, "it's special sauce made from a secret recipe."

He pronounces it *cat-sup*. Zoli-boy's a wage slave at McDonald's, so he knows his stuff.

"Yeah, special jerk-off sauce..." Ducky cuts his sentence short, glancing down at the last bite of Big Mac between his thumb and index finger.

Buoy screeches with laughter again, and Ducky's getting wound up. Through the rear-view mirror I can see his face clench.

"Nobody jerks off during work," Zoli-boy retorts to the insult.

He's full of shit. Everyone's always jerking it.

Ducky grumbles something and stuffs the rest of his Big Mac into the ashtray.

There's no music for a couple of seconds. We slide soundlessly through the night. Then, when the next track starts up, Buoy asks:

"Hey, Zoli-boy, who was that bitch?"

"Which one?" Zoli-boy asks.

"The redhead at the ice cream machine," I say, and Buoy nods.

I noticed her too. Why she's busting her ass at Mickey D's when she's got tits that size is beyond me.

"That's not ice cream," Zoli-boy corrects. "It's called a sundae and you can get it with hot fudge or strawberry sauce."

"Sure, Zoli-boy, a sundae," Buoy nods like an old professor. "But why don't you tell us about the chick instead?"

Zoli-boy clams up.

Buoy turns around. His pupils are the size of the Great Lakes.

"You'd bone her, right?"

Zoli-boy gets all embarrassed, he stammers, I can't catch a thing, and then he falls silent.

"The matchstick with the huge knockers?" Ducky says, joining the conversation. "I'd bone her," he adds with a crazed grin, and then accidentally turns on the windshield wipers. He swears, feeling around for the switch, he signals right, signals left, flashes the high beam—a deer or wild boar seems to stare back at us from behind a bush—until finally he floods the windshield with wiper fluid. When Buoy's had enough of his dicking around, he reaches in front of Ducky and turns the wipers off. Before, you couldn't see from the smear of bugs. Now, the wiper fluid is trickling down nice and slow. Buoy turns the windshield wipers back on instead. We keep at it like this, but the rubber blade's drowsy scrubbing starts to hypnotize Ducky. His head moves right to left at a steady pace. I reach forward and tap Buoy on the shoulder, and when he looks at me, I point at Ducky. Buoy gets the drift and quickly turns the wipers off. Then he waves his hand in front of Ducky's face till the kid jolts from his trance and shakes his head.

I was gonna say something before about the redhead or the lettuce, but I can't decide if I actually said something or if I just imagined saying something. When I finally get to thinking that I probably just convinced myself that I said something, I suddenly realize what I did want to say, or what I thought I wanted to say, but by that time I'm not in the mood to say anything anymore. I look up and the high beam illuminates a huge stop sign with a man-sized fluorescent hand. The hand's not there 'cause it wants a high five, that's for sure. Ducky's taken the wrong lane or maybe he just doesn't know what it means. He was probably absent the day they covered traffic signs. The grey pavement shines wet, like a giant slug. My brain keeps making up shit like that. Not so long ago we swiped a sack of escargots from the gypsies, lugged it over to a plant nursery, and dumped it over the fence so the little bastards could gorge themselves. I was in the neighbourhood a couple of days ago and the sign was still hanging on the gate: *Closed due to technical issues.* It's weird that the guardrail is to the left, but whatever, 'cause the bypass is totally deserted, there's not a single oncoming vehicle, not even a snoozing Romanian trucker or a Ukrainian van with curtained windows.

Ducky starts groping around again. He presses a button, and as the window slides down, he grabs the leftover fries in his right hand and tosses them. Meanwhile, the car starts drifting towards the ditch. My palms get clammy. I see my face reflected in the window. This can't be me. I don't want it to be me, despite the smile. The face is way too freaky. It's too old, or too young, I can't decide, and it's staring straight at me, grinning, but I'm not grinning, that's for sure. Then it turns into a sparkly skull—a huge, grinning skull—and I face forward, locking my gaze on the backrest.

"Stay on the road," Buoy says to Ducky, and then he starts feeling around for the button to roll down the window. I've still got the joint. I take a drag. Buoy finds the button. Now that both windows are open, crazy airstreams form in the interior. Strands of my hair scratch at the cool air. Zoli-boy clasps his hands over his ears and begs us to roll the windows up. Buoy presses the button. As the window slides closed my ears get plugged up, but when I try to pop them, I freak out. What if my eardrums get ruptured and my brains spill out? You can clean fake leather pretty easily though. The music is a dull thud coming from the speakers. Either that or we're gonna have a fucking mega-storm. Buoy grabs the monster drink cup teetering on top of the dash's centre panel, which he's been propping up with his knee till now 'cause it didn't fit in the cup holder. He manoeuvres the straw into his mouth while his cheeks get all dented as he sucks on the drink. Automobile factories can't seem to keep pace with fast-food joints. My mouth waters. I look out the window. The face is gone and I start to think about how the universe is expanding at a fucking mind-blowing pace, but I'll bet that some fast-food chain already has dibs on all the lots out there and when the first astronaut shows up, they'll already have a couple of McSpaces open so you can tear into a double cheeseburger with large fries and large coke right away, 'cause that's the best meal deal.

I lean between the seats and stare at the speedometer. The numbers blur on the digital display, but then everything's clear again for a second and I can see we're barrelling down the bypass at 177 kph. It's like we're shooting straight ahead, but I think the road's actually curving. I lean back to one side and my face presses against the cold window. Ducky pushes down even harder on the accelerator. The engine's strong. The car pulls intensely and I'm thrust back into a leather seat the colour of runny shit. We all chipped in so the gas tank's topped up. I'm already sorry I did 'cause I sure as shit don't wanna die broke. Last summer a couple of guys from near the lake went shooting out a curve by that door-and-window factory and wrapped themselves around an old millennium oak tree that had survived hundreds of storms, two world wars, and even the highway construction. They'd filled the tank full of 99 octane V-Power fuel right before, and they fucking exploded. The tree went up in flames. An eye-witness told the local cable station that one of the guys managed to climb out of the wreck. His hair and clothes were flaming as he wobbled through the wheat field like a Vietcong who'd just gotten slammed with napalm. Twelve acres of corn were destroyed in the blaze by the time the fire department showed up and got the flames under control. Another curve. Ducky's not slowing down. His family's loaded. His old man just opened a cross between a pig farm and a slaughterhouse right next door to the Krishna retreat. Those poor bastards holed up in that godforsaken valley thinking they could pray till their holy cows came home, and then Ducky's father stuffs the neighbouring lot full of fuzzy pigs. Right now he's trying to make a deal with McDonald's to be their domestic supplier. One time our class took a field trip to a slaughterhouse. We got to check out the EU-regulation slaughter hall and the EU-regulation carcass pit. The butcher guy said the place was so clean you could eat off the floor.

"Ducky," I say.

"What?"

"Shift up."

"Huh?"

"Shift gears."

Ducky looks down at the lever. He clutches it, but then he gets the joke.

"Up yours, asshole. You know it's automatic."

Suddenly the car lurches and everything's hushed. It's like we're all swallowed by a big, soft animal. My eardrums reverberate. I vaguely recall someone mentioning the place we were going when we got in the car, but no one remembers that now. Actually, maybe we never had any idea in the first place. We've been cruising around the city and the neighbouring villages for hours, and no matter which way we go, we always end up on Youth Street with its ten-storey projects and blinking yellow traffic lights. There's a shitload of roundabouts here. You get dizzy as fuck.

Niki lifts her head from my lap and asks Ducky if he maybe could drive like a normal person. As she pushes back her long brown hair, the dashboard's bluish-green light illuminates her face. Her lips are wet and shiny. She swallows. She sucked off Ducky and Buoy in the parking lot behind the McDrive while we were waiting for Zoliboy. I mean, I didn't actually see it because I was in the bathroom, but it's pretty likely, 'cause when I got back in the car and looked at her, she just said, hold on a minute because my throat hurts, which made Ducky and Buoy crack up. Niki and four dudes, and all of them are latched onto her. Like I'd ever manage to drive around with four chicks who all wanna get with me!

"Did it smudge?" she asks.

"What?"

"My lipstick."

"No."

It's probably blowjob-proof, I think to myself, but I keep my mouth shut, 'cause the guys are gonna make fun of her bigtime anyway.

"Sweet," Niki says with a smile, then continues at a bitchy volume. "Gimme that joint!"

"What? Ain't you done enough sucking for one day?" Ducky asks.

"You're such a dick!" Niki says, but she's just being extra. She's got a crush on Ducky and always sucks him off first. And her little sister too. I mean Niki's little sister. I mean her little sister sucks off Ducky. Zoli-boy hasn't dropped any nasty comments yet. He wants his turn with her too. I pass the joint to Niki. She takes a long hit, it flares up, and then a slick blue snake slithers out of her mouth.

"What you put in this?" Niki asks.

Now that she brings it up, it really did taste weird.

"Chocolate straight outta Tibet," Buoy says.

"Milka?" Niki asks.

"Milka is Swiss," Zoli-boy pipes.

"It's just like weed, except it's hash," Buoy explains.

"All the Dalai Lamas use it to chill," Zoli-boy adds.

"Uh-huh, got it," Niki says, taking another hit, then passes it to me.

She leans forward, trying to tilt Ducky's head into her own. She wants to blow the smoke into his mouth. She probably saw it in some Johnny Depp movie. Or no, wait, it was a James Franco movie. Ducky's not down with it. He stares ahead stubbornly. Niki sulks. She looks at Zoli-boy and smiles. Zoli-boy's had a boner for like an hour. He might jizz himself just from Niki staring at him. The whole time we've been in the car, he's been leering at her to see when it'll be his turn, but somehow he always misses out. Niki positions herself so that if Ducky glances into the rear-view mirror, he'll see her. Then she slides her hand into Zoli-boy's pants and gives him a slobbery kiss. Ducky runs the car onto the shoulder, Niki's hand slips, and Zoli-boy yelps.

"Sorry," Niki says apologetically.

Zoli-boy tries to muster a smile, but it comes out an awkward, weary grimace. Niki peeks at the rear-view mirror and her eyes meet Ducky's in the mirror. Niki turns towards Zoli-boy with a smile, then plunges down onto his cock. Zoli-boy's eyes roll back. He's probably thinking about his mom so he can hold out longer. Zoli-boy's got the ugliest mom on Earth. Her face is scarier than Freddy Krueger's. I always think of Zoli-boy's mom when I wanna keep from coming. Ducky takes his foot off the accelerator and pushes down on the brake, which makes the automatic engine shift down and screech. As we thrust into the next curve, I get pushed up against Niki's ass and she deep-throats Zoli-boy. She croaks something, but there's no way to understand what she's saying. She wants me to get off her.

"Don't talk with your mouth full!" Ducky calls, and just then, we come sailing out of the curve. I feel like we survived something again. Buoy's grumbling, or maybe belching, 'cause the speed's working his nerves. Zoli-boy whimpers while Ducky messes with the rear-view mirror to see Niki better. The headlights suddenly shine on something in the middle of the road, but even if he'd noticed in time, there's no way Ducky could've swerved. There's a hard, dull thud and the car goes flying. Zoli-boy howls—his dick still in Niki's mouth—and I drop the joint between my legs. I try to brush the burning ashes onto the floor. Ducky slams down hard on the brakes, I go splat against the front seat, Buoy head-butts the dash, and Niki tumbles onto the floor. Zoli-boy is still howling like a jackal. Either he came or Niki bit off his dick.

"Holy motherfucking shit!" Ducky roars.

"Back up!" Buoy says, patting his forehead.

"My old man's gonna slit my throat if I fucked his car up. Shit."

Niki clambers up from the floor. She blinks anxiously, like a deer caught in headlights. Her hair's a mess and her lipstick's smudged.

"Are you out of your mind, Ducky?!" she says, sounding more scared than angry.

"Shut the fuck up!"

Niki frowns, sulking, and keeps on grumbling, but I can only make out the words *asshole* and *scumbag.* Zoli-boy whimpers quietly. The car's slid into a ditch, its nose facing some big-ass farm. The engine's stopped. Smoke and fog swirl in front of the Matrix LED headlights. Ducky's still stomping the brakes. I turn around. The red glow of the brake lights outlines a dark mound and the double skid marks. The only sound is the crackle of the cooling engine. Otherwise, you could hear a pin drop. I get out. The air is chilly even though it wasn't cold when we left. I feel dizzy. I lean on the car for a second, and then I walk over to the body lying in the middle of the road. I crouch down. The guy's on his stomach, wearing a thick wool coat, and I'm trying to figure out why anyone would wear this thing in such weather. I don't really do much for a while, I just stare, but then as I turn him onto his side, he starts to moan. He's stubbly and sixtyish. Or fortyish. He stinks of booze. He's got a deep gash on his forehead and his face is covered in blood. There's a black hole where his nose used to be, gushing blood at an angle so that it trickles right into his mouth. His eyelids tremble as he tries to open them, but all the blood pastes his eyelashes together. A bubble of spit forms on his lips and pops. He's still breathing. I've never seen a corpse before, and what's scaring me isn't that soon I probably will, but that all this, with the blood and the red shine of the brake lights, seems kinda pretty in a way. I hear shuffling behind me. Ducky clambers out of the car and slams the door. He walks over to the front of the car, crouches down, and scowls as he examines the bumper and pats the radiator grille. His face is pale. The headlights cast radiance on his curly hair, as if he had a halo. He stands but doesn't move. The headlights have blinded him. He rubs his eyes, then heads towards me, squinting.

"Let's get the hell outta here."

"We should call for help."

"What for? The car's all right."

"Not for the car, you dumbass."

"Why the fuck would you wanna call for help?"

"He's still breathing," I say.

"I don't give a shit."

"Let's call an ambulance," I say.

"Shit, man, did you really bash your head that hard?" Ducky gurgles.

"No."

"Then why the fuck would you wanna call an ambulance for a wild boar, huh?"

"That's no boar."

"What is it then?"

"It's an old man."

"Like fuck it is."

"I'm telling you."

"Shit, man, it was a wild boar," Ducky insists. "Most def."

"No fucking way," I say.

Ducky steps closer, looks at grampa, and prods him with his foot, prompting him to wheeze. Ducky recoils and starts screaming. I never thought he could make such a high-pitched sound.

"Why in fucking hell does this piece of shit fuckface have to go lying down in the middle of the road? Stupid cocksucking faggot dickwad bastard faggot."

"Let's just call an ambulance already," I say.

"Is your fucking record broken, man?" Ducky bellows. "Chill the fuck out!"

"Call an ambulance."

"Why don't *you* call one?" Ducky says, waving his phone around.

"My phone's in the car."

Ducky stares at me. He understands he has no other choice.

"Fine, goddamnit, I'll call your piece of shit ambulance," Ducky grumbles, and I just stand there, staring at him. "Drag him off the road in the meantime," he adds after a beat, and pokes grampa's crushed head with the tip of his shoe.

"I can't do it alone. He's too heavy," I say, and suddenly I feel exhausted. It's quiet as fuck out here in the middle of nowhere. No grunt from any wild boar. There's nothing. Not even a fucking owl hooting.

Ducky walks back to the car and gets in, and I'm thinking, what if all this isn't really happening to us? That we're actually someplace else right now? But I try to convince myself there's no point, 'cause I damn well know that we're not getting off that easy. A couple of seconds later Buoy and Zoli-boy get out of the car. Zoli-boy grabs his crotch and Buoy massages his forehead. They come over. Gravel crunches under their feet. They stop next to me.

"What's this?" Zoli-boy asks, suspecting something's not right, but by the time I can answer, Buoy starts explaining.

"My brother does a lot of hunting," he says. "He told me that during mating season, older boars sometimes lose it and go charging at cars."

"What's this?" asks Zoli-boy again, staring rigidly at the old guy.

Buoy gets a little pissed that Zoli-boy interrupted his story, but then he gets that something's off, and takes a closer look at the dark, bulging mound on the pavement.

"Didn't we hit a boar?" he says, rubbing his forehead.

"No," I say, and swallow hard.

"It's a grampa?" Zoli-boy asks.

"Yeah," I say.

"What the fuck's he doing in the middle of the road at this hour?" he says, starting to get panicky.

"Don't ask stupid fucking questions," Buoy snaps, starting to get aggro too, even though he's way better at handling stress than Zoli-boy.

"Get off my back," Zoli-boy growls.

"Let's pull him off the road," I interrupt.

"What do you want to do?" Zoli-boy asks, alarmed.

"Buoy, grab his legs. Zoli, let's take his arms."

Zoli-boy stands there looking scared as shit. He stares at the old man. I wait a bit, then try to jolt him back to his senses.

"Zoli, grab his hand, okay?"

"Huh?"

He's totally spaced out.

"His hand."

"What about his hand?"

"Grab it."

"Why?"

"We'll pull him off the road." Zoli-boy stares at me blankly. "He can't crawl away on his own," I say, but he still doesn't get it. An immense calm fills me. I am The Zen Master. "If we don't move him, he's gonna end up a pancake," I explain.

"He's gonna die?" Zoli-boy asks.

"If we leave him on the road he will for sure," I say.

"Okay, okay, I got it now," Zoli-boy splutters.

"We lift him on three," I say.

“Why do I have to hold his legs?” asks Buoy.

“Aw, come on, Buoy, don’t do this.”

“What if he’s got athlete’s foot?”

“For fuck’s sake, man, just grab his legs.”

“No.”

“Buoy!”

“*You* grab them, if you’re so into it!” Buoy steps back and pockets his hands, sour.

I switch places. I grab the old man’s legs and Zoli-boy holds his two hands. As we lift him, the guy moans and Zoli-boy freaks out and lets go. Grampa slams face-first into the concrete. Something goes crack, his cheekbones I guess, ’cause his nose is gone already, and his throat rattles.

“Fucking hell, Zoli, quit being a dumbass!”

“Sorry, I thought…”

“Don’t think,” I say. “Just grab his legs.”

Buoy is doubled-over laughing. He takes his phone out.

“Say cheese!” he calls, and we look up at him. The camera flashes.

“Are you out of your fucking mind?!” I yell, and let go of the old man’s legs, going straight for the phone in Buoy’s hand.

“Hey, chill dude!” Buoy says, seeing that I’m dead serious about taking his phone. He lifts it above his head and steps back.

“Give it to me,” I say.

“No,” he says.

“Give it to me!”

“No.”

“Then delete the picture.”

Buoy thinks about it, then starts tapping the screen hella salty.

“Fine, asshole, I deleted it.”

"Show me."

"I can't fucking believe this."

"Show me," I say again, but then, as Buoy extends the phone towards me, I snatch it from his hand and start running toward the fields. As I move further away from the road and the car, it gets darker. I trip on the field's ridges and furrows. Buoy's behind me, but I know he can't catch me. After about thirty metres, I stop with my back to the road. I hide the glow of the phone screen under my jacket, so Buoy won't see me, and start looking through his folders.

"Shit, man, I won't hurt you, just gimme my phone back," Buoy shouts. "I swear I'll delete it."

I'm scrolling through Buoy's phone but it's hopeless. I can't find that fucking picture for the life of me. All I flip through is a whole collection of naked chicks the asshole secretly took in the girls' locker room, so I just go ahead and delete the whole folder. The bastard deserves it anyway.

When I finish, I look up, but I can't see a thing. I'm seeing spots from the fucking phone screen. After I'm finally able to roughly pinpoint where the road is, based on sound, I head back.

Zoli-boy hasn't moved from the grampa's side. But Buoy's still wandering around in the field, so Zoli-boy and I lug the old man into the ditch. Zoli-boy's eyes are big and round as he yanks at the guy's arm, and I keep thinking that Buoy wasn't so full of shit about that athlete's foot after all 'cause the stench that's rising from the old man's boots is something fierce. Ducky gets out of the car and heads towards us.

"What's the number of the ambulance?" he asks when he gets back.

"Nine-one-one," Zoli-boy blurts.

"You're a dumbass, Zoli-boy. It's seventeen sixty-nine," Buoy shouts from behind.

That means he's within earshot. Better watch our backs. Ducky quickly taps in the number and holds the phone to his ear. He's quiet for a while, then he takes the phone away from his ear and stares at the screen.

"It's a phone-sex hotline, you dick!" he shouts toward Buoy.

"One-oh-seven," I say. That's the cops' number and I mean it as a joke, because I seriously doubt someone could be that dense, but Ducky's already tapping in the number, then turns around without a word and starts back towards the car. In the meantime, he's mumbling something into the phone, but I can't hear it. As he opens the door, the interior lights go on. Niki's fixing her make-up in the rear-view mirror. Ducky gets in. Meanwhile, Buoy finds his way back to the road and demands his phone. I hand it to him. He's happy to see that there's not a scratch on it. He's gonna be pleased as fuck though when he notices that I deleted all his voyeur shots.

Ducky gets out of the car again and starts towards us.

"They're coming," he says.

"He's still breathing," Zoli-boy confirms, white as a sheet.

"I know, you idiot," Ducky says. "Why'd ya think I called an ambulance? Now let's get the fuck out of here."

"Did you delete the pictures?" Buoy asks. He can't believe his eyes.

A wise man is a silent man.

"Shouldn't we wait till they get here?" Zoli-boy asks.

"No," Ducky blurts out.

"I think we should wait for them too," I say.

"Shit, man, you deleted all the pictures." Buoy messes with his phone, more livid every second.

I pretend not to hear him.

"And what do you wanna do till then? Tell him a bedtime story?" Ducky asks.

"I dunno," I say. "We could bandage up his face."

"I'm gonna kill you, you fucking faggot," Buoy strides towards me, breathing heavy. "You deleted my pictures, you piece of shit," he adds. When he gets in this mood, it's better not to obstruct him from moving freely, so I start to back away.

Ducky turns to him.

"Chill out, dude, can't you recover it from the trash folder?"

Buoy stops. He thinks for a moment. Then, he flashes me a wide grin.

I'm gonna kill him if he posts the picture.

"What'll we use to bandage him up?" Zoli-boy asks.

The kid's off on another planet now.

"Bandages," I say, but keep my eyes on Buoy, who is caressing his phone screen and mumbling, *yeah, that's it, fucking sweet, that's it.*

"You got bandages on you?" Ducky asks.

"We can take it from the car's first-aid kit," I say.

"I haven't done the first-aid course yet," Ducky says, shrugging uncertainly.

"I'll bandage him up," I say.

"Why don't you operate on him too while you're at it?" Ducky asks. "The paramedics will be here any second."

"I really need to piss," Zoli-boy pipes up.

"Your dick's still attached?" Buoy asks.

"You're not going anywhere, Zoli," Ducky snarls at him.

"I'll just be a sec," Zoli-boy says. He dashes off into the

field, and then falls on his face. He swears, then shouts from the darkness. "I found a bike!"

"Don't touch it!" Ducky hollers, but it's too late.

Zoli-boy steps out of the ditch holding a pulverized grampa-bike.

"Why not?" he asks.

Ducky doesn't answer, he just wrenches the bike from Zoli-boy's hands, pulls a linen handkerchief from his pocket, and starts to wipe off the frame. The back wheel is twisted pretty bad. It kinda reminds me of the Möbius strip that cocksucker Lázár showed us in math class.

"Ooooh, I get it now," Zoli-boy nods.

"You don't know your ass from a hole in the ground," Ducky says, and tosses the bike in the ditch.

We go back to the car and get in. Ducky starts the engine, puts it in reverse after a short struggle, and tries to back the car out of the ditch by flooring the accelerator, but of course it doesn't work. The wheels spin and Ducky just keeps pumping the gas full force until the tires start smoking.

"Hey, how about we push it out?" Buoy suggests when he sees there's no fucking way that this is happening.

Ducky doesn't say anything, he just nods, and we get out and push the car out of the ditch. Then we get back in and drive off. We go on like this for a while. Everyone's got their mouths shut and I start feeling real funny. At first I can't put my finger on what's bothering me, but then I realize that no one's gotten a notification on their phone in, like, forever. I glance at my screen 'cause maybe the signal's fucked up. Two bars, that's totally okay. It's really creepy that no one's calling anyone.

At the next long, straight stretch, Ducky looks into the rear-view mirror and tells Niki off for touching it. When he tries to readjust it, he almost swerves into the ditch again, but luckily Buoy manages to steer the car back into the lane. Niki tells Ducky to shut his face and look at the road instead of messing with the mirror, and then she turns to me and rolls her eyes, going on about how it's, like, totally impossible to fix your make-up blind and all.

"Why did we stop?" she asks finally.

"We hit a..." Zoli-boy starts to say, but Ducky barks at him to shut the fuck up or he can expect a fist in his face.

"Chill out, Ducky," Buoy growls beside him.

For a little while we sail through the night quietly again. The car runs so soundlessly it's eerie. I just noticed that Ducky's forgotten to turn the music back on. Buoy stares out the window, rubbing his forehead, but then he gets bored of everyone being all clammed up and turns the radio on.

"Do you guys think..." Zoli-boy says.

"Shut the fuck up!" Ducky cuts him off.

Zoli-boy mumbles something to himself, Buoy hums the song from the radio, and Niki's puzzled blinking starts to get disturbing, especially because nothing ever fazes her. I guess she's getting nervous about nobody talking. In the end, it's Buoy who breaks the silence of the engine's monotonous rumble and the soft throbbing of the subwoofer.

"This city's so flat," he muses.

"There's no place to jump from," Zoli-boy adds.

"How about the viaduct?" I ask.

"It's too far," Buoy waves me off.

"Maybe a roof in the projects?" Zoli-boy offers his two cents.

Last year, five people jumped off the viaduct. Two I knew personally. Three went off the roof in the projects, but I didn't know them. It's a pretty slummy neighbourhood though.

"For fuck's sake, would you people shut up already?!" Ducky bellows, cutting us off. We shut up. Buoy too. He's even stopped humming. He just stares out the window at the dark farmland furrows, or at himself. Ducky drums his fingers on the wheel. Zoli-boy bites his nails, bobbing his leg uncontrollably. If we'd put a pump under it, he could inflate a kiddy pool in no time. We get to one of the bigger cities by the lake and the roundabouts are coming one after the other. By the time we get to the third or fourth one, I totally lose count. Ducky's getting pretty dazed too. He's gone around the full circle twice, and then we come out at the wrong exit. I don't tell him. I couldn't care less.

The road's getting shittier. Ducky drives into this huge fucking pothole, and of course he gets heated again, but he really flips out when he almost crashes into an unlit concrete Jersey barrier. He slams on the brakes. We slide towards the wide concrete block, but finally we manage to stop a few centimeters in front of it.

Ducky starts banging on the wheel with his fist and screaming *where in fucking hell are we* at the top of his lungs.

"Turn on the GPS," Zoli-boy suggests.

Ducky tells him off automatically, but then he fishes the contraption out of the glove compartment. Buoy helps him get it working. It's set to the slutty voice, and she moans, "put the gear in reverse and back up a hundred metres." There really was something else in the hash because I get a boner just by listening to her.

We manage to find our way back onto the main road after another half an hour even though we were less than a quarter of a mile from it at the roundabout. We pass a gas station. A squad car's standing in the parking lot with two cops inside. If they stop us, we're busted. We've got, like, a shopping bag full of weed, three baggies of hash, and some pills from Ducky's dealer nobody knows anything about, plus my phone's crammed full of naked pictures of Niki's kid sister, who'll be fourteen in August. It would be really fucked up to get time for kiddie porn. Pedopervs always get taken out in the slammer.

We drop Zoli-boy off first. He lives in the projects on the tenth floor with his ugly mom and nympho kid sister. His father ran out on them. I mean, I would've bailed in his place too.

Ducky drives past his door without slowing down.

"Ducky," Zoli-boy says.

"Shut up," Ducky growls at him.

"You passed my…" Zoli-boy says.

"I fucking know," Ducky interrupts him.

He slams on the brakes. Zoli-boy doesn't move. He waits for Ducky to back up but Ducky is so fucking not backing up. Zoli-boy opens the door and the interior lights come on. Buoy squints and reaches up to switch it off. Zoli-boy extends his hand. Buoy shakes it with his left, while Ducky grunts something. Zoli-boy shakes my hand and then kisses Niki on the cheeks three times.

"Sorry about…" Niki says, which makes Zoli-boy extremely flustered. "You know, about…"

"Naw, it's cool," Zoli-boy says with a smile.

I guess that means there's no serious damage. He wouldn't be Mr Nice Guy with the tip of his dick missing.

"You're sweet," Niki says, and gives Zoli-boy a complimentary cheek-kiss.

"Catch you tomorrow?" Zoli-boy asks as he's getting out.

"Don't go running your mouth off," Ducky growls.

"Relax," says Zoli-boy.

"I'm relaxed," says Ducky. "I'm just saying."

"Five-thirty then," Buoy says.

Zoli-boy doesn't manage to close the door on his first try, but when he opens it to close it again, Ducky floors the gas pedal. Zoli-boy snatches his hand away. Before we turn the corner, I look back. He's trudging towards the stairs with his head down. He'll walk up to the tenth floor 'cause he told me once he freaks out in the elevator. Or maybe he just doesn't want to wake his mom up.

Niki's family lives across from the projects, on the other side of the four-lane road. We drive in the wrong direction down the one-way street, but it's not like it makes much difference after tonight. Ducky stops the car in the middle of the road in front of her house and stares straight ahead without a word. Niki leans forward to give him a cheek-kiss, but Ducky turns his head away and grumbles something about leaving him alone, so she presses a kiss on Buoy's cheek instead. He grins like an idiot and tries to French her. Niki gives me a peck on the cheek too, and before she gets out, whispers *it wasn't really a wild boar, right?* into my ear.

"No," I say.

She closes the door and heads up to the front gate.

They live in this massive pink crib with a big, green garden. Her father's a contractor, like one of those SUV-driving, new-money assholes. They're on vacation in Thailand right now and Niki's constantly freaking out about the tsunami alert, 'cause if her mom drowns, there goes her ride to school.

Five minutes later, Ducky turns onto our street and slows down. But it seems like he's never gonna stop. Finally, he parks in front of our house. I clear my throat.

"Ducky?"

"What?"

"Did you call an ambulance?"

"Sure," he says right off the bat, then mutters something I can't catch.

"Let's go down to the spa in the afternoon," Buoy says. "We can get a load of that new coat-check girl."

"Okay," I say.

Ducky revs the engine. I get out and slam the door. As they drive off, I'm hit by the smell of exhaust fumes. I walk over to the front door and fiddle with the lock a while, and after about forever, I actually manage to get the key in it. I turn it and press down on the door handle. I step in and immediately drop my keys. The light is on in the living room. Ever since my old man died, my mother can't sleep at night.

"Are you home?" she asks.

I don't say anything. The room is dim and the smoke is so thick you can cut it with a knife. I wanna ask why she can't just open a fucking window to get some air in here, but I don't feel like arguing. She's holding a book. It's open to the exact same page as when I left. I don't know why she bothers. I'd just watch TV in her place. There's a whole mound of butts in the yellow glass ashtray. The grey dust has overflown and spilled, forming a little dune on the tablecloth.

"Where were you?" she asks.

"Out with friends."

"Again?"

"Uh-huh."

"Did you drink?"

"We have a meet on the weekend."

"C'mere, let me give you a kiss."

"Aw, Ma, come on," I say, but I go over to her anyway.

Her mouth smells like smoke. My stomach turns. I carry the ashtray out into the kitchen and dump the butts into the garbage, then walk over to the fridge and open it. It feels like a searchlight shining straight into my eyes. I squint. I don't know what I'm looking for. I feel nauseous but I'm also hungry. I open the drawer. I see a piece of mouldy cheese. It's like a dead mouse. Green and furry. I almost puke into the bin, so I push it back quickly. I close the fridge door. I wipe my mouth. I walk into the bathroom. I look into the mirror. My eyes are bloodshot. I take the Visine down from the shelf. I squirt it into my right eye. The ice-cold drops freeze my pupils. It feels like I'm hanging my eyeball out the window of a speeding train. My vision clears. I squeeze cold toothpaste onto my toothbrush, clean my teeth, then go into my room, take off my pants, and toss them on the floor. I climb into bed in my boxer shorts. I find the remote and flip through the channels. Some cops in Washington shot a guy to shreds who stepped out onto his front porch with a cordless drill. They thought he had a gun. A junkie chick in New York put her kid in the dryer with the laundry and hit permanent press. Bombs went off in Baghdad. Everyone died. Two a.m. I still can't fall asleep. My head hurts. My stomach hurts. My mom's shuffling around in the kitchen. I download and watch *Omen,* the original version. Since the porn channels got coded on TV, I only watch horror movies and nature documentaries. I just saw one about Larry, a wild boar living in captivity. They wanted him to get with a whole pen of sows for some experiment, but the poor bastard wouldn't hump the females no matter what they tried, so they finally ended up knocking him out and squeezing his sperm manually. I think of Niki. And Viki. I imagine them kissing, wearing shiny leather outfits, kneeling in front of me and taking turns bobbing on my cock. I come in thirty seconds, then turn towards the wall and draw the blanket over me. I'm already half asleep when I'm jolted awake by the realization that there's no practise on Sunday. I try to text Zoli-boy so he doesn't get up at dawn, but all I manage is "no prcts sndy. u dmbass." I feel cross-eyed and I just can't find his number in my contacts. Somehow I always scroll past it. When the image of Niki almost biting off that moron's dick flashes through my mind, weird sounds gurgle up from my throat. At first I think I'm crying, but then I realize I'm laughing. The kid with the Beatles haircut is about to off his mother. I'd be up for fucking that piece of ass anytime. Not the little kid. His mom. I'll google her tomorrow.

SQUARE SILENCE

I'm sprawled out in bed practising imaginary flip-turns in a semi-daze when the Beastie Boys' "Sabotage" starts blaring, and my body floods with adrenaline. After I finally realize it's my ringtone I'm hearing, I turn on my side and start feeling around on the floor. Eventually, I find it under my t-shirt, in my shoe. It ended up in there last night, somehow. I answer. It's Buoy, he's bored and wants to go down to the thermal bath. I'm still only half-conscious, so instead of telling him to fuck off, I agree to meet him in twenty behind the old movie theatre. Buoy—judging by his voice, anyway—doesn't seem too distressed about last night's party. I don't remember every last detail, plus these nights are pretty much the same anyway, but one thing's for sure: we did get seriously shitfaced. I hang up and try to open my eyes, but it's too early. I even forgot to roll down the shutters last night.

Downtown's always like a set from *The Walking Dead* at this time of day. Main Street's the only place with any sign of life. A couple of screaming kids on tricycles zigzag around bums in zombie costumes sifting through garbage cans. Otherwise, everything's disturbingly empty. Buoy's got it in his head to take a detour towards the White Rhino, 'cause he heard from someone that there was a major fucking battle at the club last night. I'd rather just get going to the pool, but I don't feel like wandering around by myself, so I stick with Buoy.

As soon as we get there, you can tell that whoever told the story wasn't kidding when they said it was a battle. There's POLICE LINE: DO NOT CROSS tape strung around the trashed entrance, and they tried to sweep the broken window glass under the bushes, but the shards crunch loudly under my feet just the same. The walls and fence are covered with bloodstains and there must've been a couple of bigger pools of blood on the concrete that got sprinkled with sand to soak them up. Buoy heard that the gypsies stabbed someone, or the skinheads stabbed the gypsies, but whatever happened is still unclear because there was a massive crowd, and Buoy's homie, who watched the whole thing go down, couldn't see much through the mob. In any case, it's all really fuzzy.

There's blood and hair stuck to the jagged glass sticking out from the window frame. I'm lost in space for a second and can't see anything else except a dark strand of hair quivering in the draft. Buoy's voice makes me snap out of it.

"This was real hardcore," he establishes with satisfaction. "Lucky we left early," he adds.

So that means we were at the club too. I wanna ask if I was with them, but if I was, Buoy's gonna think I'm a total retard, so I keep my mouth shut and stare at the smashed door instead. I'm not sure what facial expression should match this moment, 'cause standing around on the empty street like this kinda weakens the whole horrifying effect. Still, it's hard to disassociate from the fact that someone's head was shoved through the window here. And if the glass looks like this, imagine what's left of that poor guy's head. Buoy studies the scene a while longer, then I manage, with some effort, to drag him away, and we head off to the spa. We weave our way through the cars parked in front of the White Rhino. There's a smudged streak of blood gleaming on the trunk of a white Mazda. I'm no car freak, but I have this thing for Japanese cars. Knocked-out teeth lie on the ground, but they're arranged so neatly that I bet the news crew used them for cutaway shots.

We're walking down the road. There's no traffic at all. They cleaned my favourite graffiti off the high stone wall separating the music school from the jail that read: *Prisoners of Music.* It'll have to get sprayed on again. Buoy's talking a mile a minute, and sometimes it gets out of control, but I've realized that when he's like this the best thing to do is act like Viggo Mortensen in that creepy sci-fi and just keep saying, *uh-huh*, and *yeah*. I don't really care about the kids Buoy's going off about. I don't even know half of them by name, and he's already said everything he knows about last night's scuffle. We're almost at the spa when he launches into some story about the Cloister Street Thai massage parlour and happy endings, but before I can get him to tell me more details, a water-polo girl slows down on her bike beside us. Grinning, Buoy starts complimenting her on the killer whale tattooed on her calf.

Twenty minutes later we're soaking in the thermal basin, the water gurgling softly into the overflow drain. Wrinkly old crones with liver spots surround us in the water and by the poolside, as far as the eye can see. They remind me of wallowing hippos on *Animal Planet.* I'm watching Ducky, but he doesn't notice me. His face is all red from the hot water as he looks around, his expression bored, for somebody to bang, but we got here a little early so there are no good chicks yet, just a bunch of grannies. Then again, it's always Ducky's mood and the situation that decide who he's gonna screw.

A fat kid clutches the railing as he waddles down the steps. He's barely twelve, but weighs two hundred and fifty pounds for sure. He slowly flops into the pool, floating like a baby manatee at feeding time, his soft, greasy body casting waves. The water rocks me gently while Buoy goes on about the new coat-check girl outside. He's totally latched onto her. He goes into lengthy detail about the things he'd do to her. He gets most of his inspiration from BDSM porn, adding an extra twist to make it especially sick. He's really good at this, but if it actually came down to doing that stuff, he'd probably fuck up pretty bad.

"Jugs like that you can tie up with barbed wire, no prob," he explains. "You just gotta pierce through the nipples precisely."

The chick's tits really *are* huge. Like two baby heads. A pair of one-eyed twins. You can't help but zero in on them. Buoy tried to hit on her when we arrived, but he ran out of things to ask after about ten seconds and then just stood there at the coat-check counter all bug-eyed, staring at her enormous cans. And then *he* was the one who got all offended when the stupid bitch got cocky with him.

"You gotta take a chick to the movies," I say, and yawn so big I nearly dislocate my jaw. The monotonous sloshing of the iron-tasting thermal water spilling into the basin gutter makes me super groggy. Like someone constantly murmuring in your ear.

"Don't spoil her," says Ducky, and he yawns too. "You blow a bunch of cash on tickets and popcorn, and then when you wanna cut to the chase, she pushes your hand away."

Ducky spits the water through his teeth in a thin stream, really far. He hits this little kid of about six—who's floundering around in chest-high water sporting inflatable, dolphin-print arm bands and fogged-up goggles—on the back of the neck.

"If you wanna pay for pussy, I know a few seventh-graders," he adds.

"Too bad the little movie theatre shut down," Buoy yawns.

"The little movie theatre closed?" I ask.

"Yeah," says Buoy. "They hung a sign up saying the final show was cancelled."

"They should've bulldozed that dump years ago," Ducky adds, then tries to spray the little kid with water-spit again.

The new multiplex at the mall clobbered the little movie theatre. I mean, sure, for a while the only people who ever went in there were bums and dirt-poor gypsies from the hood. The place was totally starting to look like a cross between a detox centre and a playground: the shit-faced hobos whooping and howling while the gyppos spit sunflower-seed shells all over the floor. I remember this one time some guy got knifed at a matinee, and everyone thought it was L'il Italy, or one of his pals, or somebody else. The cops hauled a couple of gyppos down to the station and then of course it turned out that it was the guy's own chick who stuck him in the eye. They had a fight over their jug wine. So basically, it took sheer talent to coax chicks out of their undies at the old movie theatre.

"They're opening a bank in its place," Buoy yawns.

"Doesn't your old man wanna open a strip joint instead?" I ask.

"He could hire those Ukrainian hookers from the truck stop." Buoy's eyes widen, sparkling.

"Yeah," I say. "We could bang sluts with your dad."

Ducky laughs. He likes the idea. I mean, I'd be willing to bet hard cash that most of Ducky's female friends on Facebook got nailed by his dad too. Suddenly, Gyula

Csák slams into the pool. That's his name, Gyula Csák, but everybody just calls him Norris, on account of his last name sounding like *Chuck.* He's a house painter, but I'll bet he's got his hands on his shrivelled prick way more than on any teddy roller. He lands in the water with a huge back-flop, then clambers to his feet, stands in the middle of the basin, and peers around. He looks like a pumped-up hairy pig. He's got a barcode inked on the back of his head. I never understood the point of tats that you can only see with the help of two mirrors. I don't dare laugh, and Ducky and the others have their straight faces on too. One time, he almost killed a buddy of ours at the mall. He didn't like the way the kid was staring at his woman. There wasn't any use saying he wasn't staring at anybody. Norris kept kicking his head and kidneys till the kid passed out. The security guards just happened to be smoking out back by the staff entrance, though they probably wouldn't have intervened anyway, and the cops arrived half an hour later from the station three blocks away, but by then Norris and his squad had split. He spins around for a little while in the middle of the pool, then gets bored and sits down next to his pal.

"So what the fuck was I talking about?" he asks.

"The black chick," his friend answers.

Norris ponders this, then nods and continues:

"Oh right, got it. So I took her into the storage room and unfolded her twat, and fuck, man, I couldn't believe what I saw."

"How come? What happened?"

"Listen, Pete, the black babe's cunt was *pink* inside," he roars.

The pool area echoes *cunt-t-t* for, like, a whole five seconds. Old ladies reeking of garlic shake their heads disapprovingly.

"You gotta be shitting me-*me-me!"* Pete tries to out-yell his buddy.

The dude's got a concession stand that sells fried dough on the beach. Last summer, Zoli-boy slaved there for two weeks but after that he was like, better Ronald McDonald than this.

"My ass is shitting you," Norris retorts. "I thought I was looking in the wrong hole, 'cause the rest of her was so dark, black liquorice would shine like a glow stick in her mouth. Then she grabbed my head and pushed my face into that huge twat. I almost suffocated, for fuck's sake. I says to her, *fuckyoubitch*, but she was horny as hell. She was grunting and everything."

"*Grunting,*" I mumble, while sounds reminiscent of pig snorts burst out from Norris's throat.

Buoy looks at me confused, but I don't say anything, I just plunge underwater. Down here it's quiet. I open my eyes. I can only see a few metres ahead in the murky water, but I can clearly make out the skull-plus-Kingdom-of-Hungary-map tat on Norris's calf. I come up to the surface.

"She didn't wanna let my fuckin' head go, so I had to bash her in the ribs to get her to chill out. Then I spun her around and banged her hard. You should've seen it, man, her fat jiggling like a sow's belly."

"Oh, by the way, when's the pig slaughter?" Pete asks thoughtfully.

I don't hear Norris's answer, because Buoy starts going on about the coat-check girl again. He's talking about what he would stick in her and where. In the meantime, Ducky starts giving one of the Paralympian chicks the eye. It's not just old bags with floppy udders that Ducky likes. Last time, he hooked up with this one-legged triathlete cunt and a deaf-mute high diver. He said it was so crazy, like, he could say whatever he wanted during sex, and she wouldn't get upset.

"I'd try and score with her," Buoy says.

"Who?" I ask.

"Erika," Buoy says.

"Who's that?" asks Ducky.

"The coat-check girl," Buoy says.

"Isn't her name Erna?" I ask.

"No," Buoy says. "It's Erika."

"I thought it was Erna," Ducky says.

"Isn't she the chick that Joci boned?" I ask.

"Who?" Ducky asks.

"Well, Erika," I say.

"Erika?" Buoy asks.

"Joci?" asks Ducky.

"Yeah."

"Who told you that?" Buoy asks.

"Joci did," I answer. "I think."

"That is such fucking bullshit," Buoy waves me off.

"You wish," Ducky snorts and dips underwater.

Buoy looks at me, waiting for me to say something, but I can't reassure him. Joci really *is* the bullshitter of the century, but he might still have totally boned her. Actually, I don't give a fuck who's hooking up with who.

"Who gives a shit anyway," I shrug.

Buoy spits and then tilts his head back to wet his hair. I bob quietly for a while, the hot water caressing my skin, the hair on my legs floating in the lazy current like pondweed, soft waves washing over me. I stare at the clock, but the hands don't want to move. Maybe time has stopped. But I mean, here in the thermal bath, time always kinda seems to be standing. Norris is still going on about black chicks. Or pig slaughtering. Ducky swims underwater over to a little girl in a pink bathing suit and floats beside her like an alligator waiting for prey. The little girl doesn't even notice. Then he pushes off from the bottom of the pool and resurfaces in the same place he went under. Niki and her kid sister, Viki, step out of the locker room. The door slowly closes behind them, then opens again, and the other two members of the 4x100-metre women's freestyle relay team, Szilvi and Fruzsi, march in. Niki and Fruzsi have towels wrapped around their waists. They think if they do this no one will see what enormous asses they have. They're always whining about their big asses or small tits. Or both at once. Viki waves and starts towards us. Niki is a few steps behind her, annoyed that her little sis cut in front of her. My whole squad's fucked both of them already. Except Zoli-boy. Nobody's fucked Szilvi and Fruzsi yet, but they go to the Catholic school. They won't let anybody touch them. An old fart watches from the cold-water basin as the chicks tiptoe along the wet tiles. The water is 18°C. Why's he got his hand down his pants? Only sea lions can get it up in water that cold, and maybe Eskimos. Niki's still fumbling with her towel, while Viki's already heading down the steps into the pool. As she wades into the water, her bathing suit dampens. She pretends not to notice that everyone's staring at her. Even Norris shuts up for a second, then says, "She's a looker, that one. Too bad she's got no tits."

As soon as Viki comes up beside us, Buoy considerately makes space for her.

"No, stay," Viki says, and Buoy is about to answer, but Ducky beats him to it.

"C'mon, there's some space over here," he says, slapping the water in front of him.

Viki pushes off from the bottom step, dips into the water, and glides over to us. Ducky tries to reach between her legs to rub her pussy, but before he manages to pull her bathing suit aside, Viki swims off towards Buoy. Buoy wants to rub her pussy too, but before he can grab her, Viki whirls around and he's only able to pat her ass. Viki looks back at Buoy, then sits down beside me and slides her hand along my thigh. I slide my hand along her thigh, too. Her long brown hair sticks together. She pushes it back. Niki finally manages to figure out where to put her towel and starts towards the pool.

"Hey, guys!" she says, but nobody pays attention to her. "*Hey, guys!*" she repeats louder, and Ducky, like someone waking from a stupor, looks at her and says:

"Come here."

Since he can't manage to get Viki to sit down next to him, he sets to work on Niki. He goes where there's less resistance. And Niki's happy to oblige. She swims over to him and sits on his lap. Ducky whispers something in her ear, all the while keeping his eyes on Viki. Niki smiles. Ducky keeps whispering and makes Niki burst out laughing. Meanwhile, I'm rubbing her pussy. I mean Viki's. Ducky massages Niki's belly, then his hand slides lower. As I stick my finger into Viki's pussy, I think of Niki's pussy. Viki chatters on, her cheeks flushed, she asks me something, but I don't say anything because I have no idea what we're talking about. Buoy keeps answering for me. Viki moves her hips gently. I slip another finger inside while staring at the chart on the wall that tells you which ions and mineral salts you get in one cubic centimetre of water. I can't read the part that says how deep the hot spring is that supplies the spa water. I only see that it's 90°C and that they cool it down before they let it loose on us. It says the water's beneficial for people suffering from circulatory disorders. And bone cancer. Or bone fractures. I need to get glasses. I stick one more finger inside Viki.

"Hey!" she hisses, appalled, her greyish-blue eyes shooting daggers.

"Sorry," I say, but it's too late.

Viki moves over beside Buoy.

Ducky is gripped by a serious testosterone attack. He tries to get us riled up by saying he can hold his breath underwater the longest, but Buoy and I laugh in his face. Probably even Zoli-boy could beat him, if he had the patience.

"You're shitting yourselves, right?" he barks, and you can tell from his eyes that he's gotten himself all worked up.

"I'd beat you anytime," Buoy says, wiping his face.

"Then why ya shitting bricks?" Ducky says, looking him in the eye.

"I'm not shitting anything," Buoy says. He's as calm as a baleen whale stuffed with plankton. "I just don't wanna embarrass you in front of the girls."

"Here," Ducky says, handing Niki his waterproof wristwatch.

I got something similar from my old man for my twelfth birthday, but the older guys took it from me at a swim meet. I was kinda sad about losing it 'cause I could press the start/stop button twice in a row the fastest, but at least I was off the hook and didn't get beat up.

"Ready?" Niki asks.

"Yeah," Ducky answers, and puts Niki's finger on the button. "Press that. Once when we start and once when we finish."

He's not taking any chances. Niki counts to three and we plunge underwater. I count the seconds in the dark for a while, but then I get a little bored and open my eyes.

The water's pretty murky. Tiny brown flecks swim and swirl in front of my face. Maybe someone shit in the pool again. Buoy floats nearby. I can't see his body. It's like his head got cut off. With his hair floating around his head, he looks like a jellyfish. Ducky's body drifts up towards the surface, but he keeps his head down, looking first at Buoy, then at me. We float motionless, like corpses. I'm at seventy. Ducky usually can't go longer than three minutes. That's a hundred and eighty seconds. At one-fifty, his lungs start to give out. Bubbles pop out of his mouth. His lungs start burning. He can't take it much longer. I drift towards the edge of the pool. I notice Viki's thighs, or Niki's. Someone's poking around between her legs and I zone out, completely forgetting about this stupid contest. Ducky's nearly drowning by the time I zone in again. That dumbass would rather kill himself than give up. Actually, there *is* a cut-off point where you can't resurface without help. I wait a couple more seconds, but when Ducky looks at me, I stick my head out. A second later he's popped up too. He gasps for air, wheezing.

"Well, how long?" he pants when he's finally able to get a word out, his face red.

"Two minutes, forty-seven seconds, fifty-two hundredths," Niki reads from the stopwatch display.

Buoy's head emerges from the water, close to Niki's hips. He spurts water from his face. He's like a whale again now.

"Well?" he asks, rubbing his eyes.

Everyone shuts their mouths.

Ducky catches on that Buoy tricked him.

"You cheated, dickhead!" Ducky attacks him. "Dafuq you swim away for?"

"I didn't swim away," Buoy grins.

"You swam away," Ducky insists.

“I didn’t swim away,” Buoy repeats with a faint smile and more emphasis.

“Bull-fucking-shit you didn’t swim away.”

I position myself so that I’ll be able to intervene if needed. It’s just the usual smack talk which hardly ever turns into a real fist fight, but it doesn’t hurt to keep your eyes open. Ducky stays stuck on the topic a while longer, but luckily Buoy isn’t taking the bait. He listens to Ducky’s baloney with a straight face and firmly denies deliberately swimming out of his range of view. Sure, he knows Ducky’s dangerous if he’s off his meds, so he’s real careful not to stupidly provoke him. Finally, his tactics pay off and Ducky slowly gets that there won’t be a round two, no matter how long he flaps his lips. No one feels like competing. Of course, in the end, Ducky can’t hold back from dropping a comment, saying that Buoy’s older brother isn’t the limp-dick faggot that Buoy is, but luckily, just then Zoli-boy steps out of the locker room and Buoy uses the opportunity to pretend he didn’t hear the insult. I mean, I can see that he’s keeping himself under wraps, because his face is all red, though only very faintly. Zoli-boy’s slippers slap loudly as he hurries towards the pool. His hair is messy and he’s got dark circles under his eyes. Ducky perks up when he sees him.

“You feel like plunging?” Ducky asks instead of greeting him.

“Huh?” Zoli-boy asks.

“Holding your breath,” Ducky explains.

“No, thanks,” Zoli-boy says.

“You shit yourself?”

“I didn’t shit myself, I just don’t feel like it.”

“The sauna’s empty,” I suggest.

Maybe they’ll bite, but nobody’s interested.

"You're chicken-shit, Zoli-boy," Ducky sneers.

He knows exactly how to get Zoli-boy worked up.

"Blow me," he growls.

"You wish, fairy-boy," Duck keeps goading him with a grin.

They go on trashing each other a couple minutes longer, then Zoli-boy cracks and gives in. Niki's keeping time again. They plunge down simultaneously. Ducky makes sure Zoli-boy doesn't move from his view for even a second, but since he's already got a round in him, the oxygen runs out of his blood quickly and he's fucking squirming after two minutes. And of course Zoli-boy wants his revenge. He dived under looking really determined. I slide up inconspicuously beside Ducky, in case he needs saving. As expected, Ducky is forced to resurface after two and a half minutes. He gasps, his face red, and when he sees that Zoli-boy's still floating motionless in the water, goes over and stops beside him. He doesn't say anything, maybe he can't, and just takes deep breaths and spits a huge phlegm glob. We're up to about three minutes by now, but Zoli-boy's still at it. He gives us a thumbs up to signal that it's okay, which gets Ducky even more annoyed, and when Zoli-boy finally wants to come up, he pushes his head down. It takes a couple of seconds before we catch on. Zoli-boy tries to back away, thrashing his arms wildly, but Ducky holds him tight. Buoy and I lunge at the same time, and while Buoy brings Ducky down with a body check, I yank Zoli-boy out of the water. He gasps desperately for air, gurgling, coughing up water, a strange terror in his eyes. I thump him heavily on the back a couple of times to get the water out of his lungs. He might not even survive this, but already his eyes are searching for Ducky. It's pretty rare to see him so furious, but I guess he's got a reason.

Meanwhile, Ducky is already fighting with Buoy, *why the fuck d'ya have to knock me down,* and when Buoy tells him in a tone of honest disbelief that he nearly offed Zoli-boy, Ducky snarls at Buoy to leave him alone already, it was just a joke, and then stomps off to the cold-water pool. I can tell Zoli-boy is pretty shaken by what happened, so I try to lead him away as far as possible from the others. I've got to get him away while I still can, because as soon as he recovers from the shock, he'll want to take down Ducky for sure.

The whole scene doesn't last longer than half a minute.

"The motherfucker tried to drown me," he grunts, after he manages to cough all the water out of his lungs.

"He didn't really mean it," I say, trying to calm him.

"Fucking hilarious joke," Zoli-boy says, wiping away his snot.

I don't know what to say to that.

"I'm going the fuck home," he says, but then Viki comes over and asks Zoli-boy if he's okay.

Zoli-boy growls some answer, but I know the gesture's made him feel pretty goddamn nice. I leave and let them talk. In the meantime, Ducky's banging Niki in the cold water, but when I tell him that the sauna's empty, he pushes the chick away from him without a word and climbs out of the pool. As I open the sauna door, the scorching air blasts in my face. We get inside. Last year, some guy I know got a heart attack 'cause he was working out in the hot sauna. He was fifteen, but by the time he revived, he was fifty. There's only a sunbed-tan fitness bitch sweating her ass off on the top bench, otherwise the booth is empty. The chick gives us the evil eye. I guess she's scared her sauna will get cold. I'm hit by the smell of lavender oil. Ducky and the others sit on the upper bench beside the chick, yakking about something, but I'm not listening. I stare out the window. Viki and her crew move from the warm water to the cold and then to the hot basin. Zoli-boy misunderstands something and gets in the cold water, then climbs into the hot just as the girls jump back into the cold, shrieking. They keep missing each other, but it's deliberate. The girls whisper and giggle, then settle down beside Zoli-boy in the hot basin. The door of the sauna looks out onto the basins, but I can't see what they're doing. A couple minutes later they climb out of the hot water and go back into the warm. Zoli-boy disappears. He's probably got a hard-on and is scared to get out. If you get an erection in the hot water, your dick stays like that a half hour for sure, and you don't wanna go running around the spa with a boner.

The thermometer reads 90°C in here. The fitness bitch asks Ducky and Buoy to scoot over, and she stretches out on the top bench, continuing to sweat with her eyes closed. Beads of perspiration slide along her neck, her arms, her thighs. Her type can really take the heat, and if they get all settled in the sauna, they won't budge anytime soon. Buoy sits one tier lower. He waits a little while, then stands and positions his ass above the chick's face. He pulls his butt cheeks apart. Meanwhile, Ducky keeps his tongue flapping. This is part of the diversion. Buoy farts soundlessly into her face, sits back down quickly, and joins the conversation. After a couple of seconds, the fitness bitch's face clenches. She sits up like Count Dracula in his coffin, then scrambles down from the shelf and hurries to the door. She starts pulling on it. Then she realizes it's a push. When she finally manages to escape, the cold air slaps her, she staggers and goes crashing down on the wet tiles. By the time the lifeguard arrives, she's managed to clamber onto all-fours. The guy helps her up and leads her to a lounge chair by the pool. I look up at Buoy. He grins contentedly. Then Ducky steps over to the stove and pisses on the hot stones. The steam rises with a sizzle. I step up beside him, pull my swim shorts aside, and piss on the stones too. Buoy covers us. A drop of sweat rolls down his forehead and into his eyes, which he squints and rubs. He can't see anything. A second later, the door opens and Norris comes in. Our eyes meet and we head out. I close the door. Look back. I see my reflection and Norris, as he grimaces in the piss smell. The ammonia burns his eyes. Then he realizes what's going on.

"Shit, let's bounce," I say.

There's not much else to add.

We dash towards the locker room. Norris kicks open the sauna door and bellows.

"I'll spit in your ass, you little faggot, and fuck you on your mother's grave."

He starts after us, but wipes out hard on the slippery marble floor, which gets him even more pissed off. He scrambles up, roaring, spit flying, but I can't understand what he's saying. We bolt through the spa's locker room. I look back. I wanna know how much of a head start we have. I bump into a grampa and he goes flying into a locker. We sprint past Erna Gigatits. Buoy shoots a greeting to the twins. We cut across the lobby, zigzagging between the palm trees and the foosball tables, then jump over the entryway barrier. Ducky almost nose dives. We rush into the men's locker room.

"Slow it down, boys," Marika the cleaning lady shouts at us.

"Hello, ma'am," we greet her in chorus.

"Gyula's coming," Buoy adds in explanation.

Marika grabs the bucket and the mop and soaks the floor. She makes our footprints disappear. We hear Norris come barging in a few seconds later. A loud crash. I really fucking hope he fell and split his skull open, but it turns out he just miscalculated the braking distance and slid full force into the counter, 'cause next minute he's already roaring at Marika, *why in God's holy asshole did you have to mop the motherfucking floor?*

"Which way did those fudge-packing shits go?" he asks, after he's done raving.

"Who?" Marika asks him.

"Those cock-sucking little shits."

"Look around the pool area," Marika answers him calmly, but you can't get rid of Norris that easy.

He heads straight into the locker room. His feet slap on the marble as he weaves his way among the rows of lockers, peering into changing booths, slamming doors, and keeping up a steady flow of curses. We're standing on top of a bench in one of the changing booths, leaning against the door from inside. Norris stops and listens. We hold our breaths. My personal record is three and a half minutes. If he checks in here, we're dead meat. My pulse is one-eighty, like after a hard round in the pool. Ducky goes pale. I prop him up so he doesn't keel over. It's quiet. Square silence. Norris walks away. On the way out, he growls something at Marika. We wait a little longer, then climb off the bench.

"Fuck," we blurt out together.

We hear footsteps. We jump back up on the bench.

"Someone hit a cyclist again on the bypass last Saturday," a voice says.

"I'm almost surprised when they *don't* run someone over," another voice says.

"Wait, but here's the catch. They rammed into the poor bastard, stopped, got out, bashed his face in, and then tossed him in the ditch."

"Fucking savages, man."

"He was lucky someone spotted his bike from the road and called an ambulance."

"Did he survive?"

"Naw, he died in the ambulance," the first voice says, then continues. "Wait, let me help."

I don't even wanna *think* about what they might be doing.

"You can come out now, boys," Marika calls.

We glance at each other. The two dudes fall silent. I didn't know faggot cops existed. We get down off the bench. Step out of the booth. I don't dare turn my back to the cops.

"Thank you, Marika," I say.

"Get on home now, before that bastard comes back."

Meanwhile, Zoli-boy comes in from the pool too. He sits down on the bench, saying something to Buoy. Buoy puts his clothes on quietly. Beside them, the two cops put their stuff into their lockers.

"Ducky?" Zoli-boy says.

"Yeah, what?"

"Did you walk here?" he says loudly, so the cops can hear too. "You could have borrowed your old man's whip."

Someone needs to tell Zoli-boy to zip it, 'cause if he runs his mouth too much we're all fucked. We dress quickly and don't wait for the girls. No chick is worth getting killed by that psychoprick. A black Volkswagen Transporter is parked in front of the pool in the spot reserved for cripples. The front of it hangs over onto the sidewalk. There's no way a wheelchair can squeeze past it.

Tinted windshields, tinted windows, rotating aluminium rims. It's got a Kingdom of Hungary bumper sticker that's been stuck on upside down. Inverted like this, it totally looks like modern Hungary with all its former territories chopped away. Ducky looks around, walks over to the car, looks around once more, then pushes the tip of his key into the enamel. The scraping sound is shrill as he drags the key along the sides of the car. Front door, back door.

Then we get the fuck out.

SHARKS

It's five-fifteen. Give or take a minute or two. I know what time it is even without a clock. I wake up at the same time at dawn every day. My mom'll come in pretty soon to wake me. She doesn't know I'm up already. She doesn't know much about me. I pull the blanket over my head. I don't wanna get up. I dreamt I was working on a whaling ship. We were slaughtering whales with a few of my buddies and also an older, soft-spoken, sinewy American dude. We speared those huge freaking animals, sawed off their fins, then tossed them back into the water while we stood on deck, covered in blood, watching them blink as they sank to the bottom of the sea. They didn't understand why we were doing what we were doing to them. One of them even snapped at us, asking why it was necessary: they can't swim without fins and can't come up for air. Whales are mammals. They drown in the mud. Though any mammal would probably drown in the mud. The whole thing felt so real that I started thinking that maybe I didn't even dream the whole whale thing, and that maybe I actually saw it on *Spectrum* or *Animal Planet*. I'm not even sure they were whales. Cable is full of nature documentary channels. Stuff about sharks is really trendy these days. At least until they're all wiped out. I mean the sharks. The other day this narrator with a deep voice explained that sharks have skeletons made up mostly of cartilage, and since they have no gills, they can only breathe while they swim, so they have to keep in constant motion. If they stop, they drop dead. If you cut off a shark's fins, it starts to sink, and then when it lands on the bottom of the sea, it drowns. Sharks always make me think of my father. He never stopped moving either, at least while he still lived at home. I have no idea what he could be doing now, but he's definitely not standing. Once, I dreamt that he came back to tell us what happened. He didn't want us to find out from somebody else. He sat down in the living room, turned on the TV, and explained that the reason he died wasn't because he stopped, but he stopped because he died. I didn't understand exactly, but I didn't wanna ask questions. Then his head turned into a shark's head, and he looked at me and said, "Keep swimming, son, even if you die trying." We never talked that much when we lived together. I open my eyes. It's as dark as the Mariana Trench. I clamber out of bed, my feet touch the carpet, I feel around for my slippers, but can't find them. Then I remember I came in wearing shoes last night and that my slippers are still out in the front hall. It's always cold at five-thirty, never mind if it's July or January, but it sucks worse in January 'cause then it won't get warmer later on, either. I pull on underpants and a t-shirt, put on my shoes, slipper-style, and turn on the light. I walk over to my desk, unpack a few textbooks from my backpack, and pack a few other ones. We have seven periods today. I'm gonna be stuck in school till two-thirty. I go to the bathroom. The light's on in the kitchen. A strange smell hits me, like something burned. Maybe my mother set herself on fire again. She did it once before. She was smoking in bed. I check the kitchen. She's sitting there at the table, not on fire. I take the lit cigarette from her hand, but before I can take a drag, she looks up. Like she's seen a ghost.

"You want breakfast?" she asks, and reaches for the pack of cigarettes.

She pulls one out, fiddles with the match, then lights up.

"No," I say. I never eat before practice. Only Buoy can eat before practice. Everybody else would just puke into the water. "I'm in a hurry."

"I'll make something for lunch."

She exhales the smoke.

"I'm eating at the school cafeteria," I lie.

I always buy weed with my lunch money. I drink a glass of orange juice and put the empty cup on the table beside the county newspaper. The whole thing is only sixteen pages, including the comics, obituaries, and want ads. It's open at *Police Reports* and there's news in it about a gang of pickpockets working the lakeshore, a stabbing incident at some village pub, and a Saturday night hit-and-run. Not that one, not *our* accident. I mean, not Ducky's. My mother notices me staring at the paper.

"Always look both ways before crossing the street," she says, dead serious.

"Okay," I answer right away, making a huge effort not to laugh in her face.

I go back to my room for my backpack and then head out.

Ten minutes later, I'm cutting across the park. Somebody shit in the Little Shepherdess fountain behind the theatre again. As I get closer, I see that the statue got a face mask too. I've been wondering how they do this, and have come to the conclusion that either they shit into their hands and then smear it on, or they carry around a sandbox shovel and work with that. Buoy's crouched on a bench's backrest at the other end of the park, looking like a grumpy buzzard with fluffed-up feathers. He's got his feet up on the seat.

"Haul your fuckin' ass already, willya," is the growl I get instead of a greeting.

He's not hurrying me because he's afraid of being late. He couldn't give a flying fuck what time we get there. He's twice as good as most of the team with half as much practise, but he hates waiting around at dawn. We shake hands and then he jumps down onto the tiny pebbles, heading towards the railroad. He's in dawn mode, moving like a tank. We walk quietly beside each other. The traffic lights blink yellow. We don't look both ways, we just cross the road. There's no traffic. It would be a true wonder if we got hit by anything. A bus idles at the station. Two losers with sunken faces climb on at the first door. They're off to the meat-packing plant to punch their cards.

"Did you read the paper?" I ask.

"I don't read," Buoy says.

"Somebody got run over again," I continue.

Buoy keeps his mouth shut. He couldn't give a shit. Doesn't feel like talking. I make one more attempt.

"They wrote about the old guy too. The one we hit."

"We didn't hit him," Buoy answers right off.

So he did hear what I said after all.

"Whatever. We were there."

"It's *not* fucking whatever," he interrupts. "It was Ducky who hit that gramps."

There's a Latin teacher who lives in our building. Or rather, an unemployed guy who used to teach Latin. This one time, we ran into each other in our building's corridor by the garbage chute and the dude asks me why I'm in a bad mood. I have no idea why, but I didn't tell him to fuck off. Instead, I told him that I'm gonna fail math 'cause one of my friends wouldn't let me copy off him. That made the guy start jabbering in Latin, something like *in anus this amiche a parent.* Or something like that. At first I thought he was talking about someone's Amish parents getting it up the ass, and I was looking at him like, *dafuq are you telling me this for, man,* and in Latin, too, but then he explained to me that it's a proverb, and asked if I was interested in what it meant. I told him to blow me and left him at the garbage chute. The next day my mother found a slip of paper in our mailbox. It said, *In angustiis amici apparent.—Petronius* I googled it. If that Roman dude was right, then Ducky is in deep shit.

We arrive at the railroad tracks. The lights aren't on in the watchman's shack. I guess he's still off in dreamland. There's no one around. This is where we take a shortcut. We save fifteen minutes every morning this way, which is an hour and fifteen minutes a week, five hours a month. Two-and-a-half days a year. It's the shortest way to the pool. If we had to go around, on the pedestrian overpass, we'd be late, and Coach Bandi would tear my ass to shreds. And Buoy would get it from Coach Tibi. Two trains idle at the station. Two freight trains. On the way home, after practice, we like to throw stuff at them. Now, we climb over the tankers they once used for illegal oil transport. It's easy because they have a little passage at the end. You just climb up the ladder, walk along the grate, then climb down the other side. Getting over the boxcars isn't as easy. First, you gotta jump up on the step, like on a dump truck, then climb over onto the buffer, which is cylindrical and slippery as hell because it's greased up real thick. Then you have to step over onto the coupling used to connect the cars, which is also sopping with lube, and in the meantime you have to hang on for dear life because the train could start moving at any second. This one time, a buddy of mine fell under the train and the wheels cut his legs off. He totally died too, though he was a pretty good guy. I'm always shitting bricks a little since that happened. Buoy pulls himself up onto the step, onto the buffer, and then slips. But somehow he manages to hold on.

"Fucking hell," he grunts.

"What?"

"I got my pants all greasy."

The train jerks heavily.

"Move your ass already," I urge him, but Buoy's just standing on the buffer, cursing the Hungarian railway employees.

"Fuck this greasy shit," he says.

A locomotive whistles, but Buoy still isn't moving, so I jump down onto the gravel, run to the other end of the car, and climb over. As the train slowly starts rolling, Buoy sticks his head out from behind the car and finally collects himself. He climbs down. The clay crunches under out feet. No need to climb over the fence. The gyppos already made a hole in it to haul out stolen wood. I slip through the hole, careful not to snag my clothes on the ends of the snipped wire. Buoy squeezes through, gets his pants caught, and they rip. I burst out laughing, but when he looks up I can see he's not in a good mood, so I keep quiet instead and head towards the pool. It's a streamlined building made of glass and steel, renovated a few years ago, but they skimped on building materials wherever they could. They did make awesome adventure pools, complete with a waterfall and an artificial cave, plus the country's steepest slide, which had some thingamajig sticking out of it that supposedly ripped off some guy's ball sack. It's lucky nobody's died yet.

The automatic doors open and we step into the lobby. The lady at the cash desk blinks vacantly behind the glass like an owl with a hangover. Her wrinkled face clashes with the lobby's sleek contours. One of the lifeguards shuffles past us in a t-shirt and flip-flops, his whistle dangling from his neck. I can tell from his gaze that he's stoned. He notices Buoy's torn, greasy pants.

"Spiffy pants," he says, gesturing towards Buoy's legs.

"Kiss my ass," Buoy grumbles back, but the dude can't hear him.

There's two lifeguards working in shifts. One used to be a sailor, but he's got a face like a kung-fu master, and he's always boring everyone with stories about the hardcore Siberian dock taverns he's been to and how a sailor pal of his got stabbed in the head once with an ice axe. Just like in some comic book. This one time, we went up to his place to get wasted and the dumbass thought he could impress us with a mounted trophy shark. It looked pretty fuckin' stupid in his one-room apartment in the projects, plus it was barely a metre long, but the dude was conceited as fuck about it. Said he grabbed it out of the Indian Ocean. More like he grabbed his dick, 'cause the shark was definitely made in China.

In between the dented grey lockers and the varnished wooden benches, the smell of feet is almost solid. Buoy walks over to his beefcake water polo buddies. Half an hour later, they're yanking each other's junks underwater to gain possession of the ball. Ducky shows up. I say hi but he doesn't answer. Thirty seconds later, Zoli-boy comes in too. His face is all red. He's mumbling something I assume is a greeting, but nobody says anything besides me. As I shove my stuff into the locker, my cell phone slips out of my pants pocket and falls to pieces on the floor. I pick it up and toss it in next to my stuff. I'll put it back together after practice. Buoy comes over from the other side of the locker row.

"You look all shrivelled," he says as he sees Zoli-boy.

Zoli-boy is about to answer when Coach Bandi steps into the locker room and roars that he's gonna shit right on our faces if we don't shut the fuck up right this minute. I'll bet he's never seen *2 Girls 1 Cup* or else he wouldn't make a threat like that. I don't know how he does it. He can appear anywhere, anytime, just like Batman, except he doesn't need a mask to disguise himself. We get thirty seconds to dress. Zoli-boy fumbles with his swimsuit, so we don't wait for him and head for the pool area. Coach Bandi likes to get physical. This one time, he smacked one of his boys so hard upside the head that his eardrum ruptured. I mean the kid's. But they gloss over these outbursts of his because he keeps churning out top results. He was Coach of the Year again last year. Ducky slip-slides in front of me on the tiles and there's a loud splat behind us. We make it upstairs to the pool. I toss my towel down on the bench, then head over to the starting block. I spit on it. I always spit on it before I jump in the pool. I squat down and stick my fingers into the water. I kneel at the edge of the pool, lean over, and splash myself. Coach Bandi arrives in the meantime and barks at me to move my ass and quit resting my shrivelled prick. I waste a bit more time though. Every second counts. Then I jump in.

It's like all sound suddenly got put on mute. I sink down into silence, the water licks at my skin, swallowing me whole. For a few fractions of a second I feel like I'll never reach the bottom, but then my feet touch the hard, slick tile. My knees bend, everything's in slo-mo, a single, continuous movement, no break in fluidity, not even at the end, when I kick off from a squat. No effort required, I allow my body to float up, my thigh muscles barely flexing. I let the water propel me and I reach up, hold my hands high, all the while blowing air out my nostrils, till I pop out above the surface and the water spits me out. After a few easy strokes, I lift my head up and spit the saliva and water collected in my mouth.

A chick swims in front of me. She spreads her legs as she does the breast stroke. She glides, then kicks again, legs wide. The string of her tampon hangs out from under her swimsuit. I can't figure out who it is. I swim closer, but still can't see anything, just that white piece of string wriggling in the current like fish bait.

An hour later, I rest, gasping by the wall. After I manage to collect myself, I take off my goggles and cap and take a leak. It's not easy to piss while you're swimming, especially if you gotta work your ass off. So I've been holding it in for a while now, and as I let it out it feels like I'm coming in the water. I clutch the rope with one hand and push the yellow cloud away from me. Then I grab the pool edge and lunge out of the water, both feet touching the ground at once. I head over to the bench, shaking off my arms and legs, and wipe my face with the towel. I'm tired, but I'm not spent yet. Coach Bandi calls me over, I guess to tell me off again.

Zoli-boy's still floating in the water. He doesn't want to get out. Ducky, who just finished, is over by the wall, gasping. Niki grips the rope, bawling; beside her, her sister is also sobbing, as are some other girls on the rope between lanes three and four. They can't take the heat. Coach Bandi signals Ducky over, but Ducky's chill. I would be too if my old man was the club's Gold Level main sponsor.

"In my office," Coach Bandi booms at us. "You got five minutes."

He starts down the stairs. Zoli-boy calls to me, asking if I want to walk to school together. You can still see the red welts on his cheeks.

"What the fuck does that old geezer want?" I ask Ducky in the locker room.

I'm wiping my feet. There's no time for a shower. I'm gonna stink of chlorine for the rest of the day, and my crotch is gonna itch like crazy.

"Dafuq do I care?"

"I'm sick of him being so mental all the time."

"Just don't give a shit," Ducky suggests, then stands and starts towards Coach Bandi's office.

I pack up my stuff fast and wrap my swim shorts in my towel. They won't dry by afternoon. I don't want to lag behind Ducky, but by the time I catch up with him, he's already standing in front of Coach's office. He bangs twice on the door with his fist, and the big man calls "C'mon in!" We step inside, and I adjust my pants. Coach Bandi's sitting at his desk, writing in a notebook, a cigarette hanging from his lips. He's the only one allowed to smoke inside the pool building. He looks at Ducky, then at me, then back at Ducky, the smoke gushing from his mouth.

"Shut the door," Coach Bandi says, and takes a drag of the cigarette.

He and my mother should have a contest to see who can pile an ashtray higher. He crushes the butt out, taking his time, then asks if we know why he called us in here. I decide to be honest and tell him I have no idea. I try to look innocent, but of course, I know that it doesn't make any difference what I do. If he wants to tell us off, he'll tell us off. Beads of cold sweat trickle down my back. Ducky plays cool and tells Coach Bandi he doesn't know why we're here, but he hopes everything's okay because we've got to get to school soon.

"Fine," nods Coach Bandi.

Then he tells us off, saying we'd better get our act together by next weekend because what we're doing is a "big, steaming pile of shit." Qualification races, rankings, Junior World Championships, and we gotta deliver results, otherwise our sponsors will stop throwing cash our way, and if the sponsors don't dish out, then we can "go fuck ourselves." When Coach Bandi pauses for breath, Ducky quickly promises that we'll whip ourselves into shape. I attempt enthusiasm, nodding vigorously, but then Coach Bandi focuses on me, so I have to say something. I swallow hard, but when I try to speak, all I manage is a choked gurgle. Coach Bandi tells us again to whip ourselves into shape, otherwise he'll rip our balls off. We say goodbye and leave the office. Zoli-boy's coming towards us from the locker room. The second he meets us, Ducky pushes him against the wall, full force. Zoli-boy hits his head on one of the hair dryers. Ducky totally ignores this and walks on. Zoli-boy pats his head, shouting *fuck* after him, then clambers to his feet.

"Let's go," I say, before he opens his mouth.

I don't want him to jump Ducky, and anyway, I wanna get going. We have a test in first period chemistry on some organic bullshit, and I promised myself mid-semester that I'd really learn it. I watched a series about a chem teacher with lung cancer who cooked enough meth to make himself filthy rich. Sure, he died in the end, but at least he didn't die broke.

Zoli-boy stops in the lobby at one of the tables and puts his backpack down. While he's adjusting the straps, the chicks come out of the locker room: Niki and her groupies, dressed in pink from head to toe. Zoli-boy grins at them, kinda like Heath Ledger in *The Dark Knight,* but they completely ignore us. Zoli-boy wants to go over to Niki, even though I told him not to give a shit about her. He's totally pussy-whipped. Though I guess I was pussy-whipped by the first girl who sucked me off too.

"You guys coming to school?" Zoli-boy asks.

He's totally zoned in on Niki, which is a bad tactic, for one, because Niki doesn't have the slightest interest in Zoli-boy, and for two, because the dumbass would have a nice hole for himself in no time if he made better choices. Take that new chick for example. She looks good, doesn't have a huge ego, and just smiles quietly, her big brown eyes glued to Zoli-boy. But of course that loser doesn't notice 'cause his boner for Niki is so hard. Finally, Niki stoops to our level and answers, telling us to go on ahead, they're still waiting for the others. Zoli-boy doesn't fucking catch on that they want to get rid of us and says we're in no hurry. I try to fix this fucked-up situation, groaning that I forgot to copy the math homework so I really have to go. Zoli-boy's already saying no sweat, I can go, he did the homework already, but I decide not to leave him here, because these chicks'll tear him to pieces. Finally, I manage to drag him away. As I lead him out, I nearly slam him against the automatic door. The girls giggle. They're always giggling. Giggling and whispering.

We trudge along in silence for a while on the promenade. Then I try to convince Zoli-boy how cute the new girl is, and that he should try her on for size, but the dumbass isn't biting.

"Did you bang Niki?" he interrupts me.

"Sure," I say. "Everybody's banged Niki," I add.

Well, it's the truth. Everyone really *has* banged Niki. Everybody in the swim association for sure, and the water-polo team too—at least the juniors definitely have, and of course the juniors' all-star team too, but everybody bangs everybody else there anyway.

Zoli-boy's face reddens.

"What?" I ask.

"Is it really embarrassing?" he asks.

"What is?"

"That I haven't..."

I keep my mouth shut.

"Don't tell anybody, okay?"

I nod, though actually I couldn't care less who he hasn't plowed yet.

"Thanks," he says, relieved.

We're already on the overpass when I hear footsteps behind me. I move aside.

"Was it true what you said about the math homework?" Zoli-boy says.

I don't get why he's so hung up about this. Who the fuck gives a shit about the math homework? As I turn toward Zoli-boy, someone starts to pass us from the left.

"Did you bang Viki at least?" I ask, which launches Zoli-boy into a fit of winks, until he starts laughing like an awkward hyena.

"What?" I ask, and he nods towards something behind me.

When I turn, I see a woman in glasses staring into my face.

"Oh, hello, ma'am," I greet her.

She teaches biology at our school. I can't remember her name though. She blushes, then hurries away. Someone mentioned recently that Lázár, the math teacher, is pounding her, but I think Lázár's a fudge-packer for sure. I stare at her ass. She could definitely star in a MILF porno, glasses and all. The things she must know about the human body! I kneel down and tie my shoe. Let's give her a little head start. Zoli-boy stares, his face as red as beets. Sometimes I get really fed up with Zoli-boy's hissy fits. If he wants to bone a chick, he should do it. Why's he gotta make such a big deal about it? As I stand up, a Red Riding Hood, one of those regional trains, scoots into the station, crammed full of moron peasants from the farmlands.

"Did you read it?" Zoli-boy asks.

"Read what?"

"The paper."

"No," I lie, even though I know what he's talking about.

"Pretty fucked up, don't you think?"

"What?" I ask.

"Well, Ducky."

"Because…?"

"What if they catch him?"

"I don't know."

"Will he get locked up?"

"I don't know," I answer. "But I think you should get off his back."

"Okay, I'll get off it," Zoli-boy nods.

"I'm fuckin' serious," I continue, 'cause I can see that he didn't really get it. "Don't fuck with Ducky."

"I didn't fuck with him," he says, offended.

"I'm not stupid, dude. The two of you are fucking with each other all the time."

"He won't lay off me," he says.

"Why?"

"I don't know."

"Then steer clear of him," I advise wisely. "And don't get all worked up. If he sees you don't care, he'll get bored of picking on you."

Zoli-boy falls silent. I guess he's obsessing about the bullshit I just told him. Never mind what he does. If he fucks with Ducky, he'll always come out on bottom. Ducky might even beat him up.

We're walking down the overpass steps when Zoli-boy pipes up again.

"What should I do?" Zoli-boy asks.

"Probably nothing," I suggest.

We walk a few metres quietly.

"I wanna bone Niki."

"You should be more ambitious."

"What do you mean by that?"

"Nothing," I say. "You should hit on somebody else instead."

"But I wanna bone Niki."

"Niki's a fuckin' black hole."

"I know," Zoli-boy nods. "Still."

I don't know what to say to that. Some people are beyond help. Whatever. He'll come to his senses when Lázár hands back our math tests. We're already walking along the main street. They built another fountain so the vandals would have something to dump laundry detergent in. The church bells ring. We won't make it by eight. I don't give a shit. I always fall asleep during math anyway.

PEARSON LLOYD

I had a dream about Sasha and Jenna, and then Stoya joined in too, I think. One of them had a hairy cooch. We were going at it on this huge canopy bed when a black Doberman about the size of a pony came barging in. It stopped in front of the bed, growling and barking, but you could only tell that from the way it was moving its head, 'cause otherwise everything was totally on mute. I pretended not to notice it, but then I started freaking out that it would bite my ass, so I tried to get away. I jumped out the window into the dark and fell into a pool full of tar, but I still couldn't shake that fucking dog. Plus, no matter how hard I thrashed, I couldn't make it out of the pool. I was scared shitless, like hardcore, and when I was out of air, I jolted awake. My sheets were soaking wet and I was gasping like I'd just run a marathon. I kicked off my blankets, blinked for a couple seconds in the dark, then turned on the light. I couldn't fall back asleep. I flipped through channels until dawn. I watched a bondage porn flick, a Chuck Norris thriller, and a documentary about Churchill.

I got a failing grade in math yesterday. The third one this semester. We were going over how to calculate the volumes of spheres, which of course made me think of Ducky's mom's gigantic tits, so I couldn't memorize anything he said. And of course, that dickwad Lázár saw I was spaced out, so he called on me to work out a problem. I went up to the board hella chill 'cause I had no chance anyway, thinking we'd get it over with quickly, but the bastard fucked with me for about ten minutes before he slapped a big fat F in the grade book. If I had to choose which of my friends' mothers to bang, it would definitely be Ducky's mom. She got her jugs pumped full of silicone and now they're bigger than the globe in geography class. She even got cocksucking lips to match. I'm not into MILFs, but you gotta admit, she's the best mami I know in the category.

I don't look at the clock. I know what time it is. I pull the blanket over my head. My mom'll be in to wake me any minute. I clamber out of bed, get dressed, and unpack my backpack. I don't care about my class schedule. I toss in the leftover weed, half a pack of King Size cigarette paper, and lay a few textbooks on top to hide them.

Like hell I'm going to school today.

I stand at the edge of the pool. The razor-sharp floodlights slash the water's reflection. The shadows of the waves are outlined on the white tiles at the bottom of the pool. Like a network of neurons. Computer graphics. The echoing pool area is an illuminated cave of stalactites. Blurred sounds. Splashing. Coach's whistle. Shouting. I pull on my silicone swim cap. It slides on easy. Mom didn't forget to baby powder it. I collect saliva in my mouth and spit into the goggles. The dehumidifying foil is worth jack shit. I suck off my cold saliva and spit on the starting block. I spit in the goggles again, lick it off, suck it out, and spit into the overflow drain. I tie, untie, then tie my swimsuit again. Procrastinating. I adjust my dick. I squat down, stick my foot in the water, then splash myself and jump into the pool. Everything goes quiet except for the cold, bubbling sound. There's a bunch of us in the water, yet it feels like I'm alone.

Warm-up is a 400-metre round of freestyle. Then we do a 10x200-metre medley. Two minutes and forty seconds for each round. I position myself behind Ducky, tailgating. He pulls me along. If you manage to gauge the distance and rhythm right, it's like being towed along by a ski lift. At the last turn, I push away from the wall so that I can see the distance between us. I've saved my strength, and I can easily overtake him at the end. I slow down for the last few metres, but make sure he doesn't get ahead of me. By the time he arrives, I take a few deep breaths, not gasping anymore, and stare blankly at Coach Bandi, who's holding a stopwatch, shouting times. I want Ducky to see me. I want the break between laps to end quick. But as I get moving again, I know the break wasn't long enough.

Coach Bandi blows his whistle. I repeat the game on the next 200 metres. Ducky's getting tired, which hypes me up even more. I can feel how easy it is to beat him. We end up in a spiral. He gets frustrated because he can't keep up the tempo and I get energized watching him tense up. But never underestimate Ducky. Not anybody else, either, but especially not Ducky. Even if he's in a losing position, he can launch his auxiliary rocket engine if he snaps. We smash against the wall. I only gave him a couple tenths of a second advantage this time. I've still got reserves, but I'm getting tired too. 3x200 metres left to go. He almost catches up with me on the last round. We come crashing in almost simultaneously. Coach tells us equal time, but I know I smashed him by at least five-tenths of a second.

I hang onto the rope. It cuts into my armpits, but I only feel it if I actually pay attention to it. Sometimes the sharp pain of the plastic jutting into muscle feels good. It jerks me back into reality. It doesn't let me slump into that sticky exhaustion you feel after pushing yourself through a hard round. I take off my goggles. Ducky clutches the edge of the pool, looking blasé. There's no use trying to pretend the swim was easy. I know he's run himself ragged. The colour of his face gives him away. I float while holding onto the rope and act like I didn't even notice that we swam together. I piss in the water. I was expecting practice to be more laid-back, 'cause the junior nationals are right around the corner. Coach probably knows what he wants. He's the one with the qualifications, after all. The chicks finish too. They haven't even stopped for real yet and Coach is already giving them hell. They get all offended and whine about something, I can't hear what, but I couldn't care less. They float slowly over to the ladder, climb out of the pool, and sit down on the bench, making faces. Zoli-boy goes over to them. I climb out of the water and jump around on one foot by the side of the pool. Right foot first, then left foot, to shake the water out of my ears. I wonder how the Paralympians do it. I mean the ones without legs. I'll bet they get ear infections a lot more often than we do. I head over to the bench. Zoli-boy is still trying to hit on Niki, but she's ignoring him. That dumbass. Giving him advice is like talking to a wall.

Ducky hasn't gotten out of the pool. He pushes his goggles up over his forehead, spits, and sloshes the big, green glob of phlegm towards the gutter, then climbs out and heads towards the bench. When he arrives, he whispers something into the new girl's ear that makes her giggle furiously. If Ducky's spewing jokes, there's at least one chick nearby who's game. The new chick recently transferred from another club. She's hoping to fit in, I guess, that's why she's trying so hard. Ducky sits down beside her and starts coming on to her. I can see that Niki wants to join them but there's no more space because Viki's sitting on Ducky's other side. Ducky leans over to the new girl and whispers something in her ear. An icy frown replaces her smile and she pulls away a little. Ducky turns to Viki and starts stroking her thigh. Zoli-boy's staring at Niki, who's pouting and getting more annoyed by the second, watching what Ducky and her little sister are up to. Ducky knows this perfectly well, too. His hand slides further up Viki's leg. Then he reaches under her bathing suit and starts to finger her. The thing that makes Niki lose her shit the most is when Ducky's getting it on with Viki. Like now. She can only stand it for about a minute. She jumps up from the bench and heads for the locker room. Ducky pretends not to notice, his hand moving in an even rhythm, and while he's whispering something to Viki, he catches Zoli-boy's eye and winks at him, making the dumbass pop up and head downstairs to the locker room too. Now it's only Ducky, Viki, the new chick, and me left on the bench. The new chick's got a streamlined figure. They usually ban big-chested girls from competitive sports. There's too much resistance. She's got a pretty cute face. Suddenly, I can't figure out which porn star she reminds me of. I look at her feet. A light pink drop of water slides down her calf.

"Did you cut yourself?" I ask.

"Huh?"

She looks at me, all weirded out. Her tone is confident, but I know she's about to break down.

"Did you cut yourself?" I repeat.

She doesn't understand. I point to her leg. She looks down. A drop of blood drips from the bench onto the tiles. She finally gets it. She jumps up and smudges the blood with her towel. The lifeguard moseys past us along the edge of the pool. His flip-flops slap against the tile in the same rhythm that Ducky fingers Viki.

"Plug yourself up next time," Ducky grins.

Viki's chest heaves, her face flushed, eyes closed. Her legs shake.

"Asshole!" the new chick says, then wraps the towel around her waist and rushes off towards the locker room. Ducky and I glance at each other. He signals for me to get lost. I growl at him to blow me, then go down to the showers and stand under the hot spray. I take off my swimsuit. I'm alone, but I don't jerk off. Then as I'm standing under the shower with the hot water gushing down on me, I think of the new chick's bloody pussy. I turn towards the wall and run cold water onto my dick. I don't wanna scald it. After about two minutes, I turn the tap off and towel down. There's only a few people left hanging around in the lobby. Everyone's fucked off to school. A few water polo faggots snort and laugh on the other side of the locker row. I only catch a few words: *with my elbow… I almost fucking drowned… I pulled the little dipshit down… cocksucking judge… I punched him in the face.*

Buoy walks towards me in the hall in his underpants, a ripped t-shirt, and worn out flip-flops. He's holding a wrinkled comic. He's totally obsessed with manga.

"You going to school?"

"Nah," I say. "We're going over to Ducky's."

"Wait for me, willya?"

"Okay," I say, as Buoy schleps into the bathroom.

Ducky always tells Buoy if we skip school. Buoy can get us doctor's notes when we're absent. Ducky gives Buoy drugs half price as payback. His uncle's a doctor, like his father, but they've got some hard feelings between them. And I guess Buoy's uncle is like, the less his nephew goes to school, the dumber he'll be. The rest of us profit on the deal 'cause Buoy can get so many doctor's notes we barely have the chance to skip enough days to use them up. Nobody at school cares where we are, as long as we're officially excused. This semester we've been at cancer screenings five times, but our homeroom teacher probably wouldn't notice even if the slip said we were at a gynaecology exam. The point is to keep friendly with Buoy, otherwise he'll jack up the prices.

Ducky turns the corner at the end of the hall. As he passes the bathroom, he switches off the light. Buoy groans heavily and roars.

"Turn the… fucking… lights… back on!"

Ducky walks on. I hear the shower start and Ducky singing. He's got a good voice. He even got into chorus. Certainly plenty of chicks to bone there.

Half an hour later, we're standing in the lobby waiting for Ducky. Grumpy old people wander around giving us dirty looks, but we don't give a shit. I never want to get old and bitter. Who knows, maybe all they need is a good fuck.

"Viki?" Buoy asks.

"What about her?" I return the ask.

"She coming?" Buoy asks.

"You want her to?" I ask back.

"We should talk her into it," Buoy says, his eyes gleaming.

"Talk to Ducky about it," I suggest.

"He needs the doctor's note," Buoy says thoughtfully.

"Then he won't mess with you."

"You think he'll let us bang her?" he asks.

"If she was yours, would you?" I ask.

Buoy thinks about this and doesn't say anything. There's only the sound of the cash register clanking in the background.

"I rest my case," I say.

Niki and two friends of hers approach from the locker room wearing identical pink tops. Niki fiddles with the wire of her pink earbuds. The other two girls are texting. Their phones are also pink. Even the look in their eyes is pink. When they notice us, Niki pretends to be surprised. They walk over to us. I mean, it's not like there's any other way to get out of the place.

"I thought you guys already left," she says.

The other two girls quietly caress their phones. They even painted their nails pink. One of them chews gum. She blows a bubble. It bursts. She pulls the pink gum back into her mouth with her tongue.

"Nope, we're still here," I say, but nobody laughs.

"We're not going to school," Buoy says.

Letting him talk was a mistake.

"What're you gonna do?" Niki asks.

I'm about to start bullshitting so she'll let down her guard, but Buoy beats me to it.

"We're gonna party a little at Ducky's," he blurts out.

"That's cool," Niki says, and looks at me.

She's mad and doesn't understand why I didn't tell her. She's always gotta know about stuff like that. Wants to look well informed in front of her squad.

"C'mon, we'll chill," Buoy winks.

"Okay," the girls answer in chorus.

"Where's Ducky?" Niki asks.

"He's coming in a minute," I say.

"Sweet," Niki says, and sits down.

I'm not happy she's coming.

"Can you get us a doctor's note?" Niki asks.

"We'll figure it out," Buoy grins.

Ducky arrives in five minutes. He looks over the crew and doesn't say anything.

"Niki's coming too, okay?" Buoy pipes up. "And the chicks," he adds.

Ducky says nothing. He just heads towards the exit and we follow.

"C'mon," Buoy says to the chicks.

"Did Viki leave already?" I ask.

Niki turns to me in alarm and says:

"She's got a history test."

A second later Viki pops out of the locker room and says, "Let's go."

We start off on foot, but Ducky gets bored fast and calls a cab. He cuts a deal with the cabbie to let five of us ride. He doesn't give a shit that, counting Niki's two pink sidekicks, there's exactly seven of us. We managed to shake off Zoli-boy. I don't really mind. He can be really annoying these days, what with him and Ducky at each other's throats all the time. The chicks get all bitchy, but Ducky tells them to shut it. They know where he lives, they can find their way if they want. They get all offended of course and storm off without saying goodbye. Ducky sits grinning in the front seat, while the four of us squeeze in on the back seat. Viki takes one for the team and sits in my lap, so I seize the chance and finger her. Buoy tries his luck with Niki, but she's not biting 'cause she's with Team Ducky. The cabbie's staring at Viki and me getting it on, and he almost sails through a red light, then forgets to yield at an intersection. Ten minutes later we park in front of the gate, so I gotta finish up the puppet show even though Viki hasn't come yet, I don't think. We all pitch in, pay, and get out.

Ducky and his fam live in a huge, bulky three-storey mansion up on the hill right beside a nature reserve. Some trendy architect from Budapest designed it, but I think it looks totally like a collapsed Imperial Walker. They had to chop down a couple acres of ancient cedars for the place to fit comfortably and to make sure the trees wouldn't obstruct the 360° panorama. The local hiking society made a small fuss, but Ducky's old man arranged for their permit to be revoked, so that shut them up pretty fast. The garage is the size of an airplane hangar, and the first storey sun terrace is as big as a tennis court. There's a four-lane, 25-metre pool in the garden. The ground floor's got a gym, another pool, a hot tub, a sauna, an infra-sauna, a salt cabin, a cryosauna, and four turbo tanning beds. One time, some hip-hop group wanted to use the place to shoot a video. Poor bastards walked up here from the hood but the security guards must've told them to fuck off. It's no wonder Ducky's old man didn't let those baboons in. The lion's-head knocker on the front door is worth more than the digs those losers crawled out from.

We trudge up the walkway from the gate to the house. No need to shit yourself about guard dogs. Ducky opens the door with a chip card and we burst into the foyer behind him. His mom's standing in the kitchen. Kleó, the Persian cat, is on the counter beside her, lapping milk from a bowl, but when it notices us, it jumps down onto the marble floor and darts behind the wine-coloured leather couch. A Havanese stands in front of the kitchen counter yapping sharply, spit flying from its mouth. Doesn't like guests. Ducky's family hasn't had proper dogs ever since their two Argentine mastiffs, Castor and Pollux, tore the dog trainer to shreds. Dude was in the hospital for a month, even though he was wearing protective gear. They should have put those beasts down, but Ducky's father rigged it so they were only offed on paper. He didn't want to lose out on his investment. Pedigreed killing machines like that cost a pretty penny. Ducky said that some hairy Serbian dude who organizes dogfights bought the mastiffs and got filthy rich off them.

Ducky's mom isn't fazed by half the school popping in during class hours. She doesn't ask questions. Maybe she doesn't even know that it's a weekday. She downs a suspiciously pale glass of OJ and smiles.

"Hello, ma'am," we say in chorus.

Jesus fuck, she's got herself some really huge tits. I can't take my eyes off them. I'm completely mesmerised for a couple of seconds, and when I look up, I see Ducky's mom watching me. She's not mad and just smiles at me, looking like she's baked. That's when I notice that the others have already cut out. They got into the elevator and are headed up to the second storey. I'm all alone with the MILF.

"How 'bout you, Gergő?" she asks, when it dawns on her that I've forgotten to move along. I don't tell her that's not my name. We just stand there in silence for a couple seconds, and when Ducky's mom gets that I'm probably not gonna answer, she continues, "Aren't you going upstairs too?"

"Sure, ma'am," I grin, trying to suck up to her.

"Don't you dare call me ma'am again or I'll get real mad."

She's flirting with me. She must be really smashed already, even though it's barely nine.

"I'm sorry," I say with a remorseful look.

"How's your mother?" she asks.

What's this got to do with anything? I don't ask about *her* mother, but I answer politely all the same. Anyway, maybe it's not even *my* mom she's asking about.

"Fine, thank you," I answer.

"It's been a while since I've seen her."

"She doesn't leave the house much."

"I understand," Ducky's mom nods, but there's no way she understands. "Please give her my regards."

"Okay," I nod, and then continue staring like an idiot, like someone still waiting for something. The size of those hooters, shit, man. I look up. Ducky's mom is staring fixedly into my eyes. It's not threatening, but more like she's racking her brain, thinking about what to do. Finally, she says with a smile, "Go on now, get upstairs and play."

"They can wait," I shrug confidently, and my eyes slide back down to her breasts.

Sure, I like playing Xbox, but I'd rather press those nipples than the controller.

"We'll talk some more next time," Ducky's mom says with a significant overtone, and all I can think of is how I'd like to tie her to the bed, or to something else.

"Okay," I say, and Ducky's mom spreads her lips, slathered with lipstick, into a smile, lowering her gaze. She's definitely eyeballing my prick. I start sweating. If she stares like that for long, I'm gonna get a boner. "Bye, *ma'am,*" I say deliberately. Maybe she'll get the drift, but I can tell this isn't the time, so I go up to the second storey instead to find the others.

I stand awkwardly at the top of the stairs for a minute, 'cause suddenly I'm not sure where Ducky's room is, but then I hear Buoy's snort and I start down the hall. As I step in through the door, Ducky's firing up the hookah his folks got him last summer in Tunisia, and pressing the phone to his shoulder as he yaps on about something. The room's about the size of our whole pad, but since there's no walls inside, it seems much bigger.

I sit on the couch and put my feet up on the table, but Ducky snaps at me to stop being such a douche and take off my shoes. I don't feel like getting all worked up about shit like that, so I throw them off and start flipping through one of the furniture catalogues. I try to identify the stuff in the room. I put my feet up on a *simple, yet refined Pearson Lloyd "Edge" coffee table with a sunken table top.* For only 1500 euros. This Pearson guy really must know something. No wonder Ducky's so touchy about this shitty table. I turn the page. Here's a "Leitmotif" pendant chandelier. Only 650 smackeroos. Why not get two while we're at it? *The Pendant Chandelier will liven up your home or serve as the perfect style accessory. Its colour and form make it the central feature of any room.* What utter bullshit. If you put it in the middle, what else could the central feature be? Of course, a single lamp isn't enough in a room this big. I noticed they tacked up a "Leitmotif Bebop" spotlight too. Maybe it'll help drive out the incredible gloom that fills this house. Actually, the one they've got here is the version for cheapskates. They basically got it for free at 300 euros a pop. *The "Leitmotif" brand's "Bebop" light is a modern* as fuck, *unique, authentic piece of design. With its unique form and colour, it is bound to be the central feature of any home or office.* Well fuck me, another central feature. I also find the five-person "Woody Maxi" sofa that we're resting our asses on. The starting price is five grand. Though I can't feel it, the catalogue says that *the great care in the choice of materials and the precision of detailed craftsmanship guarantees that each product is of superb quality for your complete comfort: from the structure to the cushioning, the seating surface and the armrest design, all the way down to the fabrics that give the sofa its true shine.* Then I find out more important details, like that the *sofa's frame is made from pine, overlaid with Technoform,* and that the *remaining components are fashioned from cellulose-reinforced wood,* while *the proper support for the backrest is maintained by propylene and latex straps,* which of course makes me think of S&M porn. *The backrest cushioning and the seating surface are constructed from non-warping foam rubber,* and I'm thinking, yeah, that's why it's so lit to get high and chill on this couch. Ducky's parents also immediately ordered five ottomans, heightening the sofa's comfort factor, but which mostly remind me of five, rock-hard, women's asses. Ducky left that catalogue out on the table for a reason. He might as well have left the price tag on the furniture. The only thing I couldn't find was the glass cabinet where he keeps his medals and trophies. They could easily have furnished the entire Museum of Natural History for what that thing cost. These furniture-store clowns really know how to lay on the bullshit, but I guess anyone gullible enough to take the bait deserves to be ripped off.

Buoy messes with the TV. Viki's lounging on a deckchair out on the terrace under two enormous palm trees and petting her phone. The terrace is a scene right out of California. Even the plants are right on the money. Niki's nowhere to be found. I guess she went to the bathroom or lagged behind and then got lost too.

Ducky presses his phone to his ear, staring into space, and then says:

"Yeah, that'd be sweet, nigga." Someone yaps something on the other end. Ducky listens for a while, then answers, "Dafuq do I know, nigga? Bring a kilo." He's quiet again. "That's too much," he says. "Whatever, just move your ass.

We're at my place." He lets go of his phone and it slides between the couch cushions. He pulls out a storm-proof lighter from the bottom of the coffee table and starts firing up the coals. It's still early, not a problem if we get baked, we'll come out of it by the time afternoon practice rolls around, and if not, we'll just have to train high. If that happens, you just gotta make sure you don't freak out and think you'll drown, 'cause then you really *can* drown. I shuffle over to the cocktail cabinet and pour myself a glass of OJ. Meanwhile, Buoy manages to turn the stereo on. Ducky left it set to the radio function turned up full blast, so when Buoy finds the ON switch, Rihanna starts screeching *Russian Roulette,* I think. The chick's annoying as fuck but I'd tap her ass all the same. Too bad she's into black dudes with huge schlongs. When she starts howling at full volume, I spill my orange juice, and Ducky is so startled he knocks over the bong. We quickly stomp out the burning bits of coal, but the carpet gets scorched in some places all the same. I don't quite understand what Ducky's yelling 'cause Buoy can't seem to turn the fucking volume down, no matter how he waves the remote around. Just to be on the safe side, Ducky pours the leftover water from the hookah's vase onto the carpet. A thin wisp of smoke rises up from the thick, green fluff. Buoy yanks the stereo's cord out from the wall socket.

Ducky stares at the carpet. His voice trembles with exasperation.

"Goddamnit, fucking hell."

For a while everyone lays low, not wanting to get Ducky even more wound up, or maybe they're getting bored of his non-stop drama-queen show.

"Shit, Buoy, I almost shat myself," I say, breaking the silence.

"You should've turned the fucking volume down, for fuck's sake!" Ducky shouts.

"Yeah, *before* you turn the stereo off, motherfucker," Buoy retorts.

Ducky keeps on swearing, then asks Buoy to help him pull one of the leather armchairs over the burned spot on the carpet. He refills the hookah with mineral water—I guess he doesn't feel like making the trip to the bathroom—and stuffs the pipe with grass.

"Just chill, all of you, okay?" he looks at us pointedly. "I don't wanna burn the house down."

He starts to fire up the coals. The burbling sound of the pipe soothes me. I close my eyes, as if I were underwater. I like using a pipe. The smoke doesn't scratch my throat. We sit down next to him on the couch and wait for him to pass the hose. It's the third round and we're sunk down real low into the smooth, cool leather when there's a shriek and clatter of something breaking in the bathroom. I totally forgot Niki's here too. Ducky and I glance at each other, then he gets up and walks to the bathroom, to bang Niki, I assume, because he sure isn't sweeping up shards of glass. Buoy and I pass the hose between us quietly for a while, then he asks what we should watch. Ducky's got an incredible collection of European Championship, World Championship, and Olympic races. And porn. He's got the porn arranged into categories so he can easily find the film that best suits his mood. Sorted according to skin and hair colour, breast size, hentai, bukkake, animal, anal fisting, puking, piss and shit, Satan's nectar, preteen, teen, MILF, BDSM, DP, TP, A2M, and a few fake snuffs. Several hundred DVDs. You could watch non-stop for two weeks without repeating a single one. We set a group record during a long weekend in February when his parents took off to Rio de Janeiro. We told our folks we'd be at a three-day race, and we moved in with Ducky. We had films running for seventy-two hours straight, and still we only managed to see forty of the fifteen hundred. One dude who was with us stayed so stiff that even though we dumped a wheelbarrow's worth of crushed ice on it, we still had to take him to the ER. Buoy waits patiently, but when I don't answer him, he starts flipping through the menu. He's at animal double anal fisting when Niki shrieks in the bathroom again, but as far as I can see, no one except me hears her. I get up and walk out onto the terrace to Viki. She's still under the palm trees, caressing her phone. As I close the door behind me, she looks up for a moment, then back at the phone.

"Texting?" I ask, but I know it sounds like some lame line Zoli-boy would use. I shouldn't hang out with him so much.

Viki drops the phone into her lap.

"Are you hella baked?" she asks.

"Not really," I say in a slushy tone.

I'm salivating as I look at Viki. Ducky added something extra to the weed, or just got the baggies mixed up. Most of the time I haven't got the slightest idea what we're smoking. As long as it gets us high, I don't give a rat's ass. We stare at each other hard. Nothing happens. I imagine her in different clothes, without clothes, with my dick in her mouth, then suddenly I'm freaking out. What if she can see what I'm thinking? It's a little windy, but otherwise everything's calm. Still, I don't dare move closer to Viki. I freeze up, and my palms start sweating. I raise my eyes. Viki's naked, or that's what I'm seeing anyway. I stare at her breasts, and then she gets up from the deckchair and starts towards me, but as my eyes slide from her breasts to her face, I recoil. It's Buoy's head grinning at me on Viki's perfect body.

"Fuck," I grunt, and then I probably ask something else, because when I come to my senses, Viki says:

"No, we're not dating."

I don't know what to say to that.

"Crêpes?" I ask.

She raises her eyebrows.

"Pizza?"

"I hate pizza," she says.

"Kebab? Lahmachun? Adana?"

"I don't like Turkish food."

"Hamburgers?"

"Stop it already."

"What?"

"With the foods."

"Okay," I nod, and shut up.

I could tear into a Texas burger or two right now. We don't say anything for a while, until Viki breaks the silence.

"I don't want to go out with you."

"No one would know," I coax.

"I don't want to date anyone," she says.

I smell honey and almonds. Viki's body wash. Her pussy must taste like almonds. I'm salivating again. Viki's talking to me. I'm not paying attention, can't hear what she's saying. I look at her. She smiles all sassy. Or maybe that's just her default smile. She walks over to the terrace railing. She steps up onto it and looks out over the city. It was built on seven hills, like Rome. I move towards her, but it takes hours till I reach her. As if the soles of my feet were smeared with glue. Finally, I stop beside her. I watch the clouds. One of them looks like a big asshole, and there's two hairy cunts too. Airbuses, contrails. It'd be great to be on one of those planes, never mind where it's going. There's a park in the distance named after a dead mayor, and a boulevard lined with trees named after a different dead mayor. From up here, the city seems like it's got no people living in it. You can even see the pool from the terrace. You can see everything from this terrace. I think of the opening scene from *Apocalypse Now,* when the Americans dump napalm on the jungle. The wind tousles Viki's hair. I turn towards the glass door to check if the others can see us. Buoy's sitting on the carpet, running his hand along the fuzz and staring at the wall. Or actually, the wall with the TV on it. He puckers his lips, his eyes bulging. Viki steps down onto the terrace floor and leans onto the railing. I haven't uttered a sound in a hundred years. I have no words.

"You don't wanna fuck, either?" I ask.

I'm hoarse. Viki doesn't say anything. She's standing at the railing as if she were grafted to it. She messes with her phone. The warm wind drifts in between the palm tree's sharp leaves.

"You wanna come in?" I ask, but Viki doesn't answer.

I start towards the terrace door, but stop short after a few paces and turn back. A strange tingle runs along my spine. Drops of sweat trickle down my back. I swallow hard. Maybe Viki knows everything. I freak out that she knows everything and wants to turn us in. I don't wanna rot in prison. I don't want them to push me down onto a toilet-brush handle. I'm afraid to leave Viki alone. I walk back and over to the railing.

"You wanna come in?" I ask.

"In a minute," Viki says, but I can tell she's annoyed.

"I'm going inside," I say.

"I'd like to make a phone call."

“Okay,” and now I really don’t want to leave her unattended.

“I’d like to talk in *private.*” She’s getting more annoyed by the second.

“But you’ll come in after, right? It’s pretty chilly out.”

Viki looks at me and raises her eyebrows.

“Are you running a fever?” she asks.

I pat my forehead.

“I don’t know,” I say.

Viki steps away from the railing, stops beside me, and places her hand on my forehead. My dick starts to tingle.

“You don’t have a fever,” she says.

I breathe in her scent. If she doesn’t get us busted, I’ll ask her one more time if she wants to fuck.

“Cool,” I say, but I still don’t leave.

I stare at Viki. She stares at me. Then she turns away and continues messing with her phone. I step slowly towards the door. Maybe I can eavesdrop and hear who she’s talking to. I squat down to tie my shoelaces. I’m not wearing shoes. I squat for a little while. A pigeon lands on the railing at the same moment Viki speaks into the phone. That damn bird is flapping so loud I can’t hear a thing. I’m gonna execute that pigeon. Meanwhile, I get to the terrace door, stop, and look inside. I see myself in the glass, and Buoy inside, as he stares, entranced, at Ducky’s TV, which is the size of a ping-pong table.

I found it in a different catalogue. LG 84LM960V CINEMA SCREEN 3D SMART LED. They give you seven pairs of 3D glasses to go with it, but there’s only four left. We sat on the others and they broke. *79.4kg, with stand. Screen diagonal: 213cm.* It cost almost 20,000 euros, not counting the extras. Buoy swings the Magic Remote Voice back and forth. It’s a movement-sensor remote control with voice recognition. *The movement-sensor control allows for menu selection by simple point-and-click.* At this very moment, Buoy is *carrying out complex commands simply and quickly* while searching the sub-folders of Ducky's porn collection. For example: switching films by waving his hand. But only Ducky can use the voice control, and he's mostly yelling about how, for twenty grand, this piece of shit should follow commands the first time he says them. I slide the door open and glance back at Viki. I don't remember what I was freaking about before. There's just this vague memory of flipping out. I step into the room. I stare at the TV. I can't figure out how many people are acting in the scene and what exactly they're doing, but then I finally get that the dude in the costume is really a Doberman. The dog yips sharply because it isn't getting the white thing that looks like an artificial bone, but which, it turns out in the next scene, is actually a gigantic dildo. I tell Buoy to turn the volume down, then sit down on the couch and close my eyes. A second later, the doorbell rings. It's a Mozart, Vivaldi, or Bach tune. This is the first time I've heard classical music stoned. My old man really used to dig those retro tunes. He was always setting his ringtone to stuff like that. Weird sounds filter out of the bathroom, like someone neighing or grunting, and then a couple of seconds later Ducky storms out wearing only a t-shirt. He's got a boner.

"Hey!" I shout at him, which makes him stop short and turn around.

"What?"

I gesture that he's got no underwear on. He looks down at his dick, then before I can tell him that the head of his cock is bloody, he cuts across the room without a word and thumps down the stairs. The door to the bathroom is open a crack. I see Niki in the mirror. Her lipstick's smeared, her mascara's running. She brushes her short brown hair moodily. She seems sad, though maybe she's just being snotty. When she notices me staring, she pushes the bathroom door closed with her foot.

The sound of a familiar voice filters in from the hallway, and a second later Mishy, Ducky's cousin, steps into the room. He's a Rastaman in khaki Bermudas, a Che Guevara t-shirt, and shades. The only thing missing is "I Sell Drugs" tattooed on his forehead. There's three letters under the Comandante's image: MAO. He's got a bunch of t-shirts like that. Lenin's face with CASTRO written underneath. HITLER and STALIN. KIM JONG-IL and KIM JONG-UN. KIM JONG-UN and DENNIS RODMAN.

"It was the best fuck I ever had on coke," Mishy explains, then, after a pause for suspense, he continues, "I told the chick I'd pay her in services rendered; that I'd fuck her if she blows me."

He punches Ducky in the shoulder, laughing like a hyena, while his cousin stares at him blankly. Meanwhile, Buoy's entire nervous system is glued to the TV. He's even drooling as the trashy porn chick bobs her mouth on the Doberman's sharp, pink rod. I can't stand it anymore. I lean back on the couch holding the hookah's hose. As I turn my head to the side, Niki stares out from the bathroom.

"That one yours, bro?" Mishy asks Ducky while grinning like crazy at Niki.

"Yeah," Ducky answers.

"I'll do her later, okay?"

"Do her," Ducky nods.

Niki slams the door. Mishy wrinkles his forehead and looks at his cousin.

"Where's the shit, nigga?" Ducky asks.

"Take it easy, Ducky," Mishy says coolly. "What's the big rush? We got time, ain't we? Fuckin' A!"

"Sure we got time, just gimme the shit, motherfucker," Ducky urges.

"I was thinking we'd smoke a spliff first, then we can get down to business."

"Well I was thinking you hand over the goods, I pay, and then you haul your ass out."

"Sure, bro, sure." It's pretty hard to get Mishy revved up. He's Rastaman to the core. All he cares about is chicks and keeping the business lively. "Here's your shit," he says, reaching into his pocket and taking out a baggie.

"Cool."

"Lean back and relax, bro. Your Uncle Mishy's here to take care of all your needs."

"Maybe you wanna blow him too?" Buoy barks over his shoulder.

"I'm gonna kick that faggot's ass," Mishy grins.

"You ain't kicking nobody's ass, Rasta-fairy," Buoy says, chill as fuck. "Peace, man."

"Tell your little friend to show some respect," Mishy yaps, but his smile's not genuine anymore.

"Knock it off, Buoy," Ducky says, trying to dial down the tension.

Buoy yawns and turns back to the TV.

Mishy reaches into his pocket again, rummages around for a while, looking like he's gonna jerk off, but then he pulls out another baggie. Last year, he was just a small-time dealer, but then they busted a couple of the homies he sold with and the dude he bought from. Like when your commander goes down on the front. But moving a few rungs further up the ladder didn't make him any less of a dickhead. Ducky thinks it's bullshit, but lots of people still say it was Mishy who ratted out his friends. Well, I don't know. This one time, someone told me about his first deal. He was delivering stuff to a couple of cockfaced English dudes. They were working at the bus depot, fixing up rusty old water-transport tanks with some high-tech sand-blowing technique and getting their dicks hoovered every night by Ukrainian sluts at the truck stop. Back then, there were so many Ukrainian chicks doing business by Highway 8 that the limeys thought they were in Russia. One of Mishy's pals interpreted for the dudes and sent out the wire that they need some stuff. Mishy got hold of 2 Gs of dry weed, cut it with some black wormwood, grabbed the few tabs of E he had lying around, then borrowed his granny's junky old car so he wouldn't have to roll out to the depot on the bus. The English guys felt so sorry for him they even tipped him.

We sit around the table. Mishy's telling his stories, but somehow the mood is off. We're way too faded already. Viki comes in, Mishy gives her the once-over, as if he's never seen her before, then turns to Ducky and says:

"Can I do her, bro?"

"Later," Ducky nods.

"Thanks," Mishy says.

If there's such a thing as eye-fucking, that's what he's doing right now.

"C'mon," Ducky says, then stands and heads out.

His old man made him promise never to sleep in the same room as where he keeps his cash. I follow them, even though I can barely get up from the couch. Rooms open to the right and left from the hallway. Ducky steps inside one of them and tells us to wait for him outside. He'll call us when we can come in. I stare at the wall behind Mishy's head. I bet he thinks I'm looking at him. He even asks me what I'm staring at. I tell him it's that fucking bigass spider that's sliding down from the ceiling, which makes Mishy jump and thrash.

"Motherfucker!" he says when he spots it.

He slaps it dead with his palm and wipes it on the wall. Ducky tells us to come in. This must be a kind of study. There's a shoebox without a lid on the table. A couple of fifty-euro notes dangle out.

"How much?"

Mishy, like some waiter, starts to rattle off the items, then, after a bit of quick mental addition, he declares the grand total:

"That'll be one-eighty, for the homie hook-up."

"That's too much."

"It's the price."

"Still too much."

"That's still how much it costs."

"You get one-fifty."

"Okay." Mishy agrees right away.

Ducky doesn't notice that he agreed without protest. While he counts the cash, Mishy flaps the baggie. It's got the works: weed, pills, acid, blow.

"Well, what do you guys wanna sample?" he asks.

"This one!" Ducky grins, then takes the baggie from Mishy, removes a dirty-white pill, and pops it in his mouth.

"Here, nigga," he says, and presses one into my hand.

"What's this?" I ask.

"I don't know," Ducky says, then turns towards Mishy and asks, "What's this?"

"My own creation."

"That's bitchin', nigga," Ducky says. Then he turns towards me. "Fuck, man, swallow it already!"

You swallow it—my dick, that is—I think to myself, then take the pill from him and toss it in my mouth.

"Haul ass now," Ducky says, gesturing towards the door.

As we head out, he quickly puts the box away. I cough when I reach the door and spit the pill into my hand. OD-ing on Mishy's designer shit isn't how I wanna check out.

Ducky's the last one to leave the room. He closes the door and locks it, sticking the key in his pocket.

"I'm taking a whiz," I say, and start in the other direction.

I seem to recall that the bathroom is this way. I get lost in a matter of seconds. I don't know what else to do but peek behind every door. I can't find the bathroom, but I do find a bedroom where everything is red and black. The curtains, the canopy bed, the shiny silk bedspread, and the walls. I walk in. There's photos on the bedside table. Ducky grinning with his parents in front of the Eiffel Tower. At the Pyramids of Giza. Outside the Sydney Opera House. And of course on top of the Empire State Building. I walk around. I look in the closet. I spot a pair of latex pants, but as I grope them, I realize that they're just plain black leather pants. Then I see a whip, but when I take a closer look, it turns out to be just a leather belt. On one of the shelves I find a massive white vibrator, the same kind they used in the doggie porn. And a black one, too. I hear someone coming. I imagine Ducky's mom finding me, tying me to the bed, and punishing me. I hold my breath. I hear the sound of a vacuum. There's no way Ducky's mom is cleaning. I peek out. The maid pulls the appliance back and forth. I wait until she's hidden by the canopy curtain. I'm about to leave when she turns the vacuum off. She sits down on the bed and pulls open the night-table drawer. She takes something out and pockets it, then looks around, stands, and turns the vacuum back on. Somebody should call the cops. On the way back to Ducky's room, I find the bathroom. I knock. There's nobody inside. I go in and almost piss in the bidet, but I see the toilet at the last moment. Ducky's mom pops into my head. Lipstick spread thick on her lips, lying on the red canopy bed in latex, or in a red babydoll, whip in hand. I step over to the sink and splash cold water on my face, then go back to the others. Mishy's explaining something really loudly. You can hear it all the way out in the hall, and when I step in, I see he's flexing in the middle of the room with no shirt on, waving something around, but I can't see what it is because he's at the wrong angle, and panting as he says, "thrilling as fuck, nigga," which makes the others laugh really hard. Only Viki and Niki seem a bit pale. They sit pressed close to each other on the couch. Nobody notices me come back.

"This, motherfucker, is a 9mm Desert Eagle," Mishy explains. "Like in the movie *Bluff*," he adds.

I finally get that this retard's got a gun. At first, I think that if Viki decides to snitch at least we'll have something to kidnap the chicks with, and then we'll fuckin' barricade ourselves on the upper floor. There's drinks and grub enough to last three months, there's Wi-Fi, fuck everything else.

"In your dreams, pal," Buoy mumbles. "That's a water pistol," he adds, grinning, which launches Ducky into a fit of screaming laughter and knee-slapping. There's even tears in his eyes from the laughing. Mishy's not a black-belt Rasta yet, so he gets kinda annoyed. But, like, it's really fuckin' stupid to get him riled up while he's still got that piece.

"The boss gave it to me," Mishy insists, then goes off on some bullshit story about how Norris realized that you can take a hit of drugs, but you can also hit it big in cash, so he decided to tap into the drug business, but Mishy's boss told him to take a hike, so Norris threatened to murder him, his *fucking dealers* and his *motherfucking family,* and that's why they had to score these Glocks. That's how Mishy ends his story. If he's *not* bullshitting, then we're all pretty fucked. I don't know where we'll get our shit if they take him out. I walk over to the fridge, get a bottle of club soda, twist the cap off, and take a swig. It feels like I swallowed a hedgehog. I want to put the bottle down, but I can't let go of it. My brain starts whirling about polar bears and global warming. Ducky's voice brings me back to reality.

"And what're you gonna do if he attacks you? Spray your water gun in his face?"

"If you spray someone in the face with this, homeboy, your digs'll need a new paint job," Mishy retorts.

I try to join in the conversation. I try to say that "a layer of wallpaper would work much better," but my mind keeps whirling, and nobody can hear what I'm thinking.

"Yeah, the damp will make the paint peel," Buoy grunts.

It seems he didn't freak out too much about the situation. He's just sitting there, his hair a mess, stroking Viki's thigh.

Kleó, the family cat, strolls into the room. It mews softly. Must want some grub.

"Y'all can suck my dick!" Mishy's getting more revved up by the minute. "Let's go out to the woods!" he says. "I'll show you what it can do." And he pulls out the magazine, empties the bullets—a metallic clinking, like bells chiming—then pushes the piece into Ducky's hand. "Take it, motherfucker!"

"Okay, nigga, you convinced me." Ducky yields, then aims at Buoy. Buoy's game: he cringes and shields his face with his hands, begging for his life.

"Don't do this, man! Don't kill me, goddamnit!"

"Shut the fuck up, you prick! Gimme the cash or I'll redecorate the room with your brain!"

Ducky shouts at the top of his lungs, then roars with laughter. But just as suddenly as he started screeching, he stops again. He looks straight at Buoy and keeps pointing the gun at him. Buoy seems to have lost his sense of humour too.

"Stop pointing that fucking piece at me."

The smile fades from his face.

"What're you freaking out for? It's not loaded," Ducky reassures him.

"Yeah, don't shit yourself," Mishy adds. Now it's his turn to grin.

"Quit pointing it at me anyway," Buoy bitches.

"Admit it, you're scared shitless," Ducky says.

"Fuck, man, I'm scared shitless." Ducky lowers the gun, and Buoy goes on: "Give it here."

Ducky hands the gun to Buoy, and now it's Buoy pointing it at Ducky. Of course Ducky just keeps on grinning. But by now the chicks are getting really fucking pale. Neither's says anything for about five minutes. Niki's biting her nails, and Viki's clutching a glass full of red-coloured whatever.

"So, how does it feel, huh?" Buoy asks.

"It's scary as fuck," Ducky snorts. "Nobody's ever pointed an empty pistol at me."

Buoy leans closer and presses the muzzle of the gun to Ducky's temple. I want to tell them that there's a bullet left in the barrel, but my mouth is too dry. I take another swig of water. Then I stare at the ice in Viki's glass. The cubes swirl like in a slow-motion shot. Sometimes they dip under then resurface from the whirlpools. I don't dare take my eyes off them.

"How do you cock it?" Buoy asks.

"It's cocked," Mishy answers.

The cat starts meowing again. Buoy points the gun at it, and Kleó darts over to the girls and rubs against Viki's legs. It's pretty far from me, but I can hear it purring.

"Quit scaring my mom's cat," Ducky warms Buoy. Kleó seems to understand and starts meowing louder. "She doesn't know the gun's not loaded."

"Right," Buoy grins, and pulls the trigger.

I never thought a pistol could be so fucking loud. I think I've gone deaf. I'm sure my eardrum's busted. A spray of blood douses the room. Clumps of fur fly all over the place. Niki screams and Viki drops a glass full of strawberry juice onto the carpet.

"Holy fuckin' shit!" Buoy grunts palely.

"I told you it was the real thing," Mishy remarks, smugly.

"Goddamn fucking hell!" Ducky bellows. "It's bloody as fuck. My mom's gonna have a heart attack when she sees this." I can't decide if he's talking about the carpet or the cat. "We gotta get rid of it."

"Do you have stain remover?" Mishy asks.

"I'm talking about the cat, you dumbass." Ducky looks at him, annoyed.

"Let's put it on the cactus," Buoys pipes up, and gestures towards the enormous cactus standing in the corner. We all turn towards it simultaneously.

"Have you lost your fuckin' mind?" Ducky seems at a loss.

"Let's bury it in the garden," I suggest.

"I'll get a garbage bag," Ducky nods.

"And a broom," Buoy says. "And a dustpan."

"You're gonna clean it up," Ducky growls at him.

"I'm not the one who left the bullet in the barrel, asshole."

"I don't give a shit."

"You got a maid, don't ya?" Buoy persists.

"How much do you think I'd have to pay for her to clear away my mother's cat?"

Kleó starts meowing desperately. She tries to crawl, but she's missing her two front legs, and a chunk from her side. We look at each other.

"Fuckin' hell, it's still alive," Mishy says.

"I can hear it," Ducky says, and turns towards Buoy. "Give me the gun."

Buoy presses the pistol in his hand, then realizes what's going on and asks:

"What're you gonna do?"

Ducky doesn't say a word. He steps over to the cat writhing on the floor and bashes it on the head two or three times with the grip. The tiny skull cracks. Warm brain splatters on my leg. Buoy stands frozen. The smile fades from Mishy's face. Niki pukes on the Pearson Lloyd table. The blood drains from Viki's face and she reels off the couch.

After I manage to talk Ducky out of stuffing Kleó down the garbage disposal, it takes half an hour to dump the corpse. Ducky leaves the room and comes back a couple minutes later with a black garbage bag and a dustpan. He kicks the dead cat onto the shovel and tips it into the bag. He scoops the bits of brain and slivers of skull off the carpet and scrapes them from the leather upholstery with a spoon.

"Let's go," he says. "We'll bury it in the yard."

The girls don't wanna come. Mishy makes a phone call. He pretends to watch us. Finally, three of us go: me with Ducky and Buoy. I thought we were alone in the house, but in the living room we bump into Ducky's old lady and her personal trainer. He's a real stud, like he just walked off the pages of GQ. He's sitting in a sleeveless shirt and shorts on one of the bar stools with a newspaper and a glass of OJ in front of him on the counter. He's feeling right at home. He doesn't even look up when we come in. Even Ducky's surprised that his mom's home.

"Did you hear that big bang?" the MILF asks, but before Ducky can answer, I say:

"Buoy killed Mishy."

Ducky's mom's eyes open wide.

"FPS," Ducky explains.

"A video game with shooting," the personal trainer explains helpfully.

"Oh, right," Ducky's mother waves, as if she knows what we're talking about. "You shouldn't play those silly games so much," she adds.

"Sure, sure," Ducky waves her off.

Meanwhile, I'm freaking out about the cat coming back to life and starting to meow in the garbage bag.

"What do you want with the garbage?" Ducky's mom asks. "The maid will take care of it."

"Something rotted and it fucking stank up my room."

"Watch your language, son," his mother scolds. She's showing off for us.

"Aw, get off my back, Ma," Ducky says, and heads towards the hallway.

I almost get left behind, but Buoy finally takes my arm and pulls me along.

"Have you seen my little Kleó?" Ducky's mom calls after us. "She hasn't finished her breakfast yet."

Ducky doesn't answer. He just keeps walking, the black bag rustling in his hand. The force of his stride makes the dead cat accidentally slap against the hall cabinet. Mama's little Kleó definitely isn't finishing her yummy breakfast milk.

"Who was that dude? Your old lady's personal trainer?" I ask, as we walk among the pruned cedar bushes.

We're looking for a spot where the security cameras can't see us, so we can dump little Kleó in peace.

"That's my older brother, you retard," Ducky replies.

"I didn't even know you *had* a brother," Buoy remarks.

"He studies in America. He just dropped by for the weekend," Ducky explains. "He's a cocksucker," he adds.

We keep walking for a while, then Ducky stops and says: "This is fine," and drops the bag. "Buoy, the shovel."

"I didn't bring a fucking shovel. You didn't tell me we needed one," Buoy says defensively.

"What did you think, we'd dig a hole with our hands, like Mexicans?" Ducky rages at him.

"I don't even know where you guys keep it," Buoy replies, offended.

Finally, we decide that since it was Buoy who offed the cat, the least he can do is go back for the shovel. Ducky explains to him where the tool shed is. I'd bet hella money that Buoy will get lost.

Half an hour later, we're back on the Woody Maxi couch, and while I puff on the hookah, I'm wondering whether we managed to arrange the turf grass well enough, but I reassure myself: no one besides the gardener and a couple of moles are gonna notice if there's a little mound on the lawn. We pretty much cleaned up the room, too. We sip mineral water. Drops of sweat slide down my forehead. I pick the soil from under my nails and think how lucky we are not to have dug someone up when we buried that miserable cat. There's only a few spots in the garden that the security cameras can't see. And Ducky's pop gets into arguments pretty regularly with his business partners, who then disappear without a trace.

Ducky examines the carpet. He seems satisfied with the result. The carpet cleaner was effective. The chicks are still a little pale, but at least Niki hasn't bawled in the last five minutes. I'm thinking about where Zoli-boy could be and about asking Ducky why the two of them are fucking with each other all the time, but by the time I organize my thoughts, Mishy's started some shitty cat story, which I've heard from at least ten other people, in ten different versions. Easy for that dickhead to flap his tongue when he wasn't the one who had to bury Kleó. The story's about how this dude's cat dies. He buries it in the yard, but then the neighbour's dog climbs under the fence at night, digs up kitty, and takes it home. When the neighbour sees the shredded corpse in his garden, he freaks out, thinking it was his dog that chewed up the cat, so he quickly fixes the fur—washes it with dog shampoo, combs it out—and tosses it back over into his neighbour's yard. When the owner finds the cat with its fur all shiny, he's got no fucking clue what's going on. He turns the cat over in his hands for a while, but no matter how he looks at it, he's gotta admit: this really is his pet. Finally, he buries it again, but the next night the dog climbs under the fence again, digs up the carcass, and takes it home. Of course, when the dog's owner finds it, he panics. He bathes the cat, combs out its fur, and flings it back into his neighbour's yard. The following day, the two guys bump into each other on the street, start talking, and the cat owner tells the other dude how stunned he is 'cause his pet died and it's no use burying it. Every morning it lies there in the garden, squeaky clean. Only Mishy's laughing.

"I'll fire up the sauna," Ducky says, and gets up from the couch.

We gotta start detoxing. Try-outs are next week.

IS THAT YOU, BALÁZS, DEAR?

Before heading out to the White Rhino, we make a pact just to play foosball. No booze, no drugs, and we'll tell any chicks who come onto us to fuck off. But of course nothing ends up like we planned and the post-practice chill sesh turns into a hardcore rager, complete with booze, drugs, and chicks. There's no trace of the clash that happened here: the slivers of glass have been cleared away, the door's glass has been replaced, and the blood's been scrubbed off the walls and sidewalk. The Rhino's got the best foosball table in the city. An original Garlando Master Champion. Only the boss and his asshat buddies can use it during the day. They think that if they practise enough, they'll be able to pound everyone at night, when the games are played for cash. The lacquered black box of the table is made of layered pine, thirty millimetres thick, rimmed with aluminium. The table legs are made of steel. The playing area is covered in sandblasted, anti-reflective plate glass. The sixteen-millimetre-long rod is also steel, with an anti-corrosion chrome coating, which rolls in a ball-bearing socket. There's an extra spacing-rubber attached to the goalie's rod. The goals are made of fiber-glass-reinforced, high-resistance polymer. The grips are professional, wood-inlaid plastic. Every table has its own serial number. They'll reluctantly give to you it for a measly 1,100 euros. I googled it.

Naturally, Ducky's got a table like that at home. We've trained to precision on it. We can't let the dipshits get cocky. We head straight over to it. We can barely squeeze through the crowd to plunk our token down on its edge. We gotta wait three matches first, so we go back to Buoy and Zoli-boy. Buoy buys the first round, coke and whisky, in separate glasses, and while we mix them, I already know there's no stopping tonight, especially if we win a few matches. We've got a pretty good chance too, judging by the teams tonight. Twenty minutes later we're standing at the table, Zoli-boy in front, me in back. We always play like this. Zoli-boy can't take the heat in back. We're not hyped up enough for the first match and they beat us by two goals. Zoli-boy has a fit. Ducky puts down a token too. He teams up with Buoy. He stands next to the table and watches the opponents. He notes every person's strength, so when he's up, he won't be caught off guard. Zoli-boy and I go back to our table and Buoy asks how many people are playing before us. We tell him, and he quickly orders another round. Two minutes later, we're fixed up with fresh shots of whisky along with fresh glasses of coke. Buoy carries one over to Ducky, who doesn't even look at him as Buoy presses it into his hand. Keeping his eyes glued on the foosball table, he downs the drink and hands the glass back to Buoy. Buoy just stands there for a few seconds, then shrugs, looks down at the other teams' waiting tokens, trudges back to our table, and sits down in the empty seat beside me so he has a view of the table.

Ten minutes later, Ducky signals to him. He stands and goes back to the foosball table. The match ends pretty quickly. They haven't had any luck, either. Ducky gets real worked up by the end and makes dirty remarks to Buoy, who doesn't give a flying fuck, of course. It's like he didn't even hear them. He can enjoy the game even if he loses. That's just how he is. The only time he goes mental is if they bust his balls about his brother. But it's true, Gabe really *was* a better water-polo centre, and played foosball better that Buoy too. Ducky puts a token on the table to hold a place for the next match. He's not done yet.

Zoli-boy and I rest up before the next match and don't fuck up this time. We actually reel in five matches in a row. All the little dipshits just stand there, blinking. We gotta watch it though, make sure we don't pound anyone too hard, 'cause then they'll lose interest and won't put their tokens on the table. Or, if they feel provoked, they'll bash our faces in. But until they're wasted, they won't risk it if they feel they don't have a chance. We gotta give them a bit of hope, so they'll at least convince themselves they can nail us. We get so wrapped up in our tactics that Ducky and Buoy almost smash us. Of course when Ducky feels like he's got the upper hand, he immediately starts trashing Zoli-boy, who revs himself up hardcore and slams them with three goals. For the next half hour we've got everyone on their knees sucking our dicks, and the tension's high. We wanna quit, and I signal to Zoli-boy under the table that it's time for a breather, but then some douche comes over and says he wants to play for money and puts the cash down on the table. We glance at each other. We could use the extra dough. Both of us are broke.

"Okay," I say, and meet his wager.

Zoli-boy nods, he's got drops of sweat glistening on his forehead. I crack my knuckles. I clutch the handle. And in pops the first ball. Zoli-boy's hyped as fuck. We liquidate the two hotshot clowns in eight minutes. They're fuckin' livid. They want double or nothing. There's two possibilities: either they're fucking with us and lost deliberately, or they're wasted and they really *do* think they've got a chance against us. Zoli-boy's probably thinking the exact same thing, 'cause he's dead serious about the match, and we pound the two jerks even worse than before. The only reason they're not crawling under the table in the 10-0 loser's ritual is 'cause I flipped the last ball into our own goal.

They wanna play another. I tell them we're sitting down now and ask for the cash. One of them starts mouthing off, cranking up the volume, and by now everyone's staring at us. It turns out he's the boss's nephew, so we end up taking on the match. Zoli-boy's starting to lose it. He can't take this kind of heat. Both of us know we gotta lose this match or else we're really fucked, but we just can't hold back. We let the two clowns shoot, but they're such losers they still can't land a goal. After ten minutes of suffering I get bored and gently nudge Zoli-boy's ankle: let's finish this quick. Zoli-boy ruthlessly slams the last goal in, we high-five. He wants to shake hands with one of the dickheads, who's already headed straight for him. His buddy doesn't even try to stop him, but it seems like Lady Luck's with us tonight, 'cause the next minute the boss shows up and peels the dude off Zoli-boy. He doesn't want a scene. If he lets his nephew knock out one of the customers, the crowd's gonna dip out of here in half an hour, and then his profit's down the drain. While the two of them talk it over, two bouncers watch us from the doorway. Finally, the boss pays the wager that the kid lost, and buys us a round on the house.

Ducky and Buoy get up for another match, but they've got no luck tonight. Two fucktards bitch-slap them again. Ducky claims it's all Buoy's fault, of course. He talks shit to him, telling him to send his brother to play next time, because at least *he* knows how to play. Buoy snorts, laughing, but I can tell he's faking it. We start buying drinks for Ducky from the winnings so he doesn't get too mental. Half an hour later, we're hella smashed. Eyeing chicks. Things start picking up. The more wasted we get, the hotter the chicks get who come over to us. That's always how it goes.

I lose track of things pretty quick. I don't know what or how much we're drinking. All I know is, there's always a full glass in front of me, the conversation keeps getting louder, and I'm thirstier than ever. I gotta use the pisser, and as I stand, the space around me tilts. I head for the john, but I run into a buddy, so we talk a little, I have no idea what about, then I hear someone put Nirvana on the jukebox, so I walk away from the dude and rush down into the mosh pit. A few more rough tracks follow. A few hammered dumbasses jump around on the dance floor. Usually, the party at the White Rhino lasts till the DJ—a fiftyish dickhead sporting a beer belly and handlebar moustache—arrives. His real talent lies in breaking up the bash in ten minutes flat. He doesn't give a shit who wants to hear what. He just cranks out the tunes, usually the same stuff, in the same order: ABBA after Boney M, with a sprinkling of Hungarian bands of every style, then, around midnight, he breaks out some Jacko, usually after a bout of singalong punk and George Michael. Pretty soon a different audience takes over. The MILFs come. Generation shift.

We kick each other around some more to Nirvana. *Smells Like Teen Spirit.* I might never get bored of this song. I get a blow to the thigh but I don't give a shit. A couple more people join the pit. A skinny dude gets pushed up against the wall, but pops right off, kicking the guy straight in the gut, making him double over while he keeps on headbanging. Someone starts screaming, like they plunged a knife in his back, but when I look up I see that he's fine, he's just happy. Nirvana ends and I stand there all sweaty. I catch my breath, getting ready for the next round of thrashing, but the boss pulls the plug on the juke and the DJ yaps into the microphone, *time to get the real party started*, and he cues in *Dancing Queen*. The regulars already know that bitching isn't gonna get them anywhere, so they slink back to their tables or try and shake it to ABBA with the blonde tanning-salon chicks who twirl out onto the dance floor, but without much luck 'cause the girls turn away and dance with each other instead. Meanwhile, one of the pogo dudes steps over to the DJ booth and vents furiously to Moustache, who ignores him, of course. Five seconds later, one of the bouncers, his back the size of a ping-pong table, is flexing beside the heckler. He leans into the dude's face and says something. The dude turns around and clears off. I watch the whole scene while leaning against the side of a booth, and when I know there's not gonna be any more Nirvana, moshing, or fighting, I remember that I was on my way to the john.

When I get back to our table, Ducky's going on about why he wouldn't bang Madonna. Zoli-boy's not around, and since I didn't see him in the bathroom either, I ask Ducky where he's at.

"He took off," Ducky shouts, and that's that. He turns back to Buoy and continues. "You still don't fuckin' get it. I dig MILFs. It's sluts I got a problem with."

"I never noticed that before," Buoy grins. "Nevermind, I'd still plow her anyway."

"I gotta admit that Madonna seamlessly made the shift to MILF," Ducky explains. He seems not to have even heard Buoy's comment. "It didn't fuck up her career. She raked in more cash this year than ever before."

"Even though her songs are way shittier," I say, trying to join the conversation, but Ducky continues like I'm not even here.

"Whatever, I don't give a shit that she's filthy rich and famous," Ducky announces flat out. "I don't mess around with sluts."

"Well, fuck, dude, if my old man had as much dough as yours, I wouldn't care about banging broke chicks either."

"Are you really that stupid, Buoy, or are you faking it? If you hook up with girls who go off with *anyone* in your league, that'd be the same as racing in a lower class."

"I get it. So we're pretending to be in the same league as Madonna?" Buoy nods. "Adds up..."

"Whatever," Ducky waves. "If you don't care that you're The Maggot's hole-brother..."

I don't feel like talking about Madonna, leagues, and fictional hole-brotherhood with Ducky and Buoy, plus the music is getting shittier by the minute. I rest a little, then go for another look around. Maybe I'll find someone. I'm already standing out by the exit when I run into my ex. She's alone too, except she's going in the other direction. When she greets me, I suddenly remember what amazing head she gives. We chat for a while on the street. I tell her I just came out for some air, and she says she'll wait for me. Actually, I *was* planning on heading home, but in the end I go back in, of course, and buy her a drink. Things work out so well that two hours later I wake up and find myself in a car. Some chick gave me a ride. I look at her, but her profile's not familiar, and she's not the chick I met at the exit. Ducky took off too. The last time I saw him was in the bathroom. He and some of his buddies were messing with a girl who was around fourteen. She was totally plastered, with enough booze poured down her throat that she wouldn't remember what happened. If she's lucky, she won't. Puke on her hair, mascara smeared, skirt crumpled around her ankles, panties torn. But the crazy thing was that, even in that state, she looked really good. When I walked in on them, Ducky was standing half naked and waving around a bloody, severed arm. At least that's what it looked like at first, but then I realized he was swinging a red t-shirt.

I look at the chick again. I don't have a clue who it is. Long black hair; small, perky, and probably firm breasts. She probably wants to get revenge on her boyfriend because he fucked one of her friends. I don't think I'm gonna recognize her face. I can't even really see it because her hair is in the way. I feel sick and close my eyes. I don't wanna puke in here. I don't know where we are. I don't even know which way we're going, but actually, it doesn't matter. Everything's reeling more violently than before. I roll the window down. It's started raining. The cold air slaps me in the face, the raindrops prick my skin. I feel better for a while, but then the chick hits the signal and turns, making me feel like spewing again. I'm about to tell her to pull over when she suddenly slams on the brakes, and I head-butt the dash. I can feel it, but it doesn't hurt. I thrust the door open, step out, and stagger to the back of the car. I pull my hand along the car's side, stop at the trunk, and throw up on the left rear tire. My head clears a little.

The street hisses. Exhaust fumes swirl into my face. I just let them come for a little while 'cause it's easier than moving my head. When I stop feeling like I'm gonna hurl, I look up. We're standing in front of a church. I don't know which one, but it's definitely a church 'cause there's a huge cross on top of it. A plane tree in front of it. Yellow light soaks the leaves. Wrapped around the tree's thick trunk is a Volkswagen Golf. An Mk6 maybe. There's people inside. As I start towards the smashed-up car, the chick who gave me a ride rolls the window down and shouts something after me, but it's raining so hard I can't understand a word of it. Drops of water patter on my skull. I shout back for her to wait a second already till I check out what's going on. If she wants to bang, she won't bail.

Golf Gen VI, a tough piece of metal, but the plane tree was tougher. I peer in through the lowered front window. Nobody's there. I lean in. Two beefy dudes, both in baseball caps, sit in the back seat. One of them's stubbly, the other's clean shaven. Thick gold chains around their necks. They seem familiar, but I can't remember where I've seen them before. I wait for them to maybe say something, but nope. They just stare. Their eyes are bloodshot.

"Should I call an ambulance?" I ask.

They look at each other. Mr Stubble shrugs, then Mr Smoothface asks:

"You got any weed?"

I nearly blurt out that I do, but then I start thinking, what if they're undercover cops, so I keep quiet instead.

"C'mon, don't do this, buddy," Mr Smoothface says.

"You guys okay?" I try to change the topic.

"Yeah," Mr Stubble nods.

His face is so damn familiar. Maybe from TV.

"We just need some weed," the other guy says.

The space back there is pretty snug for two big gorillas like them.

"Weeell..." I say. I know I fucked up 'cause now they're onto me.

"That's more like it, buddy," Mr Smoothface says, grinning at me.

I slowly reach into my pocket, though I know I shouldn't. I take out the baggie and hand it to Mr Smoothface. I'm expecting them to flash their police badges, but nothing. Mr Stubble starts salivating. He wipes his mouth. Mr Smoothface looks at me.

"We need paper too."

"It got drenched," I say.

If the cops come now, I'll say it's not my bud.

Mr Smoothface looks at his pal. They're quiet for a couple of seconds, then Mr Stubble takes out a pack of cigarettes. They roll a spliff. Mr Stubble produces a Zippo. At least they've got a light. He puts the joint into Mr Smoothface's mouth, holds the flame up to it, and the other guy inhales. Serenity descends. It's like they're chilling in the living room of some high-class mansion with a panoramic view and not inside a smashed-up car. I think about joining them, but someone honks at me just then. It's loud as fuck because there's no other sound except the hiss of the rain and these two puffing clowns. I forgot that the chick's been sitting in the car and waiting for me all this time.

"I gotta go," I say.

"Okay," nods Mr Smoothface, and exhales smoke.

I look at the baggie. There's still enough in it for at least three fat reefers.

"Oh, sorry," Mr Smoothface says, and hands it back with a smile. The smoke flows slowly out of his mouth like the Amazon River. "You rock, man," he says. "We're doin' a show tomorrow night at The Mirror. You can come in for free. VIP."

Finally it comes to me where I know them from. They're MCs from some cowpie-country gangsta-rap band. Ducky's latched onto them hard. That shit's all he's been listening to for the past few weeks. I even memorized this one refrain: *fudge packers we'll fuck you up, fuck-you-up.* I think they hate fags, at least that's what they're singing about.

Someone stops behind me and taps my shoulder.

"Relax, just a sec and we'll go," I say, kind of annoyed. But when I turn, I see that there's a priest staring right into my face. He's like, totally got the whole priest getup going. I guess these guys stay in character at night too.

"Praise Jesus, Father!' Mr Stubble calls from the back seat while he pulls out this fucking gigantic cross hanging on a gold chain from under his shirt and lays it on his chest.

"Forever and ever, amen," the priest grumbles. "I've called for help already," he adds, after giving the two clowns a long, penetrating once-over.

"Thank you," the two rappers answer in chorus.

Then we all shut up for a couple of seconds. Nothing happens. We wait. Maybe the priest has something to say but he's all quiet too.

"Well, I'll be off then," I finally say, because this heavy silence is starting to get to me.

"What's the hurry, son?" the priest addresses me.

"I gotta go, Father," I say, pointing to the car parked on the other side of the street with the running motor. The chick is looking straight at us. I wave to her. She waves back grumpily.

"You should wait for the ambulance," the priest suggests.

"There's nothing wrong with *me*," I say. "The only reason we stopped was so I could ask if they needed any help," I say, gesturing towards the dudes huddled in the back seat.

The priest doesn't say anything. He just looks down at my hand clutching the baggie full of weed. My hand's sweating. I pocket the grass. The priest clears his throat, then steps closer to the car and peers in the window. The two dudes are grinning stupidly at him. They're high as kites. The interior is filled with thick, swirling smoke.

"Is something burning?" the priest finally asks, after studying the inside of the car for a while.

"We just lit a cig," Mr Stubble answers.

"I see," the priest nods. "Does anything hurt?" he asks.

"Well... I guess not," Mr Smoothface says thoughtfully, patting his legs, while Mr Stubble nods, dead serious beside him.

The priest ponders something for a moment, then continues:

"At any rate, I suggest you get out, toss that damned joint far away, and air the car out before the police arrive."

His voice is calm, and what he's saying is totally logical, but still the two idiots freeze up. If it wasn't a priest dishing out advice I bet they'd already have their gears in motion and be doing what he says, but since it's a priest trying to yank them out of the shit they fell in, they're like deer in headlights. Though, I mean, if I wanna be honest, I was pretty surprised too. Finally, Mr Stubble collects himself, plucks the joint from the hand of his buddy—who's still staring with his mouth open, as if it was Jesus Christ himself who'd appeared to them—and climbs out of the car. Then Mr Smoothface's system boots up too, slowly but surely. At first, Mr Stubble wants to throw the butt under a bush, but the priest snaps at him, *what do you think you're doing,* so the dude starts whirling around in a panic, zooms in on the nearest garbage can, shuffles over, stubs the butt out on the side of it, and tosses it in. Meanwhile, Mr Smoothface gets all hyped up, flapping the doors open and closed, trying to air out the interior. After a while, the priest signals to him: enough now, rest.

I watch the two dumbasses and their pathetic show, then decide it's time to get lost. It'd be fuckin' stupid to wait for the cops. I guess the priest senses my intent to haul ass, so he turns to me and asks again:

"In a hurry, son?"

"Yes, Father," I answer.

"Someone waiting for you?" he says, gesturing towards the car.

"Yes," I nod.

I don't know why, but I feel super awkward. I don't usually chat with priests about chicks. Actually, I don't chat with priests at all. Ever.

He's quiet for a while, and when a siren starts blaring in the distance, he says:

"Scram, son!"

"Yes, Father."

"Come see me if you're in the neighbourhood," he says. "I'd be pleased to have you for tea."

"Thank you, Father," I blurt out, and head off towards the car.

I'm goddamn relieved to be free of the cleric. What if he's a pedophile fag who only became a preacher so he could screw little boys? Like hell I'm gonna sit around having tea with a perv like that.

"And always use a condom!" he shouts after me.

I give him the thumbs up to signal that I think that's a grand idea, and quicken my steps.

"Let's get outta here," I say after getting in.

But the chick just stares at me wide-eyed, and isn't getting us out of there. And we really don't have time for this. I don't feel like running into the cops, 'cause if they find the weed on me, I'm dead meat. I shake my hand in front of her face. Maybe she fell asleep or something, but as I'm waving she starts to blink, so she's totes awake.

"C'mon," I urge her a little louder, but she just stares at me from behind her long, black hair, like she's dumbstruck.

I mean, I don't give a shit if she doesn't feel like talking, it's just really creepy that she's not doing a thing.

"Let's get out of here!" I hurry her.

The wall of the building beside us flashes red-blue-red-blue. I'm starting to fuckin' lose it. I look over my shoulder and there's an ambulance turning the corner, sirens blaring. Just then the chick finally collects herself, puts the car in first gear, and steps on the accelerator.

"What happened?" she asks a few blocks away.

"Nothing," I blurt, as if I was talking to my mother.

The windshield wipers can barely cope with the onslaught of raindrops. And it's only getting worse.

"C'mon, tell me already," the chick begs, and when I don't answer, she adds, with a slightly accusing tone, "I waited a long time for you."

"They wrapped themselves around the tree," I finally grunt, even though I know she knows this already, so she won't let it go.

"Was anyone hurt?" she asks.

"There were two dudes in back," I say. "They were fine, I guess."

"Who was driving?"

"I don't know," I answer; then, to clarify, I add, "The front seat was empty."

She keeps asking questions for, like, another ten minutes. The whole thing's totally starting to feel like some interrogation. It even occurs to me that maybe she's a student at the police academy.

"That's pretty harsh though," she finally notes, then falls silent.

We get a red light at the next corner. As the chick starts to slow down, I'm wondering why this light is still in service when all the others are just flashing yellow. We stop. They've got minimal techno going on the local radio. The windshield wipers are set to intermittent. They've got a rhythm: on, wipe, off, pause, on, wipe, off, pause. At the third round, someone steps off the curb and passes in front of us. His walk seems familiar, but it takes a while till I identify him as Zoli-boy. He doesn't turn towards us. He moves along with his head down, hands shoved in his pockets. Everything on him is soaking wet—his sweater, his shoes, his hair—but it seems like he couldn't give a flying fuck. A couple of seconds later I realize why I didn't recognize him right away: he's walking too slow. Zoli-boy never walks like this. Some old fart would be glad to hit such a pace, but for Zoli-boy this is nearly crawling. I don't know what's wrong with him. I wanna honk the horn at him, but then I change my mind 'cause if we get caught up in some heart-to-heart now, I'm definitely not plowing this chick. And there's no way in hell I'm gonna miss this. I promised myself at the club that I wouldn't go to bed till I picked someone up. While my mind's running off on this, Zoli-boy's swallowed by the rain, which closes up after him like an elevator door in a hospital. Then the light turns green and we drive on. I look over my shoulder, but I don't see the dumbass anymore. I don't remember what time he took off from the Rhino, but I guess he didn't go home. I'd certainly like to know what the fuck he's doing around here at this hour. He doesn't even live nearby. I seriously doubt he hooked up with someone. I'll ask him about it tomorrow if I remember to.

We cruise silently in the night for a while. There's just the dubdub of the music, the whirring engine, and the windshield wipers. This chick drives too cautiously. You can tell she's had no practice. I mean, it's still better than Ducky, who only knows how to move forward with the gas pedal floored. Every once in a while, a car passes us, music blaring, packed with country bumpkins high on speed, but otherwise the night's peaceful. I don't care where we're going. I listen to the music and the rumbling motor with my eyes closed, deeply inhaling the chick's scent. I'm starting to get sleepy, so I quickly ask whose place we're going to. I try to hint that her place is where this party needs to go, but she doesn't say a thing, just smiles mysteriously. It would suck if she changed her mind just when things started getting heavy. Even though I'm sobering up, she's still cute. She looks adorable wrinkling her forehead and squinting as she's concentrating on the road.

"Where do you go to school?" I toss in a subject.

A whole round of windshield wiping is complete by the time she answers.

"I'm doing kindergarten teacher-training."

"Seriously? You're a babysitter?" I snort.

I thought she was a lot younger.

"And you're an asshole," she says, totally serious, but then she busts out laughing.

"Have you been with a lot of guys?" I ask.

I've never hooked up with a college chick before.

She doesn't answer, just keeps smiling all mysterious, then extends a pack of peppermint flavour Airwaves towards me and says:

"Why don't you chew some gum instead?"

I take three pieces out, though I like blueberry Orbit better. I start sobering up from the gum. This sucks ass because at times like these there's always a moment when I feel like shit for no apparent reason. I need something to yank me out of the slump, so I get out my weed and swing the baggie in front of the chick's nose. She doesn't say anything, just turns towards me and nods. I'm already rolling the joint. With some weed, I'll pull through till dawn, no prob. Not to mention that sex is much better when you're high. Actually, everything's better when you're high. Maybe even swimming.

I quickly finish rolling the spliff, but as I'm about to light up, the chick tells me not to smoke in the car. I'm totally focused on getting this joint lit, so I ask her to stop at the next parking lot. We park, blocked from view by a row of recycling bins, and get out. I hand her the joint and light it for her. We pass it back and forth quietly for a while. We've been standing there for about five minutes when I notice that the rain's stopped. The crickets are chirping louder and louder. By the time we finish the J, I'm really into the chick and my dick's hard. I suck the cig to the base, crush the butt out, push the chick against the side of the car, and pull her shirt up. Her nipple hardens in my mouth. I reach into her panties. Her pussy's wet and nicely shaved, with just a thin line of fuzz in the middle. I've got three fingers inside her already when the dope kicks in and she starts cracking up, laughing like crazy. I open the door and sit her down on the back seat. I pull her jeans off and open her legs, but I can't eat her out properly because she keeps laughing and tries to push my head away. I keep at it for a while longer, but when I see it's no use, I take her hand and pull her up, try to talk her into using her mouth, but she just can't stop laughing. When I finally somehow manage to get my dick in her mouth, I almost come. The chick's a fuckin' pro. She's grabbing my ass, which gets me really hot, and I start working it porn-star style. I push my dick deeper into her mouth, but she's not into that. She pushes me away and tells me to quit it. My head clears for a second, and the whole situation feels really awkward. I don't want her to get sulky and take off on me. I low-key freak out, 'cause what if I've fallen in love with her?, and while I obsess over this, she calms down and busts out laughing again. It takes a couple of seconds till I catch on that she's just messing with me. She grimaces, makes a sad face, imitating me, and keeps giggling the whole time. Finally, I can't take it anymore and burst out laughing too. Then, she takes a condom out of her pocket, dresses me up, turns onto her stomach, and pushes her ass towards me. There's something animalistic about this whole thing, and as I'm pounding her from the back, my brain clouds over again. I thrust harder and harder, but this time I catch myself and try to hold back. But she looks over her shoulder and orders me to do it already. No need to ask twice. She keeps moaning louder, the sounds erupting from somewhere deep inside her. I almost pass out when I come.

We lie next to each other on the back seat. It's a tight fit, but I don't care. I push my back and ass against the front-seat backrest so I don't crash down to the floor. We lie without a word like this for ten minutes. I caress her belly and shoulder, then suddenly she's had enough, pulls her jeans on and sits up. I try to hold her back, but she won't let me. She gets out of the car and lights up. I sit too, watching the flare of her cigarette through the window. I button my pants, then step out into the humid night and stop beside her. I obsess for a long time over what to say.

"That was awesome," I finally break the silence.

Before she answers, her phone rings and of course she

has to answer it. I listen quietly as she argues with her boyfriend, yet I'm not happy that she's not dating me. The dude's still going off about something on the other end when she hangs up, turns to me, and says, "I gotta go."

When she sees how incredibly stoked I am to hear this, she adds, "Sorry."

"Are you in a super hurry?" I try my luck.

"Pretty much," she says, messing with her phone. "But I'd be glad to give you a ride."

I'm fuckin' happy to hear this 'cause I don't feel like walking in shit weather. The rain could start up again anytime.

"I'll drop you off at the bus stop, okay?" she asks.

"Thanks," I nod sullenly.

I want her to notice that I'm upset, but it appears she's not very moved by this.

Only after she drives off, leaving a strange, sharp smell and a cloud of exhaust fumes behind her, do I catch on that there're no busses at this hour. As the two taillights disappear around the corner, the silence solidifies, and I start swearing 'cause I forgot to ask for her name.

I check the time on my phone. The rain starts up. Drops patter heavily again on the bus stop's tin roof. Everything slows down, everything becomes motionless. I'm outside of time, I guess, or time is outside of me. I should get going, but I can't bring myself to move. There's no way in hell I'm gonna stick around here with my thumb up my ass till dawn. I'd rather get fucking drenched and start back towards the city centre. Maybe I'll find someone who's willing to grab a beer with me somewhere.

I'm trudging along Kölcsey Street. I don't remember how I got here. It's a really long street. You totally can't see one end from the other, even though it's pretty straight and it doesn't rise or fall anywhere. I went to grade school here. In a square three-storey grey building that resembled a run-down jail more than a school. I haven't been in the neighbourhood for a while, but nothing's changed, except that everything seems to have shrunk. I despised going to school here. All the teachers were pricks. The Biggest Prick Ever Award should have gone to the principal, though. Even the other teachers hated him, but since he kept them hella scared they always sucked up to him. They even took his side this one time when I was in second grade and he hit me so hard I pissed myself. Maybe time blew the memory of that beating out of proportion, but nobody's beat me up that hard since. That's when Zoli-boy and I became pals. I never knew why we got our asses kicked, but I do remember standing with my back turned when that bastard whacked me upside the head the first time and started howling that we destroyed the toilet-paper dispenser. I wanted to explain to him that it wasn't us who did it, and there was never paper in it anyway, but he wouldn't let me get a word in. If we'd had a bit more practice in situations like that, we might've avoided it. Everybody knew that was the principal's hobby. He made his rounds during recess and served up a couple of knuckle sandwiches. He liked fighting. I guess that's a thing. And it's safer fighting with weaklings 'cause they don't dare hit back. Whatever. He was more in a fighting mood than usual that day, and he slapped us so hard with his shovel-sized hands that both of us pissed ourselves. Totally. Right into our pants. I know it's nasty, but, like, we were pretty small. He alternated between our heads for about four or five minutes, then dragged us back into the classroom. I was lucky, 'cause he caught me with his weaker hand, but all the same I was freaking out that he'd rip my ear off. Zoli-boy even had blood spurting from his earlobe. Then he stood us out by the blackboard and rambled on forever about how enraging it is when someone destroys the toilet-paper dispensers the school purchased with precious money, and what lowdown good-for-nothing scoundrels we were. Meanwhile, our homeroom teacher, that stupid cunt, was nodding so enthusiastically the whole time that I was starting to hope she'd get a pinched nerve in her neck again, like in first grade, when she walked around with her head tilted to one side for two weeks, and every time she had to turn around suddenly, she hissed loudly, and we kept messing with her, whoever was behind her kept asking her questions. And we just stood there in our pissed pants like two losers, our faces burning like Iraqi oil wells. My soaked pants stuck to my skin and were cooling fast. I was fucking cold, but that's not the only reason I was shaking. I was in shock too. We were scared shitless, for sure. Zoli-boy was sobbing quietly, pants pissed just the same, and each time the principal raised his voice, he flinched and cringed. The red welts on his face showed where the blows hit him. My face was an even nicer piece of work, with the back of my neck and forehead throbbing where I'd head-butted the wall when I got socked. When I finally managed to collect myself a little, I watched the class from the corner of my eye, tried to stand at an angle so that my love, a little angel with curly blonde hair, wouldn't see the stain on my jeans, all while freaking out about how, if it got around that we'd pissed ourselves, nobody'd ever talk to us again. It was fifteen minutes into math class when the principal decided he'd shot us down enough, so he said goodbye to Teacher and fucked off. We spoke in whispers for the rest of the day, and I only got to change my pants at home. The only good thing about all of it was that my old folks didn't notice a thing. Who the fuck needed another whupping at home?

That prick's dropped dead since then. That was the best thing he could have done. I heard something about him having a stroke or whatever and pushing on in a wheelchair. Or rather, he got pushed *around* in a wheelchair 'cause he couldn't even wipe his ass with those shovel hands. I should've looked him up then. I would've had a couple of ideas about how to spend some quality time together for an hour, but of course I didn't have enough guts for it. Never mind now. He lived next door to the school. I stop at the front door of his building. I look at the list of residents' names on the buzzer panel. His name is still there: Lajos Ember. There must still be somebody from the family living here. Maybe his wife. The Widow Ember. I glance at my watch and press the buzzer. If the old lady's sleeping pills didn't kick in tonight, maybe she'll hear it. I wait a minute, then lean on the buzzer again. I'm still pressing it when a female voice croaks, *Who is it?* I don't give her time to get mad. I just say that her husband was a child-molesting prick, to which she says, *What?* and *Who's this?* while I shout that her husband fucked a bunch of little kids in the ass. I have to shout because she's deaf as a doorpost, but when I shout for the third time with all my might that her husband was a perverted pig who raped little boys, she shuts up. He was a dirty perverted bastard. Mute silence. *You understand?* I scream. No answer, only a soft click. Then, someone speaks into the intercom again: *Is that you, Balázs, dear?*

I step out from the doorway. The lights in three apartments are already on. I gotta get the fuck out of here real fast before they come down or call the cops. A window opens on the first floor. I head towards the main street. It's still raining. And I'm crying, too, I think. I vow never to come around here again.

Twenty minutes later, I stop in front of the window of a pet store in a kind of alley passageway that opens from the pedestrian mall. You name it, they have it. Cages, terrariums, aquariums, birdcages. The guinea pigs are sprawled out. Two red-eared slider turtles sleep huddled under an infra lamp. I watch the fish. A few of them stare through the plate glass, while others zip around like crazy, to impress the chicks, I guess. A couple of others open and close their mouths rhythmically, floating among the aquarium plants. For a while I watch the bored-looking goldfish, the barbels, guppies, neon tetras, gouramis, danios, and catfish. And my favourites: the Siamese fighting fish. Then, and I don't know why, these colourful little critters swimming all over the place, the aquarium, and even the whole pet store, everything, start to really get on my nerves.

I look around. The street is empty. It's still raining. Across the street, under a bush, I spot what I'm looking for. I cross, pick up the brick, then turn back and stop in the middle of the street, about three metres from the shop window. I look around and bash the brick against the sidewalk. It splits. I pick up the two pieces. The first piece breaks the shop window with a loud crash, and the burglar alarm starts wailing. The second brick shatters the side of the 500-litre aquarium. The water floods the shop. Some even spills out onto the street, but most of it stays inside. The fish surf on the waves, flap their fins, and flounder around on the floor. They haven't got a chance, even though they throw themselves in the air, even though they thrash and gasp. There's no air for them here. I try to figure out what's going through their heads, but it's pretty hard, because no matter what happens, they just stare the same way. Before, when they were swimming in the aquarium, they made the same exact faces as now, lying on the floor and the sidewalk. They breathed the same way, except they actually got air then. The alarm changes tune. It'd be nice to stick around and look at the fish a little longer, but I've gotta split 'cause the cops'll be here soon. As I start off, I step on a fish by accident, and almost go flying. I manage to keep my balance. I check out the mangled fish. There's not much left of it, but judging from the colour, it must have been a leopard-patterned bushy-mouth catfish. At least it didn't suffer long. It got off easier than its buddies, at any rate.

There's not much point in thinking about which way to go 'cause the cops could come from anywhere. I dash past the porcelain shop. That place is next on my list. Fuckin' china cups. I slow down when I can't hear the alarm anymore. My favourite bakery is two corners from here. They bake the bread right in the back room and it's open 24 hours. I breathe in through my nose. The scent of bread keeps getting more intense. Zoli-boy and I usually come in here after partying. We sober up with the freshly baked stuff, which soaks up the alcohol inside us. If we're high, we just stuff our faces with hot bread scooped from the crust, chow down on three or four salty crescent rolls or something. Whatever's just out of the oven. I stop in front of the gate. I take deep breaths. I don't want any of the bakers to notice that I've been running 'cause cops come in here a lot to graze. I stand for two minutes listening, stuck hard against the firewall. Everything's deserted. Only some shit Hungarian pop song filters out from the workroom. I step out of the darkness and start across the concrete courtyard. The neon light of the bakery falls out the barred windows like a cube. I'm headed towards the window along the shortest path, but the courtyard just doesn't seem to end. There's nobody there. I ring the bell. Two minutes later a crone with a bored expression crawls out from somewhere in the back. She certainly didn't take this long 'cause some baker was plowing her. I stare into her wrinkly face. The moment I give her my order, I feel the cops. I didn't see them roll into the courtyard, but they're standing right there behind me now. I really fucking hope they're here to grub. Meanwhile, the crone totters back with the crescent rolls and the cocoa swirl bun. She says something, but I don't react. One of the young cops steps over and his hand moves in a way that makes me freak out that he's whipping out his gun. The last time I prayed was in kindergarten, but I rattle off the Lord's Prayer now in my head and glance off to the side. The cop's just standing there and fucking with his cell phone, looking all stern. As I look at him, he looks up, and I avert my eyes quickly. The woman tells me the price for the third time. I dig the money out from my pocket and scatter it on the counter. The crone counts out the price of the rolls and the bun for what seems like an eternity. It seems to take fucking forever before I'm able to sweep the rest of the change from the counter into my hand. Meanwhile, the cop steps over to the window, as if I were invisible, and places his order. I see his mouth move but I can't hear anything. One of the crescent rolls falls out of the plastic bag onto the ground. Right into the cruddiest filth. As I lean down, I notice a bit of fin stuck to the tip of my shoes. Judging from the colour, it must be from the leopard-patterned bushymouth catfish, except I don't know how it got there. If the cop spots it, I'm really fucked. He definitely knows about the pet store. Squatting next to the cop, I peek out at the squad car. I'm lucky 'cause the other cop's not paying attention. He's messing with his phone. I quickly pick up the roll, blow on it a couple of times for show, then haul ass out of there.

When I turn the corner, I start to calm down. I walk at an even pace, chewing on the crescent roll to the rhythm of my steps. Soon, the adrenalin drains from me, and I start laughing. I haven't got the faintest idea where I'm going. All I know is, I can't stop, 'cause then I'm dead. I'm a shark.

I float naked in the tar-coloured water. I left my clothes at the edge of the 50-metre pool. The guard dog's not barking anymore either. He's standing beside the pool gutter, wolfing down my leftover cocoa swirl bun. And it's not like he was barking 'cause he wanted to catch me. He was happy to see me. We're on pretty good terms. I often come down to swim at night, and then I always feed him. That pathetic beast must be bored out of his mind. After all, who wants to break into an empty pool? Swimming is the best at night. No one can see me and I can't see anyone either. I swim a couple of laps, the last one on my back at an easy pace, looking up at the moon in the meantime. I'm looking for the smiley face but I can't see it anywhere. The moon's not a smiley face, but a round, yellow skull. I float in nothingness and I remember a photo of myself sitting on my old man's shoulders as happy as a clam. I don't really remember him ever putting me on his shoulders, because I *was* a pretty hefty kid, so I'm not sure my old man could lift me. He kept the picture in his car for a long time. This one time, we were coming home from somewhere at night, I don't remember where—not like it matters—and the photo was there on top of the dash above the steering wheel, and as the streetlamps cast light on the interior at intervals, the picture kept reflecting on the windshield. Well, things were pretty fucked up by then. We didn't even talk to each other the whole way. Night swimming is cool though, everything as quiet as the grave. There's not too many people who get why this is so awesome. I don't want anybody to see me naked. But I guess it's not like it used to be when I first started coming here, freaking out about getting busted, freaking out about the black water, which is totally like a reflection of the night sky. Then, of course, things change and everything becomes a habit. Like this night swimming. I remember that night with Pop. The moon sucks me in, I totally space out, piss into the water, meanwhile, think about dumb shit like, what if there were two moons, two identical yellow disks, and they orbited together, and I turn quickly onto my stomach, but all I can see is the black water. The sun doesn't know a thing about this night swimming.

ESC

Some douchebag leans on the doorbell for the fourth time while I shoot Buoy in the head with a silenced gun. It produces a large, even hole at the back of his head. The blood shoots high up into the air like a geyser, bone splinters fly, bits of brain splatter on the wall and slide down slowly towards the floor. It's a dick move to off someone from the back, especially if it's your buddy, but if I hadn't killed him, he would've finished me off without even thinking. I peer cautiously through the doorway. Ducky's huddled in the next room behind a cabinet. It'd be a hassle to stalk him from this angle, so I decide to wait till he comes out. I flatten myself against the wall and squat down, so if he steps out, I can get behind him while also keeping an eye on the corridor. I don't have to wait long. I hear Ducky stepping towards the door. He peeks out. I'm lucky, he doesn't notice me, and starts off in the other direction. I put my gun away, pull out my serrated hunting knife, tiptoe behind him, and cut his throat from ear to ear. The skin splits, the mangled cartilage crackles, and the dark-red blood, projectile-spraying from the arteries, coats both walls of the corridor. I think only Ottó is still alive. He's hiding somewhere upstairs, but I'll find him and finish him. He's for sure scared shitless. I gotta exploit that. The easiest time to get them is when they're scared shitless. I can smell the fear. It's no wonder I'm so bomb at this game.

Ducky's swearing his head off, naturally, 'cause he got offed about half a minute ago, and he gets reborn at the far end of the course and has to run through the whole high-rise building to get his revenge. If he had patience, he could hide until someone else gets killed, 'cause something got messed up in the settings and everyone resurrects in the same place, but he's got no patience for this strategy.

These days, we don't play hockey games at all anymore. Instead, we play Bulletstorm, ZombiU, Borderlands, F.E.A.R., and Half-Life, and on the weekends, when there's no swim meet, we get down to a serious GTA party. I guess everyone's bored of jerking off, plus it's better if you don't pop all your jock pistols in the middle of competition season anyway. It's some kind of ancient superstition, and all the great stars live by it. Some doc came to our school recently to give us a sex-ed talk and said that jerking off isn't harmful if we don't overdo it. I shouted that it's totally like weed then, but he wasn't up for laughs.

Meanwhile, the asshole at the door is leaning on the buzzer again. I guess he's not gonna budge. Any idiot can see that there's someone home. I manage to hide myself pretty well, so I take my headset off, stand, and walk over to the window. An unfamiliar car's parked outside. I tell Ducky someone's here, but Buoy's being massacred just then, so he can't hear anything from the rattle of machine gun fire, the explosions, and the screams. I sit back down and write to him on chat. Just for kicks, I write, *the cops are here mofo*, but Buoy's been reborn in the meantime and rolls a hand grenade under me. Ducky writes back telling me to fuck them up. I write back to him, *they're here irl, dumbass*. Ducky looks up from the monitor, but I can tell from his face that he still doesn't get it. He turns towards me, and the right side of his face is tinted bluish-grey from the glow of the screen. I shrug. Ducky takes off his headset and tosses it angrily on the table, then stands up, walks to the window, and looks out.

"Those are cops?" he says, turning back.

"I dunno," I answer. "But they've been pressing the doorbell for about ten minutes now."

"Why didn't you tell me?"

"I thought you heard," I say, and shoot someone with a sawed-off shotgun.

"I didn't fucking hear," Ducky grumbles, and sits back in front of the console.

I'm not freaking out or anything, but I think it would be dumb as hell not to go downstairs, 'cause if they really *are* cops, and we don't let them in, they're gonna call a SWAT team and those dudes don't fuck around, they just kick the door in on you.

"Go down already," Ducky says, gaping at the monitor and shooting a bazooka.

It looks to me like he landed a direct hit to the transformer station where Ottó was hiding.

"Down where?" I ask, decapitating a uniformed guard with an axe.

"To see the cops," he says, without batting an eye, as he tosses a hand grenade into a schoolyard.

"What for?" I ask, and decide I'm not getting dragged into this.

"I need some time," Ducky says. "To clean up," he adds, and takes down a terrorist from one of the rooftops.

That's a pretty convincing excuse. If he gets busted, so do we.

"And what should I tell them?"

"Depends what they ask," he says, and when I just keep staring at him stupidly, he adds, "You're charming as fuck.

You'll think of something."

They ring the bell again. Mozart. Or Vivaldi. Or Bach. Ducky doesn't move to answer the door, but in the meantime, holding a chainsaw, he assaults the armed men guarding the base.

I don't say anything, I just stand up then start towards the stairs.

"You're a fuckin' prince, man," Ducky grins after me. "Thanks."

If I had a weapon on me, I mean, a *real* weapon, I'd kill him.

I step out of the room, walk along the hall, and go down the stairs. I stop at the front door. Maybe they really are cops, but I doubt they'd be looking for me at Ducky's. I do a mental calculation: it's been three days since I got high, which is pretty weird, but I'm real fucking happy about it right now. I pat my pockets, take out the baggie, and put it in a vase in the foyer. I delete Viki's nudes from my phone. I look through the peephole. An unshaven, cop-like dude with a stony expression stands at the door with a chick who's got brown eyes, freckles, and wavy red hair. She looks pretty hot. She reminds me of that actress I saw in a pool-table scene online. She took off her panties so she'd have something to hold her hair back with, meanwhile, two losers kept drooling and trying to steal looks under her dress. I step back to the hall mirror for a sec, fix my hair, then open the door.

"Good afternoon," the man says, then pulls something out of his pocket—maybe his police badge—pushes it in my face, and adds, "Lieutenant Faragó." Then he nods towards the babe, "My partner, Detective Szász."

I introduce myself. They ask me to repeat my name. I do.

"We're looking for Lajos Kovács," the guy says; then,

since I'm not saying a thing, he adds for emphasis, "regarding an urgent matter."

I've only ever seen real detectives on TV before, and once they came to our school to demo "so-called designer drugs," and explain their harmful effects, but those two were clowns. Someone mixed some shit in their coffee during recess, and it made them so hyper that they sailed through the lecture they planned for forty-five minutes in ten, and then pissed off.

"Are you his son?"

"Yes," I blurt out, then quickly correct myself. "Actually no, I'm his friend."

The two cops eye me suspiciously. My hands are sweating again.

"I mean, his son's friend."

"May we see some ID?" the babe cop says.

"I've only got my student ID with me," I say, and reach into my pocket.

I feel a small plastic bag next to my student card. I didn't take out all the dope after all.

"That'll be fine too," the dude says, and snatches the ID from my hand.

A tiny piece of weed sticks to the plastic card by my name. He looks at it, then tries to blow it off, but it doesn't work, so he's forced to clean it with his finger. He reads out my name. Meanwhile, I'm looking at the chick and nodding enthusiastically.

"Please tell Mr Kovács that we'd like to talk to him."

"He's not home," I say.

"He is not present in the building at this time?"

Oh man, this cop lingo is totally whacked. Who the hell talks like that?

"No," I say. "He is away on a trip."

"Wife?" the chick cop asks.

"I don't have a wife," I blurt out, but they're totally not down with my sense of humour and start wrinkling their foreheads at the same time, so I tone it down. "His wife is not at home either."

"Do you know where we might find her?"

"Unfortunately, no," I answer. "But I don't think she's travelling," I add. "She's just not home right now." I don't have any better ideas. "I guess she's gone shopping. Maybe for a manicure, or to the hairdresser, masseuse; or she's at the gym."

"Fine, we understand," the dude waves me off.

"Or at the plastic surgeon," it occurs to me.

I suppose she's gotta take those huge knockers to get serviced pretty regular.

"Thank you," the chick cop says.

She's got this dead-serious expression, even though she seems like a pretty cool person. Maybe she smiles more when she's not on duty.

Then there's a loud bang upstairs. One of those asshats cranked the volume up to max. The babe cop grasps her holster, and I automatically step back.

"What was that?" she asks.

"FPS," I blurt out. She looks at me, puzzled. "A shooting game," I sputter.

I can see she still doesn't get it. I'm freaking out that she's gonna shoot me with her service gun. Upstairs, a round of machine-gun fire rattles, then there's a death rattle, followed by someone launching a bazooka, then shrieks and snorts of laughter. The babe cop finally catches on. I exhale.

"Which member of the Kovács family is present at home at this time?" the prick cop asks.

"Ducky," I say. "One of the kids."

"Would you go get him?" the chick says. "We need to speak with him."

"On what business?" I ask, trying to stall for time.

"Don't be a wise-ass, son," the prick cop threatens. Sure, now he's getting all superior on me. If he didn't have a gun, I'd ask him since when am I his "son"?

"Could you get him, please?" The chick doesn't lose her temper.

"Will you wait outside, or do you want to come in?" I ask.

I'm starting to run out of ideas, and plus I don't feel much like stalling anymore either.

"We'll wait," the guy answers. "Hop to it, son!"

I have no fucking clue what in God's hairy ass Ducky's been doing all this time, but I'm not finding out either, 'cause as I start upstairs, I see him at the top landing. The soundtrack of *Apocalypse Now* is blaring from the stereo. The track when Bill Kilgore's copter squad attacks the Vietnamese village.

"Well, what's going on?" Ducky asks.

"They're waiting down at the door."

"Who?"

"The cops."

"Fucking hell."

"They wanna talk to your old man."

"Fucking hell."

"I told them he was away on a trip."

"He's not."

"I had to tell them *something*."

"Nevermind," Ducky says, shrugging. "This Wagner is fuckin' lit, eh?" He winks at me, then starts towards the entrance.

I stop at the bottom of the stairs to eavesdrop on what he's talking about with the cops. He opens the door, walks out, and closes it behind him. I creep over like a commando and peer out the peephole. The detectives are waving their IDs in front of Ducky's nose. He grabs them and takes his sweet ol' time examining the badges, then hands them back with a jovial half-smile. The prick cop suddenly looks at the door and I freak out that he can see through the peephole. I step away. Not like I can hear what they're going on about anyway.

I go to the kitchen and open the fridge. Next to the 2-litre bottle of coke, I find a bottle of extra-strong chili sauce. Chinese import. I put the coke and the chili on the kitchen counter, take a glass from the cabinet, and fill it. The coke almost froths over the edge of the glass, but I put my finger over it to stop it, then down the whole thing in big gulps. The fizz scratches my throat. I put the glass in the sink and the bottle back in the fridge. I pocket the chili and go upstairs.

I find Ducky's parents' bedroom. I knock. Nobody's inside. I open the door. It doesn't give off an air of Fuck Palace as much as it did last time, but the tons of red silk are still pretty wild. It feels like stepping into an enormous pussy. I pull open the bedside-table drawer. Nothing. I go to the walk-in closet. I don't have much time. I search the shelves quickly. I can't reach the top one. I get up on a chair. I finally find what I'm looking for: Ducky's mom's vibrators. The thick, white dildo. The matching black one's rolled a bit further back, but that's the one I need, so I try to reach it standing on tip-toe. After I manage to rake it out, I take the chili-sauce bottle from my pocket. I squeeze a few drops onto the dildo and spread it evenly on the black plastic surface. I don't put any on the end 'cause maybe she likes to suck on it before sticking it up inside her. I put it back on the shelf and climb down off the chair. I leave the closet. I don't remember if the door was closed or not, but I push it partly closed to be on the safe side.

I'm creeping quietly down the hall when Ottó, Ducky's homie, steps out of Ducky's room. We're not buddies 'cause he doesn't swim. He's swinging a fat joint in his hand. His face is green. Looks to me like he's stoned hella hard and wants to go downstairs. In the meantime, the front door opens, the cop's asking something, Ducky's talking, and Ottó's headed down. He's already made it halfway when I *pssst* for him to stop, but he can't hear me. I run after him and grab the joint from his hand. He looks at me. He doesn't get it. I mean, I'd be surprised too, for sure. I take advantage of his frozen confusion, and before he starts getting cocky with me, I clasp my hand over his mouth and slam him up against the wall hard. Doesn't matter if it hurts, as long as he doesn't start yapping, 'cause then we're busted.

Ottó blacks out from the blow to his head and collapses like a sack of potatoes. I pocket the joint. Ducky distracts the cops while I quickly drag Ottó back upstairs. The dude's thin, but he must be pretty dense inside, 'cause I can hardly manage. I sit him down on the floor, lean his back against the wall, and go down to the kitchen. Ducky's trying to convince the cops that there's no point in waiting around for his father because he'll be away for a week, and his mother's at the beautician's and then she's going shopping, so it'll be at least two or three hours before she's home. The cops ask for Ducky's ID. They ask if he has a driver's licence. Ducky says he doesn't.

As I put the chili sauce back into the fridge, I spot a few small labelled bottles in one of the side compartments. I take one out and look at it. There's a strip of surgical tape stuck on it with a date. I look at another one. A date on there too. I put the vials back, close the fridge, and start towards the entrance, checking into the living room on my way. Hunting trophies line the wall: a couple of elks, a rhino, and two lions. Ducky's old man shot them. He goes to Africa during the winter to hunt. This one time they even made super slo-mo videos. Looks pretty damn awesome when a lion whirls through the air, hit straight-on by a rifle bullet.

The prick cop looks up from the ID. It would be great if they finally let Ducky go. We need to finish the death match. Ducky looks at the two cops with a pleading expression. They return his ID and tell him they'll be back tomorrow. I can't decide if they're just really stupid or if they lied about when they're coming again so they can catch Ducky's old man off guard. Ducky walks them out. I go over to the door and look out. The two cops get into the Golf parked next to one of Ducky's pop's Jaguars. I wait until they drive off. I step away from the door. Ducky comes back in.

"What did they want?" I ask.

"Nothing," he says right away.

I know he's lying, but I let it go, because there's no way I'm getting anything out of him anyway. I forgot to tell him about Ottó, so on the way back Ducky trips over him and goes ballistic.

"What the fuck you have to go lying around here for, motherfucker?"

When Ottó doesn't answer, Ducky turns to me and asks: "Shit, what in hell's his problem?"

I briefly sum up the situation, Ducky stares thoughtfully,

and then says, *let's take him to the bathroom and splash some water on his face.* As we lift him, Ottó starts mumbling something about worm or a germ, but fuck if I know what he's going on about. We've barely moved him a couple of paces when the doorbell rings again.

"Oh, for fuck's sake," Ducky says, then lets go of Ottó, who falls back like a slow motion video, hitting his head again. Meanwhile, Ducky stomps down the stairs and I'm stuck here with this sad bastard. I lean closer. He's breathing evenly. I reach under his head and pat the back of it. He's not bleeding.

It wasn't the cops who came, but Mishy. As he limps upstairs, he stops beside us and pushes the hood of his sweatshirt back. He's got a fuckin' humungous bruise under his right eye, his nose is twisted to an impossible angle, swollen and purple, and he's got dried blood at the edge of his lips. We stand silently. Nobody says a word. Ducky and I lift Ottó, lug him into the bathroom, and put him down in the shower stall. We run some cold water on him, and when he starts to whimper, we turn the tap off. At least he's alive. We go back to the room. Ducky sizes up Mishy, realizing that something's not right about the dude's face.

"Who fucked up your nose, homie?" he finally asks.

"Gibbe suh ice," Mishy says in a nasal voice, then hawks deeply and spits bloody phlegm.

Ducky walks over to the fridge and takes out a bag of cocktail ice, pressing it into Mishy's hand. Mishy sits down in one of the armchairs, leans back, puts the bag on his face, and hisses. Ducky's standing beside him, staring at him fixedly, freaked out that Mishy will bleed on the upholstery.

Buoy wins the death match. He gets up from in front

of the monitor and goes over to Mishy. He's about to high five him, but when he sees the ice bag, he asks:

"Hey, Mishy, somebody fuck you up, or what?"

"No, I head-budded yo momma, asshoe," Mishy growls from behind the crunch of ice cubes.

Buoy gets that there's no point in going up against Mishy, so he doesn't shoot back, and just says:

"Okay, chill, don't get your panties in a bunch."

"Subbuddy roll a J arreddy," Mishy asks. "I wad hidig behid yo fuggen edgge fo an hou. I fought dose fuggen cobs wud nebber leabe."

Ducky starts looking for the weed. He rummages around on the table, reaches between the couch cushions, pats down his pockets. Nothing.

"Who swiped my stuff?" he asks.

I look at Ducky and spread my arms.

"Buoy?"

"I didn't swipe nothing," he shrugs.

"Then where in motherfucking hell is my green?"

I can barely keep from bursting out laughing, but I can see that, apart from me, everyone's dead serious about the state of affairs, so I hold back and zip it.

"I flushed it," Buoy finally admits.

"Whadda fug did ya do?" Mishy grunts, and yanks the ice pack off his face.

"I flushed it."

"You flushed it?"

"I did."

"Down the toilet?"

"Yeah."

"Fuuuck," we moan in chorus.

Ducky dashes to the bathroom, cursing Buoy's mother the whole way. A loud clattering sound comes from inside;

then, about twenty seconds later, the door flies open and Ducky steps out. He's howling like a crazed animal, the saliva splattering from his mouth.

"Why the cum-guzzling, goddamned fucking whore-bitch hell did you have to flush the stuff down the toilet, you lousy motherfucker?"

"The cops were here," Buoy answers and spreads his arms.

"And what in that peabrained mush of a fucking head of yours made you think they were cops?" Ducky asks.

"I looked out the window."

"And?"

"There was a police car parked outside the house."

"Did you see any inscription on it?"

"No," Buoy says in his defence, "But the licence plate numbers tipped me off," he adds quickly.

"Fugging 'ell," Mishy whimpers. "Nobunny's god any-din?" he asks. Or at least I *think* he's asking, "Nobody's got anything?"

Ottó's fat joint is nestled in my pocket, but I have absolutely no intention of offering it up for grabs. I feel sorry for Mishy, I'll bet his nose hurts like a motherfucker, but that reefer's mine now.

"Wait," Ducky says, and starts out. He turns back from the doorway, points to Buoy, and says, "Keep an eye on him so he doesn't do something fucking retarded again." And then he goes thumping down the stairs.

Buoy doesn't seem particularly upset by the events. He gets comfy in one of the armchairs and turns the TV on. Mishy adjusts the ice on his face so he can see out from behind it. We watch the water-polo match silently for a while. Buoy glances off to the side now and then at Mishy, then finally musters up his courage and asks:

"Who did it?"

"I dell you lader," Mishy says, waving him away.

A few minutes later, I hear footsteps coming from the hallway and Ducky comes in holding a plate of what, as far as I can see, is the apple-chocolate-honey-raisin space cake left over from yesterday. We were already high when we made it, so we added at least twice as much weed than the recipe called for.

"I found some leftover cake," he says, and puts the plate down in front of Mishy.

"Ay gan't joo, aazhoe," Mishy says, patting his chin.

It's getting harder and harder to understand what he's saying.

"What did he say?" Ducky asks.

"That he can't chew," I answer.

"Let's mash it up," Buoy suggests.

"Your fuckin' speaking privileges are denied for the rest of the day, asswipe," Ducky sneers.

"But…"

"If I hear another fuckin' peep out of you, Buoy, I swear I'll mash *you* up. I don't give a shit about your half-assed ideas," he adds. Then he turns to Mishy and asks, "Who fucked you up?"

"Wud ub Norriz's men," Mishy answers in his new Mishy-speak.

"What did he want?"

"Diz iz how dey wadded do led Liddlechief no e as do inglude dem in da biddnid, or eld dey'll gill ebrybody."

"Why didn't *you* kill *them?*" Ducky asks. "Isn't that why you've got that piece with you?"

"E jubbed me wed I didin zee. E was ayding id a fugging doorway," Mishy answers, then continues, "Pluz ay forgod my fuggin gun ad home addyway."

"Oh yeah, well that'll make killing them a lot harder," Ducky nods.

"Odderwide ay wud av plugged da fuggin bazdards."

Mishy continues his mouth-karate for a while. Talking so highly of himself must stroke his ego, but otherwise he should be happy he got off so easy.

We all cool it for a while. Even Ducky shuts up.

"Gibbe sub gake," Mishy says finally, breaking the silence.

I extend the plate towards him. Mishy pulls the ice pack away from his eye, looks at the cakes, takes the biggest piece and asks:

"Wad did yu pud in id?"

"Just a bit of weed," Ducky answers, "and some of the stuff that you developed."

"Bichin'" Mishy says in approval, and bites into the cake. The longer he chews, the more contorted his face becomes. "Yu gud av pud some fuggin suga in id do."

"It's got sugar-substitute," Buoy answers, but zips it when Ducky glares at him.

Mishy bites into the cake, then puts the ice back on his face and chews soundlessly.

"We should off those cocksuckers," Ducky says, and pops some cake into his mouth too.

"Wid wad?"

"I copied a key to my father's gun cabinet."

"Bidjin'" says Mishy. He doesn't want us to think he's a pussy. "Leds do id," he continues, and removes the bag from his face again. We see his nose.

We all moan *hoooly fuck* in chorus.

"Wud?" Mishy asks.

"Your nose is broken," Buoy answers.

"Why do you think he's icing it?" Ducky pipes up.

"We should reset it," I suggest.

"Yeah, there's an S-curve in it right now, Ducky says, giving his expert opinion, then he laughs.

The cake hit him pretty fast.

"Yu god a middor?" Mishy asks.

"There's one in the bathroom," Ducky answers, so Mishy clambers to his feet and goes in to take a look at himself. He curses a short round, then sticks his head through the door and asks:

"Who wads do do id?"

Silence. Like the grave. If we had a pin we would hear it drop.

I don't want to look at Mishy. We lay low, like shit in tall grass. The silence is becoming more and more awkward. Finally, I can't stand it anymore and look up. Ducky, Buoy, and Mishy are all staring at me.

"Me?" I wrinkle my forehead.

"It was your idea," Ducky says.

I saw a few episodes of that hospital show, the one where Tony Soprano's wife is the nurse, but that doesn't mean I can do a nose operation.

"Don shid yozedf, you cad do id," Mishy urges.

"I'm not shitting myself, but I'm no doctor," I say, trying to weasel out of it. "Why don't you go to the ER?"

"Shid, man, loog ad be," he says. "I gand go oud in bublig lige diz." He bursts out laughing, then hisses, and cautiously pats his nose, which is starting to resemble a fucking huge eggplant in size and colour as each minute passes. "Sdahp medding aroud, fugger, and do id arreddy!"

I guess there's nothing to lose. It's not *my* nose that'll look ugly if I mess up.

"Okay," I nod. "Get me a towel."

Ducky goes out into the bathroom and gets one from the cabinet.

"You got any whisky?" I ask, when he presses it in my hand.

"What kind do you want?"

"The kind that'll get him fucked up fast," I say.

"Ay dond dring algohol," Mishy grins.

"Then it doesn't matter what you bring," I say.

"I'll get it," Ducky nods.

Buoy watches, pale as a ghost, while I examine Mishy's nose. I'm trying to figure out where it got broken, but now I see that it looks like it's broken in several places.

Meanwhile, Ducky comes back with a bottle of Johnnie Walker Blue Label.

"Here," he says, and pushes the booze into Mishy's hand.

"You wad be do dring id?"

"Not *all* of it," I say.

Mishy unscrews the cap and sniffs the bottle's contents.

"Ay gand zmell anyding," he says.

"Don't smell it, take a swig," Ducky urges.

Mishy wasn't kidding, he really can't hold his liquor. Ten minutes later he's completely shit-faced. I help him over to a chair and sit him down, then I call Buoy to hold him so he doesn't keel over or start thrashing. Buoy clambers up off the couch. His skin is waxy and beads of sweat glisten at his temples, but he doesn't dare object. I tell Ducky to cradle Mishy's head as hard as he fucking can to keep him from twisting around during the operation. Meanwhile, Mishy starts laughing hysterically, but he doesn't feel pain anymore. I know, because when I press on his nose, he doesn't even notice. His gaze is foggy. He grins at me and says in a nasal voice:

"Wad id id, digga, wad yu waidin fo? Quid sdallin, muddafugga!"

I glance at Buoy. He looks like death warmed over.

Ducky grips Mishy's head like a vise and focuses intently.

I take a deep breath and grab hold of Mishy's dark-purple schnoz, swollen to the size of a dinner roll.

Ten minutes later, Mishy comes to, and a couple of minutes later, so does Buoy. It's hard to find words to properly describe what happened during the last quarter of an hour. As I snapped Mishy's nose back into place, it made a huge cracking noise, then the poor bastard howled and had some kind of spasm. I didn't manage to set his nasal bone properly, and Buoy started to projectile vomit, puking onto Mishy's shoulder, then passing out on the floor. By then I was covered in blood up to my elbows, and Ducky was bellowing about what a limp-dick pussy Buoy is and how he'll tell his brother to do something about him. I'm twisting Mishy's nose as hard as I can, but after a third big crack he somehow manages to free himself from Ducky's grip. Blood's gushing from his snout, tears from his eyes, so he can't really see much, he's just running around the room like a headless chicken, then he slams head-on into the door frame, staggers back, and sprawls out. He's fuckin' lucky his head hit the carpet and didn't bash against the edge of the Pearson Lloyd coffee table. Ducky tries to slap him back to his senses, but I tell him not to knock him around too much after the operation because the nasal bone can dislodge easily.

You can tell by Mishy's eyes that he's got no idea where he is. We explain it to him, then Ducky helps him up and over to the couch. Buoy's waking slowly too, but nobody's helping *him*. Mishy sits on the couch, eyes closed, head tilted back, wheezing quietly. His nose looks pretty harsh. It's about twice the size it was before the operation, and his t-shirt is drenched with blood. Buoy sits up, whimpering, blinking. He sniffs, then makes a face and says:

"It fucking stinks in here."

"You threw up on yourself," I say.

Buoy looks himself over and tries to brush the vomit off his t-shirt.

Mishy starts whimpering nasally, something about us helping him, I think, but by now it really *is* impossible to understand what he's saying.

"What should I bring?" Ducky asks.

"Middor," Mishy answers. "Ay wad do dee by bade."

I don't think that's a good idea. Ducky's not too crazy about it either, but he goes to the bathroom anyway and comes back with a shaving mirror. He hands it to Mishy, who slowly opens his eyes and lifts the mirror to his face. He looks at himself and speaks in an ominous tone.

"Ayb godda gill ebery zingle ode ob doze mudderfuggerz."

"The swelling'll go down in two weeks," I comment cautiously.

"Ayb sdill godda egzegute doze fuggin gogzuggers," Mishy says.

I'm pretty stoked not to be on his death list.

Ducky walks over to his closet, takes out a key ring, and says:

"I'll get the shotguns."

We're sitting in one of Ducky's pop's whips. We're totally starting to lose control, but as far as I can tell, Ducky & Co are not fucking woke to this. Sometimes, for whole long minutes at a time, I feel like all this isn't even happening to me, that I'm sitting in a 4D cinema with my stupid buddies watching some Z-movie action thriller instead.

Mishy's a fuckin' mess. He could barely get down the stairs but still wanted to drive. Thankfully Ducky wasn't having any of it. Now Ducky's driving, Mishy's sitting there grinning beside him, riding shotgun—he got super perky from the painkiller cocktail—while Buoy and I sit in the back. Slipknot's *Wait and Bleed* blares from the speakers. According to Mishy, this is the best music for killing. Ducky swiped two shotguns from his father's gun cabinet. He didn't find any cartridges to go with them, but he said they'd work to intimidate just the same. We'll find the prick, point the rifle at him, then beat him up real good, so he knows his place. Mishy lectures Ducky on not driving like a maniac 'cause the cops'll end up pulling us over. They're starting to freak out, but it'd be pathetic to turn back from here. We keep our mouths shut intensely for a while, then Mishy, I guess to distract us from the situation, starts talking about his new chick.

"Jeez dirdeen yeeds ode, buddafukka, and jeez indoo ebrydig," he says. "*Ebryding.* Jeez waded do be a born zdar zince jee wud a gid," he adds.

If I understood correctly, he's going on about a thirteen-year-old chick who's into everything, and who's wanted to be a porn star since forever. Then he tells us about their most recent fuck, and I'm wracking my brain, wondering if I actually know this chick or if I saw this scene in a movie. I mean, porn is a really hot item these days. Any of my friends can rattle off at least ten AVN Award-winning porn stars who earned a distinction for Best Foreign Double Anal Scene right off the bat, but can't list more than a couple of Hungary's kings.

"De besd bard is dad jee gand get knogged ub, guz jee didn ged id yet," Mishy explains.

"Yeah, I like chicks like that too," Ducky grins. "You don't have to spend money on condoms."

We drive past a pastry shop, which reminds me that we

forgot the leftover space cake out on the table and Ottó in the bathroom, unattended. We'd better get back before he wakes up and devours it all.

The GPS-slut is explaining which way to go. Mishy made a few calls and found out where Norris's henchman lives. Ducky tapped the address into the GPS and now we're sailing across the city. The slut just keeps running her mouth. If we survive this, I'm borrowing this gadget from Ducky. I've never jerked it to a GPS before. I've done it to a telephone operator, but I was really low then.

Buoy's head is pressed against the window. A thin stream of saliva trickles from his mouth. I guess he's conked out.

"Durn ride ere," Mishy gestures, and the GPS-slut affirms, saying *Turn right here, baby.*

If I wasn't shitting bricks, I might already have a boner. Ducky turns without signalling. Some douche honks behind us.

"Dage id eady," Mishy says, so Ducky slams down on the brakes. We start off again. "Diz id id," Mishy points to one of the huge pads.

Ducky removes his foot from the gas pedal. We roll slowly past the house. There's no movement inside. Mishy tells Ducky to drive on and find a parking space across the street. We find an empty place nearby. A tractor-trailer could easily fit in the spot, but of course Ducky can barely park. He turns the engine off. We decide to wait until that cocksucker comes home. I jab my elbow into Buoy's side. He's got the hats with holes cut for eyes that we're gonna wear as disguises. He stirs awake, mumbles something, rubs his eyes, then sits up, and stares silently into space for a few minutes. We spend the next ten minutes laying low. We don't speak or move, we barely even breathe. We sit in the car like a cluster of statues. Finally, Mishy breaks the silence.

"Whadda fug? Joo guyds shiddig yoselbs?"

"If we beat the dude up, it'll be a war," I say.

"Dafug? Ids arreddy wad," Mishy says, gesturing towards his nose. "Iv joo guyds ade shiddig yoselbs, ay wid do id adone."

"I'm not shitting myself," says Buoy.

Bullshit. I know he's scared shitless. *I'm* scared shitless. *Everyone* is scared shitless and everybody *knows* that the other person is scared shitless, but pretending not to be.

"Dugy?" Mishy asks.

Ducky doesn't answer. He hesitates, therefore he's scared shitless.

"What?"

"Ade joo shiddig yoselb?"

"You're shitting yourself, not me," Ducky growls, but I know he's shitting himself.

"I've got an idea," I say before Mishy can ask me if I'm *shiddig myzelb* too.

This one time, a buddy of mine got into a fight with a cabbie 'cause the dude wanted to fleece him. They found out where he lived and wanted to spray paint ESCARGOT FOR SALE: WE BUY SNAILS! on his house. In the end, they only got to writing out ESC, but that's not the point. We've got paint. We brought it to spray on the surveillance cameras.

"Joo ade ad idiod," Mishy says.

"What'll Littlechief say when he finds out you beat the shit out of Norris's henchman?" I ask.

Mishy seems uncertain, but then says:

"Ay dond gibe a shid. Ees nod da wud oo god beed up."

"If we grab the guy now and kick his ass, Norris'll kill you," I reason. "So will Littlechief."

"Ay don gib a shid," Mishy's balking, but his tone tells me that he's not so sure of himself either.

"It'll fit perfectly on the wall," I continue, after looking at the stone fence. "Let's spray it on. It'll drive him fuckin' crazy when all the gyppos and winos start hanging around the gate, hauling him escargots by the bagful."

"Good idea," Buoy says, clearing his throat.

I'm waiting for Ducky to tell him off, but Ducky doesn't say a word. He stares into space, drumming on the steering wheel with his fingers.

"Gib be da at," Mishy says, turning to the back seat. Buoy shoots me a bewildered look, then reluctantly hands him the black hat with the holes. Mishy pulls it over his face and turns to Ducky. "Ged dressd, digga!"

Ducky doesn't say a word. He just reaches in the back and Buoy presses the hat into his hand. As Ducky adjusts the mask over his face, a yellow light at the gate starts flashing. Then, a couple of seconds later, a huge-ass jeep slows down in front of the house.

"Eed ere," Mishy says, as the jeep turns into the driveway.

He grabs one of the shotguns. He wants to get out. I lean forward and put my hand on his shoulder.

"Lebbe go, muddafugga, guz ayl bage yo fade ib!" he growls at me.

He's about to open the door when Ducky, without much beating around the bush, rams him hard on the chin with his elbow. Mishy's jaw cracks loudly, his head slams against the window, then stays that way. KO. His nose starts bleeding. It leaves a red smear on the glass.

"Fucking hell," Ducky mumbles under his breath. "I don't wanna get killed," and with that, he turns the key in the ignition and steps on the accelerator. But the car won't move, only the engine roars like a motherfucker.

Ducky starts jerking the stick shift, finds first gear with great difficulty, and rams his foot down on the gas pedal.

The tires shriek, the car jerks, and the engine stalls. The smell of burnt rubber hits my nose. The jeep's tinted windows roll down slowly and a bald dude in sunglasses stares out at us. Someday I'm gonna find out where they breed their kind. We really need to get the fuck out of here. Ducky restarts the engine, but forgets to put it in neutral, so we stall again. Meanwhile, I keep staring at the jeep dude. I don't want to take my eyes off him, hoping that if I keep staring hard at him, maybe he won't attack us. But my mind-control attempt doesn't really work, 'cause the next minute the jeep's door opens, the dude gets out, and starts towards us. He's striding towards us confidently, but in no hurry. He seems calm, all his moves completely deliberate.

"Fuck, he's coming over here," I punch Ducky's shoulder and he howls.

I doubt it hurt. I didn't hit it *that* hard. More like he was startled.

Buoy looks out the window, sees Mr Clean, and launches a mantra.

"Fuckin' drive. Fuckin' drive. Fuckin' drive."

"Fuckin' drive," I urge Ducky too.

He starts the engine a third time, he pumps the pedal—this worked before—and then, somehow, he manages to get us rolling. The car jerks a couple times, but at least we don't stall. I look over my shoulder. Wall-to-wall-muscle-dude's picked up speed meanwhile. He's about twenty metres from us. He reaches into his jacket.

"Fuck! Fuck! Drive! Drive!" I scream, but the car's pretty bad at accelerating in third gear.

Ducky grips the wheel, his forehead sweaty. He looks in the mirror and signals right.

"Don't turn anywhere, motherfucker, just go straight!"

I shout at the top of my lungs.

I don't dare look over my shoulder.

Ducky floors the gas pedal. Finally, the engine's starting to rev up. We shoot straight through the junction. I look back. The bald dude's standing in the middle of the street. He pushes his sunglasses onto his forehead and grins as he starts to wave.

Luckily, I took the licence plates off.

4X200

It's five a.m. We're sitting at the back of the bus like a flock of hung-over sparrows on a wire. We can see everything from here. Can keep an eye on everyone. Zoli-boy doesn't wanna sit next to me, and for once I'm really happy about it 'cause I'm not in a good mood and I don't feel like listening to his bullshit the whole way. He's two seats in front of us, not squirming, just staring out the window. He's not even munching on anything. Not like I give a shit anyway. All day yesterday at school he was on my back and up my ass about wanting to talk about *something*, but I always shook him off, and he didn't come to practice, where I might have asked him what he wanted. It didn't really seem like he was pissed off. He said hello and all, but it's weird that he isn't talking to anyone. He didn't even ask if there was room in the back with us. Of course, there's always the chance that Ducky will tell him to fuck off. Zoli-boy isn't stupid. Maybe it was just that he considered the odds and didn't feel like getting slugged before the race.

Ducky, on the other hand, is hyped as fuck. It's like he snorted a snowman-sized speedball for breakfast. His pupils are bigger than his eyes, he's smacking up the little kids like it's already later on tonight, dropping rude comments, groping the chicks, sticking his hand between their legs, pawing their tits, badmouthing the bus loud enough that the driver can hear it too, of course. Most of the others, though, aren't going at it like that. Everyone's totally out of it. Which is no surprise at five in the morning. They listen to music, gnaw on sandwiches, watch a film, mess around with their phones and tablets, or try to sleep. I despise these dawn bus rides. The seats are uncomfortable and the whole bus is saturated with the smell of salami sandwiches, fuel oil, floor wax, and bad breath. Times like these I wish the race would get cancelled, or the bus would break down, so we'd never get there, or the maintenance crew would fuck up again, like last year in Eger, when they combined industrial amounts of bleach and sulphuric acid and flooded the pool with chlorine gas, but so hardcore that disaster management had to come in and air the place out. The *News* was helpful in giving us the exact recipe: sixty kilograms of bleach combined with three kilograms of sulphuric acid. I wrote it down. But of course we always get to where we need to go, and by then I don't mind that we're there anymore, 'cause I wanna win.

Moms wave their kids off with teary eyes—'cause they haven't got the slightest inkling what their little boys have in store for them at initiation tonight—and dads smoke cigarettes with bored or sleepy faces. As the bus rolls out of the parking lot, Ducky's already telling all the clowns about what happened after we dropped Mishy off behind the hospital and went back to his place to clear away the traces.

"My old man, shit, he got so glazed from the space cake. He was rolling around on the living-room floor counting his fingers, but could never get all ten. He was hella wasted."

Ducky's old man is a stoned ATM machine.

We had to reconstruct the events afterwards, like an episode of *CSI,* but basically what happened was that while we were making asses of ourselves with Norris's henchman, Ottó regained his senses, went downstairs, and sat down to watch porn. Then Ducky's old man walked in and asked Ottó where we're at, but he couldn't say, then his pop started badgering Ottó to watch the game with him, but Ottó asked if maybe he wanted to watch porn instead, so Ducky's old man plopped down on the couch and polished off the rest of the space cake in front of the TV. We packed it chock full of weed. It would've been enough to last us the whole of our four-day class trip. The only reason you couldn't taste the weed was 'cause we made half the dough out of sugar-substitute. When we got back home, Ottó and Ducky's pop were rolling around, screeching on the Persian carpet, while we just stood there, staring at them, not suspecting that this was just the beginning, 'cause the next minute Ducky's mom stormed out of the upstairs bedroom, making straight for the bathroom, rubbing her twat like crazy and shrieking, *aaah, shit, shit it stings, ow, ow, fuck it stings.* The old bitch sprinted so damn fast I was scared those amazing jugs of hers would rip off her chest. Ducky was just staring, like a snowman in a tanning salon. I could tell by his face that he was totally whacked, but when he was still there just standing like a dick half a minute later, I told him to use this opportunity to bring the guns in from the car, 'cause there's no way in hell he was gonna get an easy break like this again. Amirite or what? His dad's squirming around in the living room, high as a kite, and his mom's scratchin' her pussy like a turntable record and running around upstairs. All he's gotta do is mosey on in with the guns and that's it. No way they're gonna notice. Ducky pulled himself together and went out to the car, took the two shotguns out, but of course he didn't get a chance to sneak them back into the gun cabinet 'cause his dad noticed at the last minute. Luckily, the dude was so out of it that when he saw the kid with the two massive rifles, he burst into such a fit of laughter he almost choked. Thank the fucking Christ he didn't remember any of it the next day.

Ducky just keeps going on and on about it, like a wound-up toy, and I'm starting to get drowsy again. I'm watching Zoli-boy. He's not really in great shape these days. He's acting like a dumbass all the time, talking bullshit, and then he's all surprised nobody'll fuck him. Before we left, Viki came up to me and asked what Zoli-boy's problem was with Ducky, and when I said *fuck if I know,* she told me that *somebody* said that Zoli-boy's acting like a dickhead with Ducky or something, but they couldn't say exactly what was going on, 'cause the chick—or dude—who was "blabbing" didn't quite get what was going down. *Blabbing.* That's the word she used. I told Viki she should drop it and chill 'cause there's no way Zoli-boy's being a dickhead to Ducky, first of all, 'cause he's broke as shit compared to Ducky, and second, 'cause Ducky'll bash his head in if he fucks with him too much. So I told Viki to back the fuck off, and now here I am getting all obsessed over it. I mean, no matter how much I wrack my brain, I just can't figure out what the fuck is up with Zoli-boy. After a while I get so confused that I can't fall asleep, and then I gotta piss real bad, but of course you can't use the toilet. I've never in my whole life been on a bus where the toilet was working.

Meanwhile, Ducky starts to hassle Zoli-boy.

"Hey, Zoli-boy, listen," he calls to him, and Zoli-boy slowly turns but doesn't say anything, just looks at Ducky with this droopy-ass face.

Ducky goes on.

"It'd be killer if you didn't fuck up the relay this year."

Last year we blew the 4x100-metre 'cause of Zoli-boy. The referee said that the dumbass left the block too soon, so we were disqualified. Everybody was raging 'cause we beat that cocksucking Kaposvár team by two body lengths and of course they had to rub it in by laughing in our faces when they found out we fucked up. Ducky went batshit crazy, he was ready to pulverise Zoli-boy. The only reason he didn't punch him was 'cause Coach Bandi came over and dragged the dipshit off. After all, he couldn't kick his ass right there by the pool. There would've been too many witnesses. I totally thought Zoli-boy would quit swimming, but come Monday morning, he showed up at the pool and trained like nothing had happened. Since then, Ducky takes every chance he gets to mention it, otherwise everybody would've forgotten about it by now.

Zoli-boy still says nothing. Somehow the silence is starting to feel weird. Ducky's on his case exactly 'cause he knows the kid's gonna explode in one second flat, scream with his face all red and throw a tantrum. He even bawls sometimes, but this isn't what's going down right now. A sick smile spreads across Zoli-boy's face as he stares at Ducky, and he doesn't seem tense at all.

"Chill, Ducky, I won't fuck up," he says finally.

Even his voice is all mellow. I'll bet he popped some of his mom's meds.

Ducky's so shocked he forgets to go on busting Zoli-boy's balls, and just says:

"Fine, fuckface."

Then he leans forward and pats Zoli-boy on the shoulder.

Zoli-boy says nothing again. He turns away and stares out the window. Ducky's hand hovers in the air for a sec.

Then he slowly retracts it, and smiles. He's kinda lost. I guess Zoli-boy's tactics can kick in too sometimes. Either that, or his mom's got some bitchin' meds.

An hour later I really need to piss again. Another half an hour later I can't stand it anymore and I think about asking somebody for an empty plastic bottle. But then I go up front instead and ask Coach Bandi when we're gonna stop, but the old man barks at me to haul ass back to my seat and tie a knot on my dick. On the way back, I take a little girl's drink. Of course she bursts into tears, but I don't give a shit. It's an emergency. I drink the OJ as I go, sit down in my seat, and try to piss behind the cover of the backrest. The others mess with me, push me, give me shit about my dick—like they've never seen it before—and the chicks start giggling when they realize what I'm doing. It's the driver who's fucking with me the hardest, though he's got no idea I wanna piss. It's like he always finds a pothole right when I manage to aim into the mouth of the bottle. Whatever, he's gonna have to clean up the spill. I get the hang of it by the time I finish and succeed in getting most of the piss actually *in* the bottle. Just as I wring out the last drop, Coach Bandi starts hollering at the top of his lungs. His voice crackles like it's coming from a PA system, but he doesn't need a mic. Everybody can hear him loud and clear.

"We're stopping at the next gas station. You get eight minutes. *Everybody* pisses."

Fucking hell.

Coach Bandi probably miscalculated at this morning's grocery run and didn't get to fill his hip flask properly. Drinking hard liquor in a gas station at dawn is level hardcore. The old man'd better take a nip of some rotgut fast, otherwise he's gonna be super uptight by the time we get there, and that makes him deal out the blows double time. The kids stand in line at the door of the bus, and the driver's deliberately taking half an hour to park. I can see on his face that it's on purpose and he's having a fucking ball. Nevermind. The cocksucker's got it coming tonight. Finally he manages to stop, and everybody wants to jump out the door at once. Coach Bandi whips us all into shape. The little dingbats stampede into the convenience store as if their parents hadn't packed enough cold rations to last them a month. Now that I'm in no hurry anymore, I wait until they get off and put the bottle of piss away. I read somewhere this one time that an ancient and legal way of improving your performance is to drink your own urine. There's gotta be something to it, 'cause I heard on the news that a couple of Chilean miners drank their own urine after an explosion and they were rescued from the mine shaft.

We go to a lot of swim meets, and I'm used to the countryside gas stations and the country-bumpkin asshole gas-station attendants, plus you can always find some pretty awesome graffiti in the bathrooms. I take a picture of Jesus's head with a huge, smoking joint in his mouth, sprayed on with a stencil, with the words, *"Would Jesus do it?"* I snap a couple of pics with my phone, then I'm about to head over to the store to swipe a couple of candy bars when Ducky moseys past me and into one of the stalls with his phone pressed to his ear. It takes me one second to figure out that he's talking to Buoy. I don't follow exactly what they're going on about, but I do get that there's some deep shit going down, 'cause Buoy's been banned for the next ten matches. I wash my face and Ducky flushes the toilet, so I can't hear what he's mumbling. Then he steps out of the stall and I stick my hand under the faucet, which quiets the gushing. Ducky tells him to chill. His brother'll smooth things over somehow. Then he hangs up while I put my hands under the dryer, pretending not to have heard anything.

I go back to the shop, fill my pockets with candy bars, then walk out the automatic doors, board the bus, sit down, and shove a couple of them in my face. Meanwhile, the others slowly start drifting back. Coach Bandi's losing his shit 'cause we're way past eight minutes by now. Ducky's the first one in from the back row. He grabs his bag, rummages through it for a while, then turns towards me, jabs his finger towards Zoli-boy's water bottle, and says:

"Give it here."

"What for?" I ask.

Instead of answering, Ducky starts waving a blister pack of meds in front of my nose.

"What's this?" I ask, and hand Ducky the bottle.

"Cialis," Ducky grins, then looks around and starts shaking the potency enhancer into the bottle.

"You've lost your fucking mind," I say.

Ducky doesn't seem to have heard. He's jamming the pills into the bottle with a crazed look in his eye.

"We should crush them up," I suggest.

"What for?" he says, looking up.

"They'll dissolve faster."

Ducky looks at me, then shoves the bottle in my hand and says:

"I'll crush a few. You keep shaking."

While I shake the water bottle, Ducky grabs a Swiss army knife from his bag and starts hacking up the pills on the seat's armrest. He's not being stingy for sure. If he downs this whole drink, he's gonna jizz in his pants every five minutes all weekend. It's easier to get a boner on the bus anyway 'cause of all the bumping around.

"They're coming!" I warn Ducky.

Ducky looks up for a second, then dices up one more pill in a flash, like Gordon Ramsey with a garlic clove. He grabs the bottle from me, sweeps the crushed potency enhancer in, shakes it up vigorously, and puts it back in its place. He then plops back down in his seat, pulls out his cell phone, and starts fucking around with it, as if he'd been at it this whole time.

Zoli-boy's one of the last ones back. The spiked apple juice has settled by now, so he won't taste the Cialis. He sits down, doesn't look at anybody, doesn't say a word. He's hardly ever this mopey. A bit of potency enhancer might even do him some good.

The bus rolls out of the parking lot. I'm guessing we're off the fucking hook for once 'cause Coach Bandi's managed to up his blood-alcohol level and he'll be resting a bit now. Ducky's still petting his touch screen while glancing at Zoli-boy every once in a while. Zoli-boy doesn't reach for his bottle for a long time, but then, an hour later, when we speed past the Great Plains, he drinks the whole thing straight down in big gulps. He makes a face at the end, and turns around, so I close my eyes fast, and pretend to be sleeping. Zoli-boy doesn't ask anything. I count to sixty, then open my eyes. Zoli-boy's staring out the window. The landscape is flat as fuck. There's a grey cloud swirling in front of a barn. At first I think it's a swarm of locusts, but it turns out to be just horseflies. Then I spot a lake of red water, but that turns out to be a red sludge reservoir or some shit. This place needs a couple of well sweeps, a herd of grey cattle, and those cool horsemen with their stripy bellbottoms, but all you can stare at from the highway are the endless plains.

I'm watching Zoli-boy from the corner of my eye. He's tense, like a porn star in a confessional. He's probably thrown off by this unexpected onslaught of horniness. Maybe he suspects his tight pants, or the bumping bus, or the smell of the girls' sickly sweet spray-on deodorant wafting towards him from their direction, which many wrongly think is pussy smell. I didn't think the stuff would kick in so fast, but it's logical after all: if you wanna fuck and your dick ain't hard, there's no time to twiddle your thumbs. Meanwhile, Ducky's looking at hardcore porn sites, and naturally, he's got the tablet at an angle where Zoli-boy can see the dominatrixes—gigantic tits, whips in their mouths, dildos up their asses and all—even if he doesn't want to. By the time we arrive, he's jizzed himself at least twice. Half an hour later, when we park in front of the pool building, he gets off the bus with a red face, holding his bag in front of him. He avoids the girls. Actually, he's avoiding everybody, but that's pretty hard in such a crowd. As he's shuffling around with his bag, Ducky walks over and starts hassling him in front of the girls, asking stuff like why is he using his hands when he could hold up the bag without it, and some other shit. The chicks are shrieking. I guess Ducky's already let them in on it.

As we step into the lobby and the smell of chlorine hits me, my brain clicks into a different state of consciousness. My stomach clenches for a second, then I take a few deep breaths, but secretly, so no one sees, and my tension starts to ease. By the time we get our locker keys in the changing room, all I can think about is the 200-metre freestyle. I swam the length a couple of times on the bus, imagined the start, the flip-turns, and the streamline. I counted the strokes and pushed myself in the third fifty really hard. I pack my stuff in the locker, tie my swimsuit, and put on my bathrobe. I'm headed up to the pool area to warm up when the cocksucking Kaposvár guys come barging in. The rival relay team. It's been counterstrike attacks for years. One year we win, the next year it's them. Last year they had it lucky, so this year we need to throttle them.

"Hey there," one of the cocksuckers says, the one called Nándi, trying to get chummy. We grip each other's hands, our finger-bones cracking. We slap each other on the back. Nobody's being soft about it. Our fingers leave nice welts. You could carve the testosterone in the air with a knife. Nándi won a silver in the 400-metre freestyle at the Junior European Championships last year, and ever since he's been surfing an ego trip that would put Ronaldo to shame.

"How's it hangin', Ducky?" he asks. "You got the butterfly down yet?"

The dude's harmless, but you don't mess with Ducky before a race. You don't mess with him period, but especially not before a race. He starts psyching himself up real early, so that when he gets up on the starting block he'll really believe he can mow everybody down, that he *has to* mow everybody down, including us. Sure, everybody's like that, but Ducky's the most serious about it.

"Suck my dick, asshat," Ducky answers in a bone-chillingly calm voice.

He doesn't even glance at the kid.

The dude tries to brush it off with a lame comment. Ducky looks up. He smiles coldly, the air freezing around him. Nándi doesn't know what his next move should be. It really *was* just an innocent joke and dumbass Ducky's being all tough guy on him. The grin fades from the dude's face. This is what Ducky's been waiting for. He bursts out laughing and slaps him real hard on the back a couple of times, till the kid chuckles awkwardly. Then the others join in, everybody talking shit to everybody else, everybody laughing. Ducky peers around slyly, thinking nobody can see him. He leans over to Nándi and whispers something in his ear. The kid freezes for a moment, and when he comes to, he grabs his stuff, sits down on another bench, and packs his stuff in another locker. He doesn't look at Ducky again. Ducky puts his things neatly away and heads out to warm up.

I'm glad Ducky's so calm. This one time he got into a fist fight because of some similar shit, but of course I wouldn't want him to chill *too* much and get all Zen master on us, 'cause if the Kaposvár team does end up beating us in the relay, we're the ones who'll get our asses kicked, not him. Meanwhile, Zoli-boy rushes to the toilet, to jerk it real quick, I'm guessing. Maybe then he'll get through the warmup without coming in the water. When he returns, he hides behind a locker to change. The 4x200-metre freestyle relay's in the afternoon. Maybe by then the drug will have cleared from his system. The more I think about it, the more I realize that I still don't know why we had to mix the potency enhancer in his drink. Sure, it's a funny prank and all, but what's really going on here is that Ducky's trying to get Zoli-boy kicked off the relay team. If the dipshit can't race, Coach Bandi will be forced to put someone else on the team. I hope Ducky considered the fact that Zoli-boy's in fuckin' awesome shape, and that no matter who takes his place, we end up worse off.

Coach Bandi already told us back home that everybody's swimming the whole "menu." And this goes down at every swim meet. Everybody swims all styles so we can build up a proper race routine. Things went pretty well in the morning. We delivered the times expected of us, which of course doesn't mean that Coach was satisfied. He always tells everybody off, even if we're on the podium: if your time is good, if you don't position your hand properly at the stroke, if you roll onto the wall too early at the turn, if you meet the water at too sharp an angle when diving, if you don't streamline long enough after the turn.

We eat lunch in a fast-food joint at the base of a long housing block. I fish a dinosaur-sized cockroach out of my goulash, send one of the little kids to fetch bread, and when he walks off after moaning and groaning, I put the bug in his soup. I mash it up, 'cause if I leave it in one piece, he'll definitely notice it. I even manage to pick out the exoskeleton before the dude comes back with the bread. After lunch we go to our lodgings and rest up, except for Zoliboy, who doesn't get to rest, naturally, 'cause he's gotta run out to the bathroom, like, every ten minutes. Ducky's already hyping for the relay. We look at the morning's lap times to know who's in what shape. Based on the results, the Kaposvár team fucked up the tapering, so I don't know what they were so high and mighty about in the locker room. Considering what they showed—and what we did—we've got the relay in the bag, so long as Zoliboy doesn't fuck up, of course. Walking back from lunch, I subtly asked him what was wrong. He said he must've eaten something that didn't agree with him and not to worry, he'll be all set by this afternoon. His bullshit was so brilliant I almost praised him, but came to my senses at the last second. I'm sprawled out on my bed listening to the most recent Lostprophets album, but can't detach myself from the thought that the singer raped babies, so I just delete the whole folder instead. Luckily, I took the whole file from a torrent site, otherwise I'd be mad as hell right now knowing that I was stuffing that cocksucker's bank account with my purchase. I switch to Slipknot and swim the afternoon's races in my head a couple of times. I'm doing a mental flip-turn when Coach Bandi comes barging into the room without knocking. We all sit up in bed simultaneously, like Count Dracula in his coffin. Only Zoli-boy doesn't notice that Coach is here. He lies motionless on the top bunk, turned against the wall. He's listening to music too, and if he's got any brains, he'll skip all the female artists. There's a huge colour poster on the wall, and if he opens his eyes, he'll find himself face to face with a blonde, complete with fake tits and BJ lips, being pampered by a huge black dude from behind. Ducky designated that one as Zoli-boy's bed after he scanned all the bunks and posters. I guess this seemed the wildest option, 'cause the poster I had showed a stupidfaced actor dude in a leather jacket staring seductively from the hood of a fire-red sports car. Maybe I'm in some faggot's bed? I poke Zoli-boy to rouse him, but as I touch him, he jolts, then, when he turns, he sees Coach Bandi. I root for him not to freeze up from the shock, but luckily he sits up immediately.

"I'm glad your siesta is so nice and pleasant," he begins, nodding towards the poster. Then continues: "If you fuck up the relay this year too, son, I will personally rip your balls off. Am I clear?"

Zoli-boy hiccups something, I don't understand what, even though I'm sitting right under him. If that doesn't make him tense up, nothing will. It'll be a miracle if he doesn't fuck the relay up outright.

"Something the matter?" Coach Bandi looks at him piercingly.

"Yes, Coach," Zoli-boy finally groans. "…Or actually, no… I mean, everything's fine."

Ducky seems disappointed. He looks at Coach Bandi and says:

"Zoli-boy's got the runs."

"Huh?" Coach says, turning towards him angrily.

"Zoli-boy," Ducky repeats. "The runs."

Now I'm sure that he really wants to get Zoli-boy kicked off the relay team.

"You got diarrhea?" Coach Bandi asks Zoli-boy.

"I'm fine," Zoli-boy answers, but doesn't sound too convincing. "I had a stomach-ache this morning, but everything's okay now."

"Don't mess with me, son," Coach rumbles. "You can't swim the relay if you're sick."

"No, I'm really feeling better now," Zoli-boy insists. "The coffee must have set it off."

"Is that why you're running off to the john every five minutes?" Ducky grunts.

"That's not true," Zoli-boy says, defensive and desperate.

"It's really not," I say. "The last time he went out was half an hour ago."

Of course that's bullshit too, but I do kinda feel bad about the Cialis, and I don't want Coach to kick Zoli-boy off the team.

"Shut up!" Coach Bandi says. He's near the end of his rope. We know what's coming, so we zip it and listen. Coach Bandi sizes Zoli-boy up, time seems to come to a standstill, maybe we've been here for days, we'd be ready to scream if someone came in the room, then Coach continues: "Whip yourself into shape for warm-up, son, otherwise Kishorvát's gonna replace you."

When he leaves, I check my phone. Coach's visit lasted three minutes.

My eyes meet Ducky's. He seems disappointed, but doesn't say anything. He just shrugs and leans back on the bed.

The next-to-last race is the 4x200-metre freestyle relay. After that, there's just the women's 4x100. We're in the final with the best time and will be swimming in lane four. You can keep a close eye on everybody from there. You alternate looking right and then left at turns. The outer lanes are shit to swim in 'cause you get the waves straight-on, and even in crystal-clear water, you might not be able to see to the other end of the pool, and then it's impossible to catch someone gaining a lead. Unless, of course, it's you who's sneaked off in the lead. As the start of the race gets nearer, my consciousness narrows and all I can think about is that we gotta kick everybody's asses. We made it to the finals with a pretty big advantage, but until the last guy on your team hits the wall, you can't know if some cocksucker on another team wasn't taking the whole field for a ride in the prelims. It's kinda hard, though, to mislead the others in a relay, 'cause it's four people who've gotta be in on the tactics scam, but you can work it if you really want to.

Zoli-boy doesn't jump the gun this time, and he even swims his best time this year. With a hard-on. It's only 'cause of the flying start that a new national record isn't set. I'm the anchor, diving last with a body-and-a-half length's advantage, and shoot off even more on the first fifty metres. I pace myself, saving my strength for the second half of the distance. If the Kaposvár team's kid in lane five starts coming up, I can upshift. He's basically got zero chance of gaining on me. This isn't mind-over-matter anymore. In the 200-metre race, a three- or four-metre advantage is more than enough. I'm about to explode. I cut through the water with long strokes, my reach stretching nice and long. My muscles aren't burning, I don't feel tired, and streamline lengthily underwater after the final turn, while the others are just now reaching the wall. I swim the last twenty metres in a delirium, barely breathing, and almost shatter the touch pad as I slam into the wall. We beat the team in second place by two body lengths. The dude from the Kaposvár team petered out by the end. Even the Szolnok team beats them at the last catch. Ducky's in ecstasy, jumping up and down and hollering at the pool's edge, even though he swam pretty shit time. I don't look at the scoreboard, but for sure it was at least half a second less than what Coach Bandi asked of us. Ducky swam first and the dude from the Szeged team he hassled in the locker room most def came up on him four or five tenths of a second. It's not much, but it was still us who had to work it off. If you fuck up in the relay, it's *you* who fucks up. But if we win, then we win *together*. I grip the rope. I'm in the same place I started out. I take a deep breath. When the last team's anchor reaches the wall, I'm not panting anymore. I'm mute and cold. The others are hugging each other by the pool, high-fiving, shouting. I take my goggles off and glance up at the stands. Coach Bandi's looking at his stopwatch, then he wrinkles his forehead and writes something down on his pad. Even from here you can tell he's not happy. The Kaposvár team's kid clutches the other rope, then comes over to me and we shake hands. He gasps for breath. He ran himself ragged. He slips under the rope and swims to the ladder. I grab hold of the poolside by the block and lunge out of the water. I'm barely out when Ducky's got his arm around my neck, screaming into my ear, "We fuuuuckin' destroooooyed them!" I look over Ducky's shoulder. A competition referee is staring at us, looking strict. I pretend not to notice. Meanwhile, the Kaposvár team slinks away. I know their coach. They're really gonna get it later. I mean, they deserve it though. They were weak. We gather up our stuff, I put on my robe and head down to the showers. There's plenty of time till results are announced.

As the speaker blares our names, we step up onto the podium. The four of us barely fit, and we shove each other around a little before everyone finds their place. Ducky's hogging the area up front, completely blocking out Zoliboy, who, for once, has no objections to this. I think about pushing Ducky off, maybe he'll fall on the County Assembly Sports Committee's Vice-Chairman, who is distributing the medals. The dude's got a huge double-chin and his face is all red, like he just stepped out of a sauna. He definitely flunked PE in school. We lean down one by one, hogface breathes heavy and loud as he drapes the medals around our necks, gazes earnestly into our eyes, congratulates us, and shakes our hands. Ducky tries to get the attention of the chick carrying the silver tray of medals, *pssst pssst,* but she can't hear him 'cause the announcer starts listing the Szolnok relay-team members' names. Then it's the Kaposvár team's turn. They've managed to collect themselves enough that you can't tell they're disappointed. Everybody shakes with everybody else. We're all sportsmanlike homies. Ducky can't resist dropping a comment though: *nice job, fellas.* They know he's messing with them, and they just murmur something in reply. I'm still up on the podium but I take off the medal. I don't care about all this fuss. I'm here for the adrenaline.

The chicks flopped bigtime. Coach Bandi was livid,

'cause he expected them to bag first place no prob, but in the end, they almost lost the medal even. They're still sulking as they stand around looking blasé on the podium. They congratulate the winning team, but would rather scratch their eyes out. I know them. What I don't get is why Coach Bandi's surprised. Everybody knew they'd swim like shit. It was last year at the Junior World Championships that things started getting bad between the girls—though they weren't too crazy about each other before either—after it turned out that Ducky fucked all of them, one after the other, at training camp. Of course, nobody would ever have found out, but the dumbass got so wasted at the banquet from the free drinks, he started mouthing off about how he's the only guy who's also on the women's relay team. Like Robbie Williams in *Spice Girls*. Naturally, the girls immediately pounced on each other, tearing each other's hair, scratching and clawing, you name it. They had to be pried apart. Meanwhile, Ducky was standing at the counter, laughing.

At dinner, I ask Ducky what's up with Buoy 'cause I can't reach him on the phone. I pretend not to know anything, and he tells me that Buoy got busted for doping at some international water-polo meet, and is probably gonna be banned for several months, and not even his brother, a member of the water-polo federation board, will be able to gloss things over. I murmur about how that sounds really fucked up, but considering the amount of EPO Buoy was doing, I'm surprised he lasted this long. The funny thing about the whole thing is that it's exactly *because* of his big brother that he even started that shit. Everybody was always hassling him about his brother. Chicks used to sleep with him 'cause they thought they'd have a better chance of hooking up with his polo-star brother for a night. Sure, Buoy had a goddamn blast for a while, but then he realized what a fucking loser it made him. One night he got smashed real bad at the Rhino, and he laid out his plans, telling me how he would surpass his brother's achievements. I already knew that he wouldn't have an easy time, 'cause the dude had been to two Olympics already, but I was like, whatever, it's none of my business.

I'm pushing around the neon-pink square of cake on my plate while we discuss tonight's initiation. All the little kids are on our list. Ducky says that one of the fat, blond kids made some snide comment to him on the bus so *leave him to me*. It'll be *exclusive* treatment, he grins, pointing the kid out. The kid looks pale and squishy, not dangerous or one to make snide comments. At least he never messed with *me* before, but you never know with these little snot-nosed toddlers. Fatso looks real innocent from over here, but he could be a spoiled little cocksucker. This one time at initiation, a dude tried to threaten us, saying that his dad was a cop and he'd lock us in jail. The only thing he achieved with this was to get a treatment twice as special as the rest. Still, he just couldn't shut the fuck up, so after lights out, Ducky went to his room and whispered that he'd cut the kid's throat in his sleep if he dared to rat us out. I wouldn't have put my life on it that Ducky really would've done it, but you gotta admit: he can be pretty convincing. The poor little bastard staggered around all morning the next day at the pool with huge bags under his eyes, and every time he sat down, he drifted off to sleep. A year later, he was the biggest asshole at initiation.

We wait until the corridor quiets down, then go visit the little kids, armed with slippers, towels, and flashlights. Ducky's even got a plastic bag, for what I don't know, 'cause we've never used one before. We knock quietly on the girls' door and invite them to come with us as judges, then head over to the kids' room. They blink sleepily in the lamplight. One of them slips his hand out from under the covers. Ducky shines the flashlight on him and tells him to quit fapping, which makes everybody laugh while the kid turns beet red. Ducky quickly orders him up and the chicks sit down on his bed. Then we line the kids up by the wall, tell them to pull their pants down, and we slap their asses one by one with shower slippers. Ducky attends to the blond kid, and naturally he gets twice as many slaps. I didn't think they'd take it this well. Only a couple of them start blubbering, and actually, it's just one who gets really whiny, but we shut him up real fast. Now it's time for the towel. We twist it, wet the end under the tap, and snap at their backs till they've got welts. A few of them burst into tears again, the blond kid too, but he gets twice as many whips again from Ducky, who finally walks over and hands him a tissue. The kid's surprised, reaching gratefully for it, but Ducky drops it on the floor at the last second, and when the towhead looks at him all puzzled, Ducky booms at him to pick it up. Then, as he leans down, Ducky lifts his foot and tells him to lick the bottom of his shower slippers clean. At first the kid thinks it's some kind of joke and starts giggling awkwardly, but Ducky just pushes his slimy slippers in his face and repeats the order. Someone snorts, laughing, and porky starts bawling. He gets that this is dead serious. He really will have to lick the crud off. I'm starting to feel sorry for the poor thing. He's a fuckin' mess, even without knowing that Ducky intentionally went into the men's room before we came over here. Next minute, one of the bigger dudes steps over to the kid and bitch-slaps him real hard, so finally he starts licking the bottom of the slipper. Of course my cell phone has to ring right at that second. I check the display. My mom. Maybe she only just realized that I'm not home. Otherwise I don't have a clue why she'd be calling me at this hour. I turn the sound off and watch the little kid's clean-up job. He spits and gags, but licks faster and faster. I guess he realized that the quicker he finishes, the quicker he's free of this grinning psycho who's shining a flashlight in his face.

I'm starting to get bored of the show. I look around. The little boys are deathly pale, staring saucer-eyed. They have some idea of what's coming. They've heard the horror stories.

"Let's see you lap it with your *whole* tongue, shithead, or you'll be licking the dingleberries from my asshole in a minute," Ducky threatens.

My phone rings again. Mom can't seem to chill. I decline the call and pocket the phone, but then I realize that I should probably just talk to her before she starts calling Coach Bandi.

"I'll be right back," I say to the dude standing next to me, who's watching Ducky in amazement, then I quietly step out into the hall and shuffle back to our room.

Zoli-boy's out cold, turned towards the wall. He's whimpering in his sleep. I didn't even notice that he wasn't at initiation. I fish out a secret stash of weed from my bag. Somehow I'm not in the mood for all this anymore, so I go down to the backyard instead and step behind a row of garbage containers to roll a J. As I take the rolling paper and the weed from my pocket, the top of a container bursts open with a loud clatter and a grubby-faced guy with a beard climbs out of the garbage. It's like he's emerging from a tank, exactly like that dude with the leather cap in *Kelly's Heroes.* But his clothes look like he swiped them from the set of some zombie flick. As he scrambles out of the reeking garbage and lands beside me, I slowly look him over. He really *does* look like a zombie, except maybe his face is kind of in better shape. He shakes a couple of potato peels from his hair, looks at me, and says:

"Greetings, young Padawan. May I have a toke of your cigarette?"

All this is so weird that I wouldn't have been surprised if the old dude's words appeared in a thought bubble. I tell him sure he can, but I can't really talk by this point. My mind's all hyped up at times like these. I don't even try to follow my train of thought. I listen to the fella. We kill the joint, and he goes on about how he feels like he's finally found a person to share his views about the apocalypse with, or something. First he tells me not to worry about the homeless. They'll be all right. Moreover, since humans are cranking out more and more garbage, quality of life will become increasingly better for winos, since they know perfectly well what to look for and where. And everything's gonna be destroyed by the apocalypse pretty soon anyway. I try three times to say the word apocalypse, but I just can't get it out, so homie lifts his finger and simply whispers:

"Armageddon."

"Bruce Willis." I nod. "That's a badass dude."

The guy wrinkles his forehead, and when I don't say anything, he shrugs and asks me:

"I'm hungry. Would you like to have dinner with me?"

I know it's impolite to decline such an invitation, but two chicks gave me their dinners at the restaurant, so I wolfed down three portions of fried cheese, and I'm still completely stuffed. I tell him I just ate, but thanks anyway. Homie smiles and says no worries, your loss, then scrambles up onto the container's top, looks back one more time, then disappears through the opening, closing the cover over him.

I stand around for a little while longer beside the container, listening to the sounds of the dude shifting around inside, then head to the building entrance, freaking out a little, 'cause what if Coach Bandi's gotta piss right now. My bowels start rumbling at the stair landing. Like distant cannon fire. It's dead quiet on our floor. It feels like the initiation was a thousand years ago, but there's no way they're gonna be done so fast. They're probably doing some quiet torments. I hurry it up so I can get to the bathroom in time. Somebody left the light on. I can't decide which stall to use, but I'm about to shit myself. I shuffle around flustered for a while, then take a deep breath and enter the stall at the far end, with pussies, cocks, names, and numbers scrawled on the door.

Ducky stands in front of the toilet bowl, his back to the door, sticking a fucking enormous hypodermic needle to the hilt into his ass. His butt cheeks are full of needle marks. I guess I never noticed before because I don't spend too much time staring at his rear end. The door detaches from my fingers and keeps swinging open. Ducky pushes the contents of the hypo into his glute, then yanks the needle out. Now I can really see how incredibly long it is. The door knocks against the wall. Ducky looks up.

"You could have locked the door, for fuck's sake," I say, glancing at the hypo.

Ducky seems flustered for a sec, then turns towards me and hides the hypo behind his back.

"I saw what you did," I grin.

"Buoy's aunt prescribed it," he tries to put up a front. "My fuckin' ears hurt like hell."

I know he knows I know it's bullshit. I stare at this poor bastard as he's standing there with the needle hidden behind his back, and the image of his pinpricked ass flashes through my mind, and I just can't hold back the laughter anymore, which actually comes out sounding more like a mew. Ducky's looking at me odd, like he's scared, while tears well up in my eyes, and I just keep screeching, and I just can't stop. I don't know how much time passes like this, but Ducky collects himself and says:

"Fuckin' hell, stop it already. You'll wake Coach."

This just fuels the fire. I start whooping again, and can't stop for, like, two minutes, and meanwhile I'm freaking out that I'm gonna be laughing for the rest of my life. Ducky finally gets that there's no point in shushing me, 'cause I'm not shutting up. I know this expression of his. Now comes the part where he starts losing his patience. He takes a step towards me, and I leap aside like a bullfighter. Ducky shakes his head, looking at me. He shrugs, then leaves the bathroom. Wiping my tears, I step into the empty stall and squat over the toilet bowl, but there's no way in hell I can squeeze the fudge out, I'm laughing so hard.

4X100

As Zoli-boy swims up to the wall, I lean down confidently and grab hold of the starting block's rubber-lined edge with both hands. It's like I'm seeing Zoli-boy on footage that's moving slower and slower, but maybe he's coming in more sluggish as the acid builds up in his muscles, as his arms and legs start to tense up. The water foams around him, the splashed water droplets spark in the cold glow of the spotlights. The shouts become softer and the noises duller, as if I were under a bell jar. For a moment I feel like Zoli-boy'll never make it to the wall, while the others are still shouting behind me at the tops of their lungs. There's nothing much they can do now. They've already swum their laps. I'm the only one left. I'm the last person. Referees stand on either side, watching with strict faces to see if the changeover takes place by the rules. I'm dead calm. Our advantage is huge. There's no way that any of the relay teams straggling behind us can shave off the time needed to close the gap. Ducky was the first, and he shot off like crazy, slamming the field with a body-length-and-a-half advantage. Then came our weakest man, but even he managed to keep the lead, while Zoli-boy pushed yet another half metre away from the others. The only way you can screw up with such an advantage is if you change over badly. It's never happened to me before, and we practise it a whole lot during training. The changeover is the easiest thing ever: you don't push off till the other guy touches his fingers to the wall. Continuity is the key. You aren't two people. You pretend you're one with your changeover partner, as if you were an extension of him, and the two of you are a single, continuous movement. Sure, it's always a little different at a swim meet. You're more hyped and all. You wanna win. I've never screwed up the changeover, but when I start to lean towards the water, I can already feel that I launched the jump too fast. Until Zoli-boy's finger touches the wall, my feet have to stay on the block. The timekeeper will signal if I push off too early. A few years ago, it was the referees who determined if someone jumped too early, but nowadays, it's computers that decide. It's as if I were frozen in mid-air for a fraction of a second. Maybe the tip of my toenail is still touching the rubber coating. The world moves even slower now. The last sound I hear before I slam into the water is Ducky screaming, "Go, fucker, go!" If I screwed up, it was only by a few millimetres.

I come crashing into the finish. By the time the second and third team arrive in a dead heat, I've taken my cap and goggles off, wiped my face, and am looking out at the stands. I can tell right away that something's wrong. Coach Bandi's face is redder than usual. It's nearly luminous. I clutch the edge of the pool, lunge out to my waist, then push off and step out onto the ridged tiles. As I wipe the water flowing from my forehead away from my eyes, Ducky steps over to me and all he says is, *you fuckin' fucked up*. I shrug and don't know what the hell to say, but show me a person who hasn't fucked up once in their lives. I go back to the chairs, collect my things, then head to the locker room. I can see Coach Bandi shouting and waving, but I don't give a shit. Hell if I'm gonna go over there.

Instead, I just bow my head and move on, right past the stands, then down the stairs to the showers. Down here it's quiet. I get in one of the stalls and open the tap. I turn it hotter and hotter, the water gushing on my head increasingly harder. I can't hear anything. I can't see anything. Then, as I step out from under the spray and feel around for my towel, I suddenly touch someone. I wipe the water from my face and open my eyes. Ducky's standing in front of me. He doesn't say a thing. He just punches me once in the face. For a second I don't know what's happening. I reel, but manage to keep my balance. As I lower my head, drops of blood explode everywhere on the wet tile, coming down thick, like a carpet bombing. Pain spreads across my face like a spiderweb. I look up. Ducky's standing a few paces from me. He's about to slam his fist into me again, but Kishorvát holds him down. I start towards him to hit him, but as I lift my hand, someone grabs my arm and twists it behind my back. Zoli-boy walks me to the first-aid room. The doc—a young dude wearing glasses and flip-flops—wipes the blood from my face, studies it for a while, cautiously pats my nose, my jaw and cheekbone, then tells me not to worry. It's not broken, just bruised. If it were *his* nose that was bruised, I bet he wouldn't be so calm about it. I almost talk back, but I can tell he's not a douche, so I don't say anything. He walks over to the fridge, takes a bag of ice from the freezer, comes back to the exam table, and places it on my face. The cold feels good. Like sticking my head in an ice fishing hole. Meanwhile, my mind's already going off on how I'm gonna murder that prick. Broken nose or not. I ask the doc to let me lie there a bit longer on the table. He nods, tells me to make myself at home, then walks over to the tap and washes his hands with disinfectant.

They disqualified the team. Why else would that prick jump me? I'm mostly freaking out about my face, 'cause sure, I'm icing it but it still hurts like hell. That asshole popped me hard, and I'll probably get a punch to match from Coach Bandi. I mean, there's not gonna be any scandal, but I'll be curious to see how they gloss it over. Ducky won't be suspended. I'm willing to bet good money on that. Only Zoli-boy saw the brawl, and Kishorvát. They'll just threaten Zoli-boy and say he's dead meat if he rats them out. Kishorvát they can just pay off and he won't squeal. I got no chance against Ducky's pop's lawyers. Those dudes would figure something out even if that asswipe had socked me on the stands in front of five hundred eyewitnesses: he tried to hug me but slipped on the tile; I wanted to beat him up because I can't stomach failure, so he was forced to defend himself.

Sure, I could bust him if I wanted. He'd deserve to get suspended. He's lucky there's no doping test for junior competitions. They say it's too expensive, but what they really mean is, ain't nobody got time for that, or feel much like hassling kids. Let them bumble along nice and easy. They'll grow up soon enough anyway and then the WADA will round them up. They'll be sent home from training camp or pulled from some international competition and suspended for a couple of months. But while you're a junior, you can shoot whatever you like, or can afford, or your coach manages to get a hold of. Nobody gives a damn how someone gets to be a national champion at sixteen.

The door opens, the sounds from outside are amplified for a moment, then everything quiets down again. Someone comes towards me. I don't look, can't open my eyes with the ice pack on them.

"What happened?"

I hear Coach's hoarse voice. He's standing beside the exam table, leaning over me. As I lift the ice off my face, the pungent smell of BO hits my nose. I feel nauseous, so I put the ice back down and arrange it until it's no longer hanging over my mouth. I want to give coherent answers.

"He punched me," I say in a nasal tone.

"You know why, right?" he asks.

"'Cause he's an asshole," I answer, and smile contentedly at my comment, but then a sharp pain shoots through my nose, so I stop grinning.

"Don't be a wise-ass, son, 'cause you'll get one from me too," Coach Bandi growls.

"I don't know why he hit me," I answer.

"You know what place we came in?"

"No."

I pretend to have no clue that we were disqualified.

"Zero place, son," he says. "*Zero,*" he repeats in an ominous tone. "You fucked up, son. You fucked up really fuckin' bad."

"But..."

"Shut your face." His tone is louder now, but he's not yelling. "The relay team was disqualified because of you."

"I'm sorry."

"You bet your ass you're sorry," he says. "That's the last time you swim on this relay team. I won't let you fuck up other people's chances. Not again. I should rip your balls off and stuff them in your mouth. That's what you deserve."

I don't say anything. I know they're just empty threats. He wouldn't kick me off the team. I'm the second best on the two hundred. If I'm not on the team, those pathetic asshats are never getting up on the podium again.

"You better do some soul-searching!" he warns.

I can tell he's forcing himself to stay calm, even though

he's livid. I wanna tell him not to get so worked up 'cause he'll end up getting a stroke, but I keep quiet instead, so he doesn't think I'm provoking him. Not like I'd give a shit if he croaked. Then suddenly I feel something really strange. I don't really get where it's coming from, but I feel sorry for this sad old bastard. Coach Bandi turns and steps over to the door. I hear him stop for a moment. Maybe he's got more to say, but then he presses down on the door handle and walks out. As he exits, the noise of the pool area, the splintered sounds of splashing water, the loudspeaker listing the names of people in the next heat intensifies again, everything echoes, and then quiets again. I close my eyes and fall asleep with the ice on my face.

In the end, I don't have to go to the hospital. The doc says it's not broken, maybe just fractured a bit, so the bone doesn't need to be popped back into place, but they can't do much else with it. Whatevs, it doesn't hurt so much anymore, and I sure as hell don't need my brain flashed with a jolt of X-ray radiation. On the way home we're carefully separated. I sit in front—Coach mumbling behind me with the assistant coach—while Ducky's in his usual place, playing hotshot in the back seat. He's started being Mr Nice Guy with Zoli-boy, but he's definitely stringing the kid along just to kick him harder later on. Zoli-boy's gonna be really sorry, that's for sure. Stupid kid trying to be all blasé, but I can tell he's happy as fuck about it. He can sit in my place beside Ducky and the chicks. Ducky might even arrange a blow job for him on the way home.

The swim meet ended late, and afterwards we went for a bite to eat, so we're gonna get home after dark. At times like these, it's a free-for-all: they don't turn the lights on in the bus. There's only floor-path illumination between the aisles. I don't turn around. I know what they're doing.

It's always the same. They mess with their phones in the gloom, or watch films, staring at the touchscreens with blue faces, as if they were masks, while others use the opportunity to make out. A couple of weeks ago—I forget where we were coming home from—Niki gave Ducky and two other guys handjobs, and then Ducky talked a new girl into giving everybody handjobs 'cause "that's the custom around here." Meanwhile, a row ahead, two dudes were fingering Timi or Viki, I forget who. We were having a ball, but then one of the fugly chicks threw a tantrum 'cause nobody wanted to make out with her, which was true, but well, poor thing really was hideous, so we tried to talk Zoli-boy into it. It's dark anyway, no prob, but the dumbass wasn't game, and the chick kept whining louder and louder, and we didn't want Coach Bandi to come to the back, so finally we ended the make-out session and watched a bondage porn flick on Viki's tablet instead.

I feel like tearing my hair out thinking about what I'm missing 'cause of that cocksucker Ducky. I don't fucking get why I'm the one paying for this when he was the shithead. My face is still aching, but nobody cares about that except me. They'll gloss over the fight, you can bet your life on it. Coach Bandi already greased somebody so they wouldn't file a report about what happened at the pool; and at home, his word is law. As for my mom making a scene... not a chance. But God forbid she *does* try to complain. Coach will just explain to her that it's all my fault, and Ma will just give in and nod, like she always does.

I could rat on Ducky 'cause of the drugs, but that would be douchey, and I'm no douche.

I hear Zoli-boy's voice. I turn around and see that he wants to come over here, but Coach Bandi stops him and asks what he wants. And when Zoli-boy explains that he wants to talk to me, Coach orders him back to his seat. Zoli-boy doesn't argue. He heads back. The road is winding, and I follow Zoli-boy's swaying figure with my eyes. As he sits down in his place in the back row, my eyes meet Ducky's. He grins at me and draws his index finger along his throat. I'm about to flip him off, but a sharp turn makes Ducky keel over into Niki's lap. They burst out laughing. Let them laugh. I don't give a shit. I face forward and stare out the window. I don't know where we are. The bus's engine is a monotonous rumble, tiny dots of light appear out of nothingness, and next minute they disappear in the great blackness, like they never even existed. I'm bored out of my mind up here, alone. I stare into space, and make up various methods of execution. I steal ideas from the *Saw* films, but I always try and add an extra twist to them. I'm really getting into it. The killing techniques are clear and chiselled, more and more artistic. Finally, I fall asleep, and continue in my dreams. Ducky has died a thousand deaths by the time we reach home.

I wake to someone turning on the overhead lights. I squint in the brightness, then see everybody gathering their stuff. Coach Bandi's standing next to me, ordering someone to hurry it up. He's not swearing so much right now 'cause the parents are waiting out in the parking lot. They haven't seen their babies in two days. They're all excited to hear what happened, as if they hadn't called every five minutes to check in anyway. As I head for the exit, Coach grabs my arm and tells me not to go anywhere, he still wants a word with me. I sit back down in my seat and watch everybody file off the bus. Ducky passes me like I don't even exist, and sure, I try to ignore him too, but as he approaches, my blood starts to boil and I toy with the idea of hitting him. But Coach Bandi's watching. I know the old dude. He gives me same spiel about how the team was DQ-d because of me and that I should do some soul-searching. He's never gonna roast Ducky for the brawl. At most he'll call him into his office, give him a dirty look, and tell him not to do it again. And Ducky'll be snickering to himself 'cause he knows that if his old man stops pumping cash into the club, then they can close shop. That's why he gets off the hook all the time. 'Cause of his dad. 'Cause of his dad's cash. After everybody gets off the bus, Coach Bandi leans over to me and says that he knows that I fucked up the relay race on purpose. I'm kinda surprised by this, 'cause even *I'm* not sure I fucked it up on purpose, so how the hell does *he* know? I don't say anything, and he doesn't expect me to. Then he growls at me again, telling me to whip myself into shape, blah blah blah. He wrinkles his forehead, knits his brows, stares into my face, and strongly suggests that I think up some believable story by the time I get home in case my mother starts asking questions. Otherwise he'll kick my sorry ass. My nose starts throbbing, even though he hasn't even touched it. He finishes by threatening to rip my balls off if I don't show up to practice tomorrow morning. I just nod like an idiot, and meanwhile, I feel like the old man's in a weird, chummy mood. He even slaps my back when he says *haul your ass home now, son, your mom will be worried.*

Go fuck yourself, I think to myself, but of course I don't say anything.

When I get off, I can see the huge crowd clustered in the parking lot. I walk over to the luggage compartment, and when I lean down to take out my stuff, Zoli-boy whispers *psst* to me from the other side of the bus. I pretend not to hear him, but he's hissing so loud now there's no way he'll believe I can't hear him.

"What?" I ask.

"I wanna talk to you," he says.

"Blow me," I say.

"It's really important," he says, ignoring what I said.

I can tell from his face that it's something serious, but he was a dickhead after the fight. Kissing up to Ducky. He can go fuck his ugly mother.

"I don't care," I say, and pull my bag out.

My bag's the last one. The driver steps up beside me and is about to close the luggage compartment. I snap at him, 'cause why's he closing it on me? He barks back at me, saying *hop to it then*, and that he hasn't got all night to fuck around with us, which makes me lose it completely and tell him to suck my dick, that's what he gets paid for, and anyway, he should be grateful he's got work, and other shit like that, and by this time the dude's really getting revved up. He's about to jump me when a mom appears and asks where her little boy's backpack is, 'cause they can't find it anywhere. The driver is distracted from the argument, and I quickly grab my bag, sling it over my shoulder, and head home. I don't shake Zoli-boy off so easy though. He circles around the bus and comes after me. Nobody's come to pick him up, either. I start towards the inner city. Zoli-boy wants me to stop, so I tell him to get off my back. A car approaches and Ducky's mom brakes beside us. She's driving with her little boy next to her. There's two girls in the back seat, I think, Niki and Viki, but I can't see very well 'cause of the tinted glass. Ducky rolls the window down and tells Zoli-boy to hop in, they'll drive him home. Zoli-boy is flustered, he seems nervous, but I guess he doesn't wanna be impolite, especially now that he and Ducky are such great pals, so finally he climbs in the back. Ducky's mom asks if I need a ride, but before I get a chance to say *no thanks*, Ducky tells her that I live nearby, and they sail off. I stare at the outline of Zoli-boy's head, and the heads of the two chicks. I know it's stupid, and I don't really get why the fuck this pops in my head, but my mind latches onto thinking: what if this is the last time I ever see that dumbass kid?

On the way home, I cut through skid row, hoping someone will pick a fight with me, and then I won't have to lie about my broken nose. This neighbourhood got nicknamed "The Bronx," and it's where they hauled all the gyppos when they renovated the downtown area. The place isn't really so bad, it's just got a bad reputation. At any rate, I keep glancing over my shoulder to see if anybody's following me. The streets are pretty quiet, with the sound of shouting or babies crying from a few windows, dogs barking in a couple of yards, pigs grunting, and, at one house, a braying donkey.

Just as I come to one of the quieter parts, a junker with a broken exhaust pipe whizzes past me. I look in the window as it hurdles off. Two savage-looking dudes sit inside. One of them looks straight at me, but it's like he doesn't even see me. He's about sixteen and his buddy's twenty. They slow down about a hundred metres away, stop at the next corner, in front of the 24-hour convenience store, and jump out, one from the front seat and one from the back. I just noticed that there's three of them, not two. The third guy was probably stretched out on the back seat. The driver stays where he is and keeps the motor running. Both of them are hulking mountains of flesh, so it's no wonder their ride was sitting so low on the pavement, but now the bigger of the two dudes stops in front of the service window and starts waving something black around. I can see his mouth moving, his voice is reaching me in snippets, but I can't hear what he's really going on about.

The light of the neon sign paints their faces red and blue. I finally get that this is a heist, and the black thing the brawny dude's waving is probably a gun.

Suddenly, I go fucking apeshit. Fuck all these motherfuckers. I don't give a flying fuck. They can shoot me if they want but I'm not gonna cross the street to steer clear of them. I'm not gonna hide in a doorway and wait till they rob the store and piss the fuck off. I keep moving forward. The store's only fifty metres away. The two gorillas are still clowning around at the window, getting more and more annoyed, and the clerk is either really lame or a huge badass, 'cause he could have run a whole inventory of the store by now. My heart's pounding as hard as it does after the 10x400 butterfly at practice, and a hardcore jolt of adrenaline kicks in, making my dick tingle. The robbers are still hollering, my phone starts ringing, and I look at the screen. Zoli-boy's calling. I look up. There's this weird silence. The two dudes aren't shouting anymore. There's only the sound of the engine. My heart rate goes up another notch, I'm striding forward, and if they don't finish with the robbery, I'll be forced to cut in between them 'cause I've already decided not to cross the street. The street is totally empty. Not a single dog walker, no cars, no police. There must be some athletic event going on somewhere. Or some TV show. I'm twenty paces away when one of the cocksuckers looks up. Our eyes meet. I don't look away. Fuck your mother, I think to myself. Maybe he can hear my thoughts or can sense how furious I am and so he knows it's not worth fucking with me. Ten paces. Beefcake turns away, grabs his buddy's arm, dragging him away from the store, but the dude's cursing for the other guy to let him go, they need the change too, but he gets shoved into the car. They thought I was a ghost.

Or thin air. As I get to the store, the driver starts revving the engine, and one of the motherfuckers rolls the window down and barks that he'll kill me if I rat them out, so I bark back at them to haul their rotting carcasses back to their mommas' dirty cunts. He stares at my swollen nose, my bloody t-shirt, but doesn't get out of the car, and doesn't wanna beat me up. Then the engine roars and they drive off, rubber screeching. I look in through the glass door of the store. The clerk is a chick. She stares out blankly. She's totally in shock. A TV screen vibrates above her head. Barcelona is kicking Real Madrid's ass. I ask if she's okay. She mumbles something haltingly, then grabs the phone and calls the cops. In the meantime, a young chick walks past me with a dog. She's got earbuds in. She stops at the window, leans in, and asks for a pack of Marlboro Golds. I start off in the other direction. Fifteen minutes later, I turn the key in the lock and remember that I didn't call my mom back.

ZOLI-BOY'S KID SISTER

I'm standing in front of the mirror trying to imagine looking at myself from the other side. I stare at my scraped chin, my swollen nose. Thank God Ducky's a lame-ass fuck and can't even land a proper right hook. Luckily my mom's totally out of it and didn't even notice the size of my nose, so at least I didn't have to make up an excuse. I mean, when she's rock-bottom like this, she never notices anything. Or she notices, but she doesn't care. Of course, if she'd asked what happened, I could've fed her some bullshit story no prob. I don't usually freak out if some part of the story doesn't add up or if I get lost in the details. There's holes in every story: usually all you gotta do is scratch the surface and the bullshit starts to seep through. Sometimes I really don't get my mom. If she'd ask details, she could corner me easy. She'd just have to ask the right questions. I mean, you can get really unnerved when you're cranking out BS and you realize there's no way in hell things could have gone down that way. Times like that, don't panic, 'cause if you panic, you start to rush through it, and from that point on the reins start to slip from your hands. If you notice you took the wrong exit off the highway, there's no point in obsessing over how to find your way back. The best thing to do is floor the accelerator and move forward. And anyway, grownups don't give a shit what you're talking about anyway. It makes their own lives way easier if they just believe your bullshit. When I got home, my mom started telling me off about not calling her back. I don't know what came over me, but I apologized, which took her so off guard that she wouldn't get off my back for the rest of the night. An hour later, I was fed up, so I told her I was really beat and that I was going to bed, but of course I couldn't sleep. I just lay there, staring at the ceiling, my mind latched on Zoli-boy, wondering what he wanted to talk to me about. I even called him, but he didn't answer the first time, then he rejected the call, and later, his phone was switched off and I never leave voicemails. Then I called my favourite crisis hotline, asked for my favourite crisis operator, rattled off some bullshit story about how my pop beat me again and how I wanted to commit suicide, and while the chick consoled me, I jerked off.

Early the next morning, we swim long laps. I'm not in a good mood, bored of practice, so I mess with Ducky a little. I keep up with him for two-thirds of the distance so he'll believe he can crush me, but then I kick the shift into high and sail past him. I make sure to beat him by just enough so he knows I'm fucking with him, and he's got no chance. And I don't even have to make an effort. Ducky gasps for breath at the wall, his face all red. It feels good to see him suffer. I harass the shithead quietly so the others can't hear. I ask him if he forgot to shoot up today and snicker when he can't even manage to get an answer out. Things go on like this for about an hour. I can tell he's about to explode, but he doesn't dare make a scene. He's happy he got off so easy after the race. I guess he was shitting bricks that I'd rat him out. We haven't talked much since.

I get dressed and head to school. I wanna get there early 'cause I still gotta copy some four-eyed dork's math homework. Zoli-boy didn't show up to practice again. I called him early in the morning, but his phone was off. I guess his battery died. Whatever. His mom lets him leave the house without his phone. I don't remember the last time I went to school without him. Better alone though than with Buoy. He was feeling super shitty this morning. But, I mean, it looks like his bro will arrange for him to get off with a short suspension, and he can still practise with the team till then, but they lost again on the weekend, and the championships are almost over, and those pathetic morons are about to lose their place in the league.

One of the overachieving nerds from my class rushes past me outside school. I haven't spoken two words to him in three years. He comes in from whatever village, always arrives first, then sits at attention, reading or memorizing at his desk. I spot Lázár in the hall, grinning, stoked to hand out a bunch of Fs again I'll bet. I hope one of those big, heavy-framed class photos falls on his head. I dart behind a locker so he doesn't notice me. He's a nasty bastard. His ears are hairier than his head and he's constantly sweating, like he was in a sauna, and his nose hair's so long it could pass for a moustache. He's like a pedophile serial killer, except he's better at math. Come end of term, he's gonna fail some people hard, and it's not just the total retards who're gonna go down, that's for sure. I guess that's his secret perversion. Maybe he pops a boner every time he pens an F on a report card or something. At any rate, you can tell from his face that he gets a real kick out of it. If I get an F on my final test, he's gonna fail me too, but Zoli-boy's doing way worse. Basically, it doesn't much matter what he does, he's gonna be spending his whole summer with his nose buried in a textbook anyway. But he dug his own grave. He should've whipped himself into shape way earlier. I haven't got the slightest idea why he didn't do it sooner. He's not a complete moron when it comes to math, and it was obvious that Lázár was out to get him. He wanted to fucking fail him last year too, and then, at the end of the semester, he showed the poor kid some mercy. But this time, he hasn't got a chance. Lázár moves past me like an Imperial Walker, disappears into the faculty lounge, his leather satchel under his arm chock-full of our graded tests. He'll hand them back to us during fifth period. That'll be the moment of truth.

When that cocksucker Lázár steps into the room, everybody shuts up. He distributes the tests in grave silence. You can totally tell from the sniffling which of the chicks got Fs. Lázár gets to my desk, puts the paper down in front of me, then looks at me meaningfully, and moves on. At first I don't believe my eyes. He must've miscalculated or made a mistake. I quickly add up the points for each test question in my head, but he didn't miscalculate. I got a C. I don't get how it happened, 'cause I copied off my desk mate and he got a D. He's a little annoyed too when he sees that I got a C. So it looks like I won't get flunked after all when end of semester rolls around. After everyone gets their tests back, Lázár goes over the answers, then drones on some more about our final grades. He lists the people who need to do make-up tests to pass, but I'm not paying attention, 'cause the girl with the biggest tits in the class is sitting right in front of me, and just then she starts to peel off her long-sleeved shirt, and you can see her bra strap. It only occurs to me near the end of class that I should ask somebody what grade Zoli-boy got. I'll bet he's shitting bricks 'cause of his math grade, and that's why he didn't come to school, but he could've said something. I don't want him to call me during recess and ask what he got. I don't feel like telling him what he already knows: Lázár failed his ass. Of course, I'm freaking out for no reason, because Zoli-boy doesn't call me. There's something real fishy about this silence. I've got no idea where the dumbass is hiding, but it's starting to make me uneasy as fuck, so I take off from school after lunch. Nobody ever notices if I'm not at PE anyway.

1 p.m. I'm standing around outside Zoli-boy's building. I call his cell, but it's switched off, and I don't know his home phone, and plus I don't wanna talk to his mom, maybe she thinks Zoli-boy's in school. I watch the windows of his family's apartment but there's no movement. I wait till somebody comes out of the building and slip in through the open door. I go up to the tenth floor, stop outside Zoli-boy's door, and listen. No sounds. I'm about to leave when I hear the safety-chain rattle and the lock click. The door opens. I don't dare turn around in case it's his mother.

"Hi!" Zoli-boy's kid sister says. Everybody just calls her Bunny. I don't even know what her real name is. She's standing in the doorway in slippers, a thong, and a crop top. "You here for Zoli-boy?" she asks.

Before I answer, I give her a good, hard stare. She's looking way hotter since I last saw her. She's chill as fuck, tits could be bigger, but she qualifies as fuckable. Every time I see her, I wonder how a woman as horribly ugly as Zoli-boy's mom could have made such a pretty daughter. I mean, Zoli-boy's a handsome dude too, and if he didn't whine so much he could have way more chicks.

"Yeah," I mumble with some difficulty, and swallow hard.

"Come in," Bunny says, and gives me the once over.

Her eyes stop for a second at cock-height. She smiles, steps back a little so I can enter, but makes sure to brush her nipple against my arm by accident.

We're sitting on Bunny's bed in Bunny's room, which is also Zoli-boy's room. It pretty much looks like we're alone in the apartment. I'm hella stoked that their mom isn't home, but I'd be even more pumped if I finally found out where the fuck Zoli-boy is, 'cause he sure as hell isn't lying in bed with a fever, and he's not shouting *I'll be right out* from the bathroom either. I ask Bunny where her brother is, but she looks at me like I'm crazy and says:

"At school, duh."

"You see that clock?" I ask.

"Yeah," Bunny nods, but you can tell she doesn't care what I'm getting at.

"Can you tell me what the time is?"

Bunny stares at the clock for a while, then says:

"One forty-five."

"Clever girl," I say. "Do you know what that means?"

"That it's almost two o'clock."

She's being a smart aleck, but I let it slide and continue.

"We had five periods today."

"So?"

"School's been out for a million years."

"Uh-huh. Awesome." She's super bored, and her eyes keep wandering to my lap as she twirls her hair, squirming on the bed. "Then he's at the pool."

I hesitate, 'cause if I let it slip that her brother wasn't at practice either, I might get the dumbass busted. But I guess if he's disappeared, then there's no point in me covering for him anyway.

"I haven't seen him all day," I finally say. "And he hasn't

been at practice even once this week."

"Seriously?" Bunny is honestly surprised. "That's fucked up."

"Yeah, I think so too."

"Mom's gonna rip his head off," she adds with a gloating smile.

It really looks like she's got no idea where her brother is.

"When was the last time you saw him?" I ask, totally sounding like I'm from *CSI* or something.

Bunny thinks about this.

"Well, last week, I guess," she answers.

"Fuck," I sigh.

"What's the matter?" Bunny coos, and edges closer to me. "You seem really tense."

As she pulls me down beside her on the bed, a pink stuffed elephant catches my eye.

Twenty minutes later, I step out the door of the building. I'm a bit sorry I let Bunny put out for me. Not like I've got a problem with somebody hooking up with his friend's kid sister, but now I've also gotta worry that I caught something from Bunny. Sure, it felt good and all, 'cause I was super tense, and now I'm not, but it's also true that I haven't found out jack shit. Apart from learning that Bunny sucks like a porn star, I didn't find out anything.

On the way down in the elevator, I try to piece together the puzzle. I don't remember the last time I saw Zoli-boy. I've called him a bunch of times since about yesterday morning, but it's no use, he won't answer. I have no idea who to turn to. I'll give him one more day, and if he doesn't turn up, I'll find Ducky and get him to help me look for the dumbass. Maybe he knows something, because they hung out a lot after the swim meet. By the time the elevator stops on the ground floor, I'm calm. This seems like a good plan.

I check my watch. I've got loads of time, I could do anything in the world, but I still head to the pool. I'll get there easily by three even if I walk the whole way backwards. I cut through the park. I kick a pebble around. I almost hit a little kid on a bike. The rock bounces off one of the spokes. He's startled, but he'd be okay even if he fell 'cause he's got a helmet on. I look around to see if anybody noticed. I only see two glue sniffers on a bench searching through a homeless dude's stuff. They even rummage in his pockets, but of course they don't find anything. I like this park. This is where I lost my virginity two summers ago. I was hammered. I don't even remember what happened, but the chick told me later. I ran into her at a house party, and she had this weird smile, so I went up to her and we started chatting. She looked pretty good, big tits and everything, so I was hitting on her and of course we ended up in the bathroom. I had serious déjà vu while we were doing it, and then afterwards the chick told me that we'd fucked before.

The kid on the bike rolls past me again. He's chasing a little girl on a tricycle and almost plows into her, but at the last second somebody shouts at him, and he manages to jerk the handlebars away to avoid collision. I don't understand how, but the memory of the grampa we ran over on the bypass flashes through my mind. It feels like none of it ever happened, or like it didn't happen to us, or, if it did happen to us, then definitely in some former life. A Buddhist said that one time on TV. I mean this whole former-life thing. But he didn't say anything about whether you're in your real life now, or still in your former one. If what the Buddhist homie said was true, then maybe ol' grampa is already scuttling around somewhere in the woods in his next life as a doodlebug and will get splattered on a car windshield one day. I haven't thought about all this for a long time, but now it sticks in my mind and I can't shake the thought of that night from my head. I guess we would've already been rounded up by the pigs if they'd realized it was us who plastered ol' gramps. But it's not like anybody gives a flying fuck about those old winos. Not even the cops. They're not gonna get worked up about finding the driver, even if it *was* a hit-and-run. Five minutes later I'm totally obsessing over this whole accident thing. I can already see the commandos yanking me out of bed and pushing me down on the floor in nothing but my boxers, cuffing my hands behind my back, while my mom screeches in falsetto, *how dare you come barging into our home like this*, and then the pigs drag me out and stuff me in the pork mobile beside Buoy, who's already been wrangled by then. I'm latched onto this, but walking too, I don't even know where, and then I hear someone calling me, and when I look up, I see Ottó. He's sitting there on a bench in a baseball cap and shades, even though it's not sunny out, and gestures for me to come over, and I'm low-key freaking out, 'cause I haven't seen him since I bashed him against the wall at Ducky's last time and he passed out. Ottó's calling me so persistently that I have to go over to him. I've got loads of time anyway. I pretend like nothing happened, but I'd be pretty surprised if Ottó had any real memory of that party, especially considering that, after the KO, he devoured a platter of space cakes with Ducky's pop. We high five and then I sit down next to him on the bench's backrest. I calm down, 'cause it really does seem like he doesn't remember anything, but I'm on my guard anyway, 'cause maybe he's just stringing me along.

"What's up?" he says, taking a nonchalant drag of his cigarette.

"Everything's cool," I say.

We're quiet for a little while, and then Ottó says:

"I got fucked over real hard."

He takes another drag. I give him a sidelong glance. I didn't notice till now, 'cause of the shades, that his face is swollen like a dinner roll. Pretty soon I'm gonna have more friends with bashed-in faces than not.

"What happened?" I ask.

"I got fucked over," Ottó repeats curtly as he fishes a pack out from his pocket, pulls out a cigarette, lights it with the burning end of the one he's already smoking, then flicks the butt away, all while telling me about how one night he and Mishy were rolling through the city when suddenly, out of thin air, a huge black Volkswagen Transporter cut in front of them. Norris and his men jump out, drag him and Mishy out of the car, and fuck them up so bad that Ottó literally shit himself, and he couldn't even call an ambulance, 'cause by the time a passer-by came over to help him, two shitty little brats had unloaded his pockets. But like, in hindsight, he was happy, 'cause even though he was super pissed at losing his cash and phone, he was stoked that those snotrags swiped all the drugs too, 'cause if the cops had found the weed and the pills in his pocket, he'd be recovering in the prison infirmary right now.

"What's up with Mishy?" I ask.

"Got his ass kicked," Ottó says. "Real bad," he adds, after a dramatic pause, then he goes on to tell me that Mishy really got taken out. First with a couple of kicks to the stomach, then when he was on the ground they went for his head and kidneys, while one of them shouted, *if you key my car one more time, motherfucker, I'll cut your head off and puke in your lungs*. That was the last time Ottó saw Mishy—when the three gorillas flung him into the Transporter. He turned up at dawn the next day and looked *really* fucked up, and now he's in the IC unit. They say he's stable, but his condition's still critical.

"That's so fucked," is all I can say.

"No shit," Ottó says, spitting out a huge glob of phlegm. Then he goes on a rant about how he's fuckin' had it with this fucking city and all the douchebags in it, and that he's gonna get the fuck out to Colombia, 'cause the coke is cheaper than smokes there, and he's gonna buy a kilo of the stuff, bring it home, and make a killing, except that the goddamned plane ticket is so expensive, but he doesn't really give a shit, 'cause he'll scrape up the dough somehow or hitch a ride or something.

"We should go to the hospital," I say, after Ottó's done with his monologue.

"Are you out of your fuckin' mind?" Ottó looks at me like I'm some asshole. "What if those pricks are watching the hospital?"

"They meant it as a warning," I say. "If they wanted to bump you off, they would've done it already."

"Well they didn't fucking inform me about what the fuck they wanted, but they were certainly convincing about it, shit…" Ottó says.

The little kid in the helmet rolls past our bench. I think about kicking him over, but then I hear his mommy screeching from the slides for him to turn back. Of course the kid doesn't give a flying fuck, peddling like crazy in the other direction, towards the road. Maybe a car will slam into him, and maybe he'd deserve it, but his mom starts running, dragging a girl of about two behind her, probably the dumbass kid's sister, howling like a jackal, "Marky, stop!" but the kid just pedals on, he's not stopping, maybe he can't hear from the helmet. His mother rushes past the bench, screaming, the little girl bawling, and she's not wearing a bra. I mean the mother isn't. The kid's pedalling like mad. He disappears behind a bush, and maybe that's the last time his mom ever sees him. I turn to Ottó, who's just staring into space. He doesn't give a shit about what's happening. Doesn't give a shit about anything. And I'm watching bike-boy's mama. She's got a pretty nice ass. She won't catch up with the kid. The kid will pedal out onto the road and that's that. Then the dumbass appears from behind the bush after all, and when his mom catches up with him, she slaps him with sheer momentum, so hard that if he wasn't in that helmet, he'd have a ruptured eardrum. As it is, only Mom is hurt, so she yanks the helmet off the kid and delivers another blow, which makes the kid start blubbering.

"Ottó?"

"What?"

"Don't you want to go to the police?"

"Are you really that dense?" Ottó asks, then continues. "And what the fuck am I supposed to say to them? That we sold drugs outside the wrong school by accident?"

I don't really know what to say. If they don't snuff Mishy out in the hospital, and he comes to his senses enough to be questioned, the cops'll be all over him, and sooner or later, that'll lead them to Ottó. He really does need to disappear fast. Even Colombia is safer than here.

"I'm fuckin' outta here," Ottó growls.

"Okay," I nod.

"You wanna give me a hundred?" he asks, exhaling smoke.

"A hundred euros?"

"Yeah."

I bust up laughing, but when I see that Ottó's serious, I go quiet and tell him, sorry, I don't have it. And anyway, the last time I saw a hundred euros was when one of my buddies tried to make counterfeit bills with a photocopier so he could buy stuff at the corner grocery run by a half-blind grampa.

We sit for a few more minutes in silence. The church bells ring. I check the time on my phone, but I don't feel like taking off yet.

"Have you seen Zoli-boy around recently?" I ask.

"Who's that?" Ottó asks.

"My buddy. He's like, this skinny kid," I say. "Talks real fast."

"Ducky's bud?" Ottó asks.

"Yeah."

"I saw Ducky yesterday," he says. "He was hanging with two chicks, and a skinny blonde dude."

"That's him," I nod. "When did you see them?"

"Fuck if I know," Ottó dodges a straight answer without even thinking. "Evening, I guess."

"Where?"

"In the projects."

"Do you know what they were doing?"

"What do you think?" Ottó looks at me like I'm retarded.

"Oh, right," I say.

The mother's coming back with bike-boy and the little girl. Both of them are bawling. The boy's face is a mess of snot and tears. He's really gotten himself worked up. Mom is at her wit's end. She's panting. Her breasts heaving fast.

"Then what happened?" I ask.

"They took off," Ottó answers.

"Where?"

Ottó looks at me as he answers, "I don't know."

We sit quietly for a few minutes. I've got no idea what Zoli-boy was doing messing around with Ducky, but if

Ottó's not bullshitting, then it could be that Ducky's the last one who saw the dumbass. I gotta talk to him.

Crying kids, shouting, squeaking swings. I'm starting to get fed up with the park.

"Okay, I'm outta here," I say, even though I know that Ottó doesn't give two shits about what I do. I get up from the bench, we slap hands, and I head over to the pool. I look back from the edge of the park. Ottó's sitting motionless on the backrest like a statue or a corpse, then lifts the cigarette to his lips, takes a deep drag, and exhales the smoke. Colombia. Yeah, right.

VIADUCT

I shouldn't pig out like I did tonight, 'cause then it always takes me forever to fall asleep, and I have totally fucked-up dreams. In one of them, it's night and Zoli-boy jumps off the fucking viaduct, gets caught on the security fence, a piece of metal that's poking out cuts his neck, and he starts bleeding, and it just doesn't wanna stop, the whole valley fills up, the lake of blood rocking like the waters of Lake Balaton, while Zoli-boy's hanging seventy metres in the air, and no matter how much he flails, he can't climb back up onto the bridge, and he's terrified he'll fall and drown in the blood, but he's afraid to shout, plus there's no point, 'cause I'm the only one who can hear, and then he slowly bleeds to death, and the whole time he's gripped by the thought that now he's definitely gonna die a virgin, while the chicks are lying around on a huge, pink air mattress floating on the lake, soaking up the sun themselves, rubbing their pussies like crazy, and I'm lying there next to them, but when I see myself, I jump off the mattress into the cold blood, and thrash my arms and legs, as if I couldn't swim, but I finally manage to flounder onto the shore, and, as I drag myself out, covered in blood, Ducky's there in front of me, and it's like I'm fighting fog, I can't hit him, and he's just grinning, knowing that my struggle is pointless, and then he flicks me with his finger and I crack, and he flicks me again, and then I fall to splinters, and I have to get away, but I can barely lift my backpack, and then when I open it, I see that somebody's filled it with dead fish, and colourful barbels, guppies, neon tetras, gouramis, danios, and catfish, and the Siamese fighting fish slither under my skin, flap their fins, then gasp mutely, slowly sink into the black void, and I reach into my pocket because I really have to make a phone call, but my phone is soft and wet, like milk in a plastic bag, and when I try to dial, there's only my mother's number in the contacts list, but I wanna tell somebody the shit that's going down, and I get more and more irritated, then I wake up, call Viki, and tell her that I dreamt of her, and ask her to tell me what she knows about Zoli-boy's death, and she's kinda surprised, and says she didn't even know that Zoli-boy was dead, but she promises not to rat me out to the cops, and then when I ask her if she'll sleep with me, the line gets disconnected, and I wake up beside Ducky's bed in the hospital, the nurse saying that he's better now, he can pack up his things, and we call Ottó to bring some drugs, then wait for him behind the garages, and then when he gets there, we get all riled up 'cause of something, but finally everybody calms down, and we smoke a joint, and Ducky starts laughing, looking more and more like the Joker, then he waves his hand, smokes one of the viaduct's support beams, and turns into mist again, which makes Zoli-boy burst into tears, while Viki gets up from her knees and wipes her mouth, and then I wake up again, and of course I can't fall asleep, so for a while I think about the last time I had a dream without porn stars in it, then bike out to the viaduct in my mind. I've wanted to climb out on the bridge since they built it. As I step over the safety barrier, the wind tousles my hair, and suddenly I can't breathe, just like that winter the year before last when I swam under the ice for a bet, and I almost drowned, because I could barely find the ice hole in the filthy water. Stig Severinsen swam seventy-six metres under ice in nothing but a speedo. He's one of my role models. The wind's blowing, I gotta hold on so it doesn't blow me off. I don't really feel like dying half-asleep. After I manage to steady myself, I look up. Too bad it's dark 'cause you can't see the view, only the quivering lights of a couple of houses in the dark. There's not even any cars around. Actually, it's not so bad that the sun's gone down. There's something chillingly calm about this endless blackness. I lean forward, and peek over the edge of the safety fence. There's nobody on the road. No reference points, nothing to compare to, just the black depths swirling under me, but I'm not terrified of it anymore. A couple of cars whizz past behind me. They can't see me from the road. The headlights don't penetrate the safety barrier or the fence. I moseyed on out here without anyone stopping to ask what I was doing. I wanted to imagine a star-filled sky, but it's totally cloudy. Then lightning strikes me. I get charred against the safety fence and jolt awake for a second, but when I get that this is just a dream, I relax, and sink back in. I'm standing there on the viaduct again, feeling colder by the second, and yet I start undressing. First, I throw my coat hella far. The wind catches it, lifting it a little, and then it disappears into the deep, like Batman. Then my shoes go, then my socks and pants as I hurl them all into the deep. It starts drizzling, even though I try to stop it. Then I take off my t-shirt, and as I throw, the wind catches it, flutters it over the safety barrier, and slaps it against the windshield of a truck that's speeding by. The driver floors the brakes, and the trailer swerves sideways onto the road, blocking both lanes. There isn't much traffic, but the trucker switches on his hazards, then opens the door and jumps down onto the blacktop. A dude in his fifties, wearing a cap. He walks over to the front of the transport, steps up onto the bumper, and pulls the shirt off. When he figures out what he's holding in his hand, he looks around, and I come to my senses too late, forgetting to duck down behind the safety barrier. The trucker starts shouting at me, in Ukrainian I think, and waving his arms like crazy. I don't understand a word of what he's babbling, but from his gestures I assume he's telling me I'm a motherfucker and to get my ass off that fucking barrier. As he rushes over to me, another car almost slams into his truck. The driver honks and shakes his fist, maybe the dumbass thinks that'll make this monster disappear, while the trucker barks back at him, gesturing towards the barrier, so the dickhead puts his flashers on too, and gets out of the car. The trucker comes towards me, and I quickly scare him a little, as if I'm on the verge of jumping at any moment. I manage to freak the dude out, so he stops short while the other dickhead's messing around with his phone. All hell's gonna break lose here in a matter of minutes, even though I wanted to think all this through quietly, not like that dude from Ghana who climbed up on the Eiffel Tower butt-naked and did a pike dive onto the pavement from three-hundred metres. Meanwhile, the rain starts coming down harder, even though I try to stop it. I'm just shaking, wearing nothing but my underpants on the viaduct, while the Ukrainian keeps mouthing off, even though he should know that I don't understand a single word of what he's saying, while the dickhead ends his call, so I guess he's managed to reach the highway police or the fire department—they're the ones who usually pull people off bridges. I try to block the whole thing out of my mind. I stare at the road. There's more traffic moving towards the sea. The cars are already jammed bumper-to-bumper, the brake lights heaving like a burning lava flow. The dude with the phone heads towards me, going off about something, but the wind's howling so loud I don't hear what he's saying and I can't read lips. I lean onto the dark air. The Ukrainian's facial features aren't smooth at all. He's bellowing as if I already jumped, waving my shirt around, like some white flag, until he gives up and squats down beside his truck. The line of cars gets jammed in the meantime. They slow down with their emergency lights flashing, the passengers get out, and when they realize what's going on, they whip their phones out, hoping to video me as I jump. I spot the first blue-and-red strobe. The cars try to pull over beside the two safety rails, but at the same time a bunch of people are already gawking, and it takes a while before they find their way back to their cars, get in, and pull over. Then a police car appears from the opposite direction. They trap me. I don't have much time, so I lean over the safety barrier before they drag me down. I want to imagine Zoli-boy hurling himself into the deep, and I stare into the big black void again, because I simply can't get it through my head how the dumbass had the fucking guts to go through with it. He definitely didn't mess around too long, just walked out here and bam! I tilt a little, which makes everybody start shouting again behind my back. I'm like a rock star. The more I lean forward, the louder the audience shouts, so I play around with this for a while, swinging back and forth. Let them shout. Meanwhile, the first police car arrives. What a goddamn fuss, man. I'm starting to feel like I'd disappoint them if I *didn't* end up jumping. I pull away again for a moment,

’cause super dumb shit keeps popping into my head, stuff like: what will the chicks say if they find out that I jumped off the bridge too, and how torn up my mom’s gonna be when they call her to say that her dopey son offed himself. The wind blows the rain into my face. I lick my lips. It’s got a weird, salty taste. A cop climbs out of the squad car, comes over to the safety fence, and goes about his business, ordering me to get down, but I don’t say anything, and then the wind catches hold of me, and I lean a bit so that the cop steps back with his hands up, and he keeps telling me over and over to calm down, everything’s okay, and I’m thinking that nothing’s okay at all, because if I’m not careful, this fucking storm’s gonna sweep me away. Meanwhile, the other cop’s questioning the trucker, but he just keeps waving the t-shirt, and yammering on in Ukrainian, I guess. The dude with the phone’s eager to serve and offers detailed information about everything. While that’s going on, more squad cars come coasting in, plus a huge fire engine complete with a winch and crane-suspended manbasket. It’s gotta be at least fifty tons, so I hope the bridge doesn’t collapse under us, ’cause I’ll have to take the rap for that fuckup too. I don’t really feel like standing trial for causing a mass catastrophe. One cop is on his walkie-talkie, the other is trying to get the gawkers to stand back, while the firefighters get out of the fire truck and wait. They’ve seen stuff like this before. One of them chews gum, blowing bubbles. The bubble flashes blue, then red. Another patrol car arrives, and there’s one stationed at the end of the bridge, stopping anyone else from driving up onto the bridge. There’s a young cop among them too. Super high-strung. He lights up. We lock eyes. I can see it in his eyes that he’s furious. I’m really starting to lose track of what’s going on, or actually, now I finally understand that I don't understand anything. He starts towards me, I bow my head, and when I look up, he's standing in the same place. Then, when I look down again, it's Zoli-boy who's staring back at me from the dark. It's cold, and it's raining, but I'm freaking out, and my body's flooded with a heat wave or something, and I'm sweating hard. I look up again, another police car parks—there's gotta be at least five by now—and this whole thing's starting to feel like the end of *Die Hard,* only Bruce Willis is missing now, and another cop gets out, plus a plain-clothes dude from the back seat, and at first I'm thinking, here's the psychologist who'll try to talk me out of suicide—I mean, he doesn't know that jumping is the last thing on my mind—and then as he starts towards me, I see him dragging his leg all weird, just like my old man, plus even his face is familiar, though I can't see it clearly 'cause of his hat, but like, even the hat is super familiar from somewhere, and then as he gets closer, he pushes it back, and through the sheet of rain I can straight up see his face, and I don't really wanna believe it, but these cocksuckers brought my old man here. Ol' Pops stands stock still and doesn't say a word. The rain trickles into his eyes from his forehead, he wipes it with his coat sleeve, then signals for the cops to stop, he'll talk things over with me, and he steps over to the safety fence, and I'm just standing there butt naked on the railing, holding on with one hand, and I still can't believe my eyes, and the old man's not saying anything, he just nods for me to get down, and I fling myself lightly into the void, and wake up.

The sheets are soaking wet. I check the time. It's on the hour. The two zeros stare at me in the dark like hollowed-out eyes.

CLARIFIER

No news of Zoli-boy for a week now. He's disappeared, as if the earth's swallowed him whole. When I start asking questions, it turns out that nobody's seen him, but of course nobody can say how long it's been. A couple of days, or a couple of weeks, or who the fuck knows. Hasn't gone to school and hasn't shown up at practice all week. His mom's hella freaked out and has reported the dumbass missing. The cops, the neighbourhood watch, and the police dogs searched pointlessly. They came up with nothing. Not even a bloody t-shirt or a severed finger. I get so worked up about this whole thing that one night I dream about Zoli-boy. It's creepy as fuck and the next day I go to a couple of places, hoping I'll run into him, but I just keep seeing the same faces over and over and none of them are Zoli-boy. I wanna ask Ducky too, but we keep missing each other, and after a while this seems sketchy to me, like he's doing it on purpose. When I finally manage to corner him, he refuses to talk to me, so I'm forced to bluff and say I'll rat him out to the cops about the hit-and-run if he doesn't help me find out where Zoli-boy is. He starts to threaten me, but when he sees that I don't give a fuck, he's suddenly all Mr Nice Guy, except when I start asking him questions, he doesn't answer them straight, which pisses me off and I tell him to stop the fucking bullshit 'cause he hung out with Zoli-boy non-stop after the swim meet, and there's no fucking way he didn't notice that the dumbass has been AWOL for the past week. Ducky finally gets that I'm not fucking around. He's all quiet for a while, then mumbles about how the last time he saw the dumbass was a week ago too, but he's got no idea where he is, and then he goes off on some story that sounds eerily like the dream I had: they bought some drugs from Ottó, went out behind the garages to roll one, but somebody mixed something extra into the weed and they ended up so blitzed that he was hardcore hallucinating, then he passed out, and when he woke up, Zoli-boy was nowhere to be found. He disappeared, vanished, end of story. He hasn't seen him since. He told the cops a phony story 'cause no way in hell is he getting himself busted. I mean, this basically isn't total bullshit, 'cause even these hick cops wouldn't buy a story about somebody going behind the garages just to lie down on the grass for a sec, falling asleep, and then waking up to find his friends gone.

I wake up again in the middle of the night covered in sweat, my mind starts reeling, and I'm more and more convinced that Ducky did some fucking sick shit. I'm sitting in the kitchen, yesterday's newspaper on the table. The thin paper crinkles. If I ever have my own cash, I'll cancel the newspaper subscription, drag my mother out of the Stone Age, and buy her a proper phone. Zoli-boy's on the cover. Things are getting really serious. It says they've got police dogs out looking for him. Fucking hell. But yeah, I guess we already had one child-murder case in the city this year, and that's why everybody's shitting bricks. Grown-ups are always hella freaking out about stuff like this. Sure, it's pretty hard to grasp that somebody could just get offed like that. This one buddy of mine told me about how one of his homies was beaten to death outside a disco. Dude was pretty fucking upset about it. Couldn't talk about nothing else but that fight and the cocksuckers in it, and I was just listening and nodding, and after a while I totes felt like I wasn't even there.

Before I get myself even more worked up about this shit, my phone rings. It's Ducky. He says we definitely have to meet. I try to get him to tell me what he wants, but he just says *not over the phone*, and that we should meet this evening by the clarifier. Alarm bells go off in my head, and I know I shouldn't go out there, but I just keep obsessing over it: what if he wants to tell me something about Zoli-boy? Ducky knows it too, I guess, that's why he thought up this whole thing, and of course I agree in the end, though I'd bet my life that there's something shady going on.

Last night, after practice, I smoked a joint, then made a round of all the places the dumbass usually hangs out. I started at the Rhino, 'cause that's where Zoli-boy likes to chill the most, but of course he wasn't there, and nobody'd seen him. There's hardly any decent hangouts, so I ran out of ideas pretty quick, plus I was so damn fed up with running around the city to find the dumbass, and him just not fucking turning up. I ran myself ragged and got home hella late, of course. I got myself worked up a little too, though I knew I shouldn't give a shit about this whole thing.

If I had any idea about where to look for Zoli-boy, I wouldn't care about Ducky's offer, but since I don't have a clue where he's at, I decide to go to the meeting. But I mean, I really don't get why Ducky wants to meet up out in the boonies, so I call him back and ask him why the picnic's gotta be at the clarifier, to which he says that if I'm pussying out, he'll send Buoy to the railway embankment, and he'll show me the way, or that I should bring a flashlight and then I won't get lost. When I ask him about the clarifier again, he says we definitely have to meet there 'cause he wants to show me something. If I back out now, Ducky and Buoy'll think I'm a pussy. I gotta say yes. Okay, so Buoy will be waiting at the embankment, waving his flashlight, and he'll walk me to the clarifier.

I arrive to the set place, but don't see Buoy anywhere. I check my phone display. I'm not late. For a second I'm not sure I came to the right place, but then I decide not to give a shit. If they want to find me, they will. I don't feel like standing and waiting, so I sit down on the tracks. I stretch my legs out. The embankment stones give off the heat collected during the day. It's so hot out it might as well be summer already. After ten minutes, I'm fucking bored out of my mind, so to kill time, I start throwing rocks, trying to hit the windows of a graffiti-bombed train car. I get it on the second try, but the sound of shattering glass sets off a guard dog at a nearby storage lot, so I quit throwing, and just sit in the cricket noise. I've just decided to wait two more minutes then fuck off home, when Buoy pipes up behind me and I nearly piss myself. He staggers over to me in the dark, and when I ask him where the fuck his flashlight is, all he says is, *fuck, the batteries died*, and his phone froze too so he couldn't call me.

We trip through the dark. Buoy's in front of me humming *Stayin' Alive* from the *Madagascar* soundtrack, and I get totally disoriented in this fuckin' jumble. Some entrepreneur dude bought up the land behind the meat factory and wanted to build luxury condos or an industrial park, I forget which, but then he got blown up in his car and the project went bust. This went down a few years ago. Not much has changed around here since, but the fancy GMO bamboo he brought over from China spread and grew like crazy. And, like, they planted it so densely that Buoy can only squeeze through if he turns sideways. In places where the bamboo rotted and left gaps, the stinging nettle comes up to your waist. Suddenly, I hear an owl hooting in the dead silence, and then a branch cracks. I hope they didn't import tigers to let loose in the grove. Some entrepreneur dudes have sick ideas. The wind picks up every so often and the leaves rustle like sandpaper when you rub them gently together. Buoy carelessly snaps off the branches that get in his way. If I didn't know it was him in front of me, I'd totes think he was a wild boar. He's going on about something, but I can't understand a single fucking word in all this rustling and branch-cracking, and by the time I ask him what he said, we arrive at a clearing. I've got a good view of the terrain in the strong moonlight, even without a flashlight.

A figure is scanning the clarifier, which is covered in water plants. The stench rising from the pond is like a flooded mass grave. He hears us coming and turns towards us. He's got a bandana tied over his nose and mouth, but I can tell from the way he moves that it's Ducky. He's got some long object in his hand. At first I freak out that he's gripping his old man's hunting rifle, but as we get closer, I see that it's only a thick branch. The sickening smell hits my nose at the clarifier's edge. My stomach clenches.

"This isn't long enough," Ducky grumbles instead of a hello, and tosses aside the rod he'd been using to poke around in the water.

The smell is so brutal that I get dizzy if I breathe too deep. Buoy starts gagging too. But the stench clearly bounces right off Ducky. It's as if he were standing in the middle of a wildflower field. He's probably been here for quite a while now. I take my t-shirt off and tie it over my face. I don't give a shit if the mosquitoes bite me to a pulp—better that than this stench. It's unbearable. Ducky starts towards the trees to look for a longer branch, I guess. His flashlight isn't dead, so we try our luck that way too, but we can't find any stick worthy of use. I guess the gyppos started collecting firewood early. Buoy's had enough. He stops in front of a thinner bamboo stalk, stares at it for a while, pats it, then, like a hungry elephant, he sets his weight against it and uproots it. Ducky thoroughly sizes up the stalk and finally decides that it'll be long enough, then takes out his serrated hunting knife to hack off the shoots. When he's done, we drag the trunk to the edge of the fish pond. The t-shirt over my face doesn't help much anymore. The carrion stench is so thick you could almost bite into it. Buoy walks behind me for a while, but then he starts gagging and has to stop. He's suffering real bad, but all he manages to get out is bile. While Buoy gags and gurgles, Ducky stops at the edge of the fish pond and scans the water, or rather, the thick sludge at the bottom of the hole. This fish pond isn't really a fish pond. It's more like a foundation ditch at a construction site. The edges are steep. If somebody slips into it, there's no way they can climb out by themselves. The fish were caught long ago, or they're dead. Another wave of nausea hits me, but I manage to hold back the vomit. Then I step over to Ducky, who's scanning the hollow with his flashlight.

The corpse is floating in the water face down. The flashlight's beam illuminates the green, purple, and orange patches covering the swollen body. This totally isn't what floating corpses look like on *CSI,* but I stop this train of thought 'cause maybe the bacteria here is different and makes dead bodies puff up like this. Ducky picks up a stone from the ground and lobs it at the body. The rats chowing down on the decomposing carcass scatter. Just as I happen to look over, a huge, grey rat climbs out of the gaping hole in the corpse's side. Something, maybe a frog, leaps into the water with a soft splash, and I projectile vomit the shredded cabbage and pasta I had for dinner. Ducky manages to jump out of the way at the last second. He's swearing a bit, checking to see if any of it splattered on his pants, and when he sees that it hasn't, is chill again, and says we should examine the corpse. Buoy and I grab the toppled tree while Ducky orders us around from the edge of the hole, telling us which way to push, when to lift, when to lower. We fumble around clumsily for a long time, partly because we can't really see what we're actually doing, and partly because the corpse is decomposing so badly that when we manage to reach under it with the branch and try to flip it over onto its back, its arm falls off. Finally, Ducky suggests that we saw through its neck 'cause then it'll be easier to turn the head around. He's talking like he's done stuff like this before. While he sketches out the plan, he pulls out his serrated hunting knife and a roll of black electrical tape. I get caught up here for a second. I mean, why's he got stuff like this on him anyway, but before I can ask, Ducky's got the knife pressed to the branch and is winding the electrical tape around it with a practised hand.

"Ducky, dude, this doesn't feel kosher at all," I say.

I'd rather not hack up Zoli-boy. He's our friend, and it would be messed up to desecrate his body.

"Well, I think we should get to the fucking bottom of who the fuck this is," Ducky says, and shines the light on the corpse.

A bunch of fish and a few chunky rats scurry over to the light and start nipping at the head. I never would've thought there was such liveliness in this swamp, but judging from the commotion, the frothing water, the number of slapping fins and rat tails, the biodiversity down there's got to be pretty significant. Buoy hunches over and starts retching again. The amount of bile he has is impressive.

"Let's call the cops," I suggest.

"Like the fuck we will," Ducky roars at me. "Don't start that again, okay?"

"What?"

"Your need to cumguzzle cops."

"This isn't cumguzzling, Ducky," I say.

"Yes, it is."

"No, it's not." I balk. "Here's a fuckin' corpse. If you find a corpse, you inform the police. End of story."

"There is no fucking way we are calling anybody out here until we kill the motherfucker who offed Zoli-boy."

A cosmic silence descends on the area, as if all sound had been sucked out of the universe. The leaf-rustling ceases, the crickets shut up, the rats and fish gnaw mutely on the corpse.

"*What the fuck?!*" I finally blurt.

"What?" Buoy asks.

"Who killed who?" I say, turning towards Ducky.

"Lázár killed Zoli-boy," Ducky answers.

"Pretty much," Buoy adds.

"*Pretty much?*"

I've got no idea what they're talking about.

"Yeah," Buoy nods, dead serious.

"Zoli-boy left a message on my voicemail," Ducky says when he sees the look of utter confusion on my face. "Before he died," he adds with a poker face, then extends the phone to me and says: "Listen."

I dial the number, then press the phone to my ear and wait. The robot voice lists the number of messages, the phone numbers, the dates and times. I've skipped over about five by the time I finally arrive at Zoli-boy's message. His voice is quivering. He sniffles and sometimes spits. "*Fuck, Ducky, answer already… or call me back… I'm fuckin' dead meat… Lázár fucked me up… I'm at the clarifier… I'm fuckin' bleeding… I'm scared of leaving… come here… I'm at the clarifier!*"

I can't speak. It takes me half a minute to drop the phone from my ear.

"Fucked up, huh?" Ducky says, breaking the silence.

"Did you call him back?" I ask.

"Yes," Ducky answers. "But it was a little too late."

"What were you waiting for?"

"I was at the movies, for fuck's sake," he says, insulted.

"So?" I ask.

"I don't usually answer my phone at the movies," he lies.

"That's such bullshit," I say, so he looks at me and says:

"Okay, I was with Niki," he says. "At the movies."

"You could've still answered the phone."

"My dick was in her mouth."

"You still could've answered," I repeat.

"You're fucking nuts, motherfucker," Ducky says, waving me away.

I listen to Zoli-boy's message again.

"Are you sure it's him?" I ask.

"Don't you recognize his voice?" Ducky responds with a question.

"I'm talking about the dead body," I say, gesturing towards the hole.

"Didn't you hear his message? He said he was waiting for me at the clarifier."

"There's no other corpses in the area," Buoy says, wiping his mouth. "We checked."

"Of course, if you're really curious, we could just cut his head off," Ducky suggests.

"Forget it!" I say, ending the conversation.

I want to see him. I want to look in his eyes. I want to be certain that this decomposing body in this filthy muck really is Zoli-boy. I ask Ducky to give me the flashlight and shine the beam over the corpse one more time, but his head still isn't properly visible. I start to undress. First I kick off my shoes, then peel off my pants, but leave my underwear on. I wouldn't want the fish or the rats to chew on my dick.

"Jesus fuck," Buoy grunts, when he gets what I'm about to do.

I kneel down at the edge of the hole, my back to the clarifier, and grab hold of a clump of grass so I don't go tumbling in.

"Help me," I say, so Buoy steps over and takes my hand, then slowly starts to lower me down the steep, muddy bank.

First, I dip my toes into the water. I'm expecting some thick, warm slime, but goose-flesh springs up my arm, it's so cold. A second later, Buoy starts retching and lets go of my hand. I guess he doesn't want to puke on my head, but at the moment he releases me, I keel over and land with a huge back flop into the carrion-stinking sludge. Somehow I manage to keep my head above the surface and the gunk doesn't get in my eyes. My feet touch the bottom of the clarifier and sink into the soft mud. I quickly yank them up. I don't dare think about what creatures might be hiding at the bottom of a clarifier like this. The corpse is about three metres away from me. I have to get there somehow, but I can't stomach putting my feet down, so I start swimming with my head above the water, like the garlic-reeking old-timers who swim in the side lane at the pool.

Down here, the stench is even more unbearable. I was starting to get used to it on shore, but now it assaults me again. You can't even really burp in the water, let alone barf, but something bitter comes up from my stomach all the same. I glide over to the dead body with two or three powerful strokes. There's a lot more commotion around here. The animals flit apart. All kinds of tiny, slimy, furry bodies brush my legs and arms. Fins, tails, legs, and tentacles touch my belly and back. Something nips my thigh.

I gotta hurry because I won't be able to stand this for long.

One more stroke, and I arrive at the chewed-up corpse. I feel woozy again from the stench, but I keep going. It would be dumb as fuck to give up before the finish line.

"Shine that fucking light over here already!" I shout to Ducky and Buoy, but nothing happens. They just stand there in grave silence at the edge of the hole. "I can't see a fucking thing," I say, trying to shout, but all that escapes my throat is a kind of rattle.

The flashlight's weak beam pans across the corpse floating at arm's length from me.

I can't flip him over while treading water to keep my head above the surface, but there's no way I'm putting my feet down, plus I wouldn't have stable footing in the soft mud anyway. I'd need to turn his head around somehow, and then we could finally look at his face.

As I try to grab hold of his chin, I reach into his mouth by accident. His teeth are tiny, sharp icicles. Something scurries out of his mouth. I jerk my hand away. Then I try again. This time, I manage to grab his chin. It cracks as I wring his neck. Nevermind. I can't do much more harm to him now.

As I look into his eyes, the face of Zoli-boy's mom flashes into my head, and then I think that there's no way in hell that anyone's gonna be able to tell who this is without a DNA test. All you can safely say is that this is a human head, and it might even be Zoli-boy's.

I look up. Buoy shines the flashlight into my eyes. The beam blinds me for a moment.

"What the fuck, man?!" I shout.

Then something splashes loudly next to me in the water. It wasn't a fish. It was something bigger.

I look up.

I see Ducky's silhouette in the sticky moonlight. He's lifting a huge rock or piece of cement over his head. He swings it a little, then tosses it. Directly at me.

It slams into the water a couple of centimeters from me.

The motherfuckers want to kill me.

I take a deep breath and duck underwater. I kick furiously. I have to swim out of here, as fast and as far as possible, otherwise I've got no chance. I stroke with all my might and crawl. If Stig Severinsen swam seventy-six metres under the ice in nothing but a speedo, I gotta be able to swim out of throwing-range in a clarifier. I don't count the strokes. It's like the last hurrah before the race's end. My oxygen starts to run out after about fifteen strokes. My lungs and muscles are on fire. I'm about to suffocate when I finally resurface about twenty metres from shore. They can't throw those fuckin' huge pieces of cement this far, but they can easily hit me with smaller rocks, so I only stick my head out long enough to grab some air, then I dip underwater again and swim on. A bit farther away I come up again and open my eyes, but I don't see anything. I don't take a breath yet. I squint. I try to wipe the water from my eyes. I don't hear splashes. It's a strange silence. As if the water would've completely plugged up my ears. I watch the shore. Two black figures are there in outline. Ducky and Buoy scan the clarifier. They listen hard: maybe I'll give myself away. They don't notice me. I exhale and inhale soundlessly.

Then something cracks in the thicket and a short, squat figure comes tearing out from among the trees. It's headed straight for Ducky and Buoy. They turn towards the sound, but it's too late. I'd be willing to bet the guard dog got loose from the nearby storage lot, but when I hear the sounds it's making, I realize what it is. It's squealing and grunting. Dogs don't make noises like that, not even if a truck rolls over them. Buoy starts to run, howling like a jackal, *get the fuck out of here you fucking beast*, but of course the wild boar doesn't give a shit. It catches up with him in seconds, knocks him down, and starts to maul him. I think it's even biting. Buoy calls to Ducky, shrieking as loud as he can for him to get the fucking boar off him. Meanwhile, Ducky's sprinting like crazy towards the embankment. He doesn't even look back. Buoy's screaming louder and louder, but Ducky gives zero fucks. Then, two more boars peek out from behind the bushes and start towards Buoy.

After the wild boars trot off and Buoy goes quiet, I swim out onto the shore. With great effort, I manage to wriggle up the slippery bank. I stagger back to Buoy. He's lying on his back, his leg twisted, looking real fucked-up. At least he's not screaming anymore. It *was* pretty annoying after a while, but as I get closer, I hear him whimpering. I guess he's not quite dead then.

While Buoy gurgles softly, I take my underpants off and toss them on the ground. While I dry off, I check to see if I have any leeches. I find a couple. I quickly rip them off. It feels like I'm waxing. Then I start shaking, and I get dressed. Buoy's in pretty bad shape. He's not fully conscious. He doesn't even notice when I squat down next to him. He might not even know somebody's here. His arm hangs limply beside his body. All around him are the rocks he wanted to throw at me. I grab hold of one of them. It's bloody. Either it's his blood or one of the boars'. I pick it up. It's pretty heavy. I stand. Suddenly the wind picks up and carries away the carrion-reek, which I don't really smell anymore anyway. As I lift the rock above my head, something starts to flash in Buoy's pocket. I lean down and pull out the phone. Looks like it didn't freeze up after all. The caller ID says: Gabe. I answer it. It's Buoy's brother. He skips the greeting and gets to the point, saying how it looks like he managed to have them gloss over the whole doping case but if he fucks up like this one more time, he won't be able to yank him out of the shithole again, and he should be happy he got off the hook this time. He goes off on this spiel for a long time, but doesn't once ask if Buoy is still on the line or not. I quietly listen to the fucker's bullshit, but in the end, he gets me so goddamn angry with his arrogant, condescending attitude that I can't hold myself back anymore and I tell him to fuck off, then hang up, then call the ambulance, let it ring, and stagger through the dark bamboo grove, back to the train tracks.

FLIP TURN

I've been hiding for two days. I'm afraid to go home and all I know is that they hauled Buoy off to the ICU and there's a huge fucking scandal. I tried to reach out to Viki a couple of times, I texted her, but she didn't call me back and didn't reply, and finally, when I'm really about to lose it, she rings me and we agree to see each other. Things aren't looking too good, but I'm really fucking happy she called, 'cause I was starting to trip that maybe Ducky bumped her off too. Viki's pretty bitchy on the phone, like she's pissed at me. She wants to meet in the park, at the fountain next to the playground, at four in the afternoon, which is just fucking perfect because the whole place is packed with people at that hour. Plus I have to cut across town to get there. Right before the cops and all the other assholes latched onto the case, I managed to creep into the Tesco and make off with a couple of things so I could change out of my carcass-reeking t-shirt and pants, so I'm not wearing the same clothes I was in when I left home three days ago. There are several advantages to this: one is that the police can't identify me so easy, the other is that the stink was starting to stress me out, and basically only the bums weren't staring at me on the street.

When I spot Viki, I instantly know we're fucked. She's sitting on the bench, staring at yellow gravel the size of shotgun shells. When I stop in front of her, she looks up. I can tell from her eyes that she's fuckin' terrified, which is especially creepy because as far as badass chicks go, Viki takes the cake. She was into seriously hardcore shit that would have made half my buddies shit bricks. I've never seen Viki scared before. She's got massive dark circles under her eyes. Looks like she didn't get much sleep last night, but just the same, she's hot as hell, and her lips don't care how much she sleeps, they're always sexy, though they're not especially plump and she's got no lipstick on either.

"Hey," I greet her, and she presses her phone into my hand. "Did it die?" I ask, 'cause I don't get why she wants me to look at this piece of junk.

"No. Check the photo album."

I really don't feel like scrolling through Viki's selfie collection, plus I've seen most of them on Facebook already anyway, but she looks like she's in pretty bad shape and I don't wanna be a jerk, so I take the phone from her and open the photo album. That's when it hits me that this isn't Viki's phone.

The first picture shows Ducky grinning at himself in the mirror, stark naked. I start scrolling through, like, tons of dumbass shots of him with Buoy and his other pals. I have to laugh when I get to where they light their farts on fire, because I was there for that, but I start to get bored after a while, and I'm about to ask Viki what I'm supposed to be looking for when I find a complete series with Zoli-boy.

At first I don't recognize the dumbass, but then I realize it's him and I get all woozy. I grab hold of the bench's backrest. I really need to sit down but I don't want Viki to notice I feel sick. I look up. I watch the kids on the swings, the jungle gym, and in the sandbox. I need some time, but I finally manage to pull myself together. The screen switches off in the meantime. I slide my finger over it and look at the pictures again.

Zoli-boy's kneeling in the grass. Ducky's got his hunting knife up against his throat. Buoy kicks Zoli-boy in the head. He stands over him with a huge piece of concrete, posing for the camera. The last picture shows Zoli-boy, his face beaten to a pulp. No wonder I didn't recognize him, but the clothes and the place where they took the pictures check out. It was Zoli-boy floating in the clarifier.

"Were you there?"

Viki's voice jolts me awake.

"Sure," I say right off the bat, but then I realize we don't mean the same thing and I quickly correct myself. "They wanted to off me too."

She's silent. I wasn't convincing enough.

"Did you see me in any of the pictures?" I ask.

"No, she says," but I can tell from her tone that she still doesn't believe me.

"Viki, I wasn't there," I say, and look her straight in the face.

"They might have killed you too," she says, easing up.

"Yeah," I nod. "But I might have been able to save Zoli-boy."

We leave it at that.

"Is it Ducky's?" I nod towards the phone.

"Uh-huh."

"Why'd you steal it?" I ask.

"I've had enough of him," she answers softly, but clearly. I wait. "He used me," she adds.

"Ducky uses everybody," I add quietly, but I don't quite get why this just now started bothering Viki.

"He fucked me over," she continues. She hesitates for a moment, then adds, "He took Niki to the movies."

"I know," the words slip out, but Viki doesn't care anymore.

"And when I found the pics, all he said was *keep your mouth shut*," she goes on. "Get it?"

"What?"

"That asshole thinks he can brush me off that easy. He just needs to say *shut up* and I'll shut up."

"Yeah."

"You know what?" Viki says, looking at me, the terror in her eyes displaced by rage for a moment. She's so pretty when she's like this. "Fuck him."

We fall silent again. I know what we're gonna do but I ask anyway.

"What do you want to do?"

"I don't know," she answers, though she knows just as well what we're gonna do.

"Okay," I nod, and pocket the phone.

I look at her face. She seems even sadder now. I want to give her a kiss on the cheek, but as I lean over, she turns and moves off. I'm struck by the honey-almond scent of her body wash again.

She's only a few steps away when I think of something and call after her.

"Viki, wait. I want to ask you something."

She stops. Turns around slowly. I hurry over to her and hand her a tissue, and when she refuses it, I wipe off the mascara that's run down her face with my thumb. I didn't think she had make-up on.

"Do you have a crush on him?" I try to keep a serious expression because it's a serious question, but I manage to hit a nerve.

"You are such an asshole," she says, then turns her back on me and keeps walking.

"Viki, this is important," I insist, and catch her by the

shoulder. "I'm not giving you shit."

"Get off me," she says, and shakes my hand from her shoulder, but then she stops anyway, turns, and looks at me sadly.

"I gotta know you're not gonna change your mind."

"Last week, we went behind the garages." As she speaks, the terror seems to creep back into her eyes. "He had a lead pipe with him." Her voice quivers, then she falls silent. I don't wanna know what Ducky did to her. She nervously wipes the smudged make-up from her face and continues. "He never took *me* to the movies." She turns away and cuts across the playground defiantly.

The days blur. I never fall asleep completely, and I'm never fully awake. I switch my phone off to keep them from tracking me through it. The world becomes a distant vision. The image clears in unfamiliar places, then plunges back into obscurity again. Sometimes I don't even know how I got to where I happen to be, but my mind keeps whirling around the thought of how to take out those two douchebags. If I want Zoli-boy's death to be properly avenged, I'm the one who needs to make a move. I know from Viki that Buoy's still in the ICU, so he probably doesn't need much, but I'm not taking any chances. Ducky will be harder to round up. Viki said he's under house arrest, and there's police surveillance on their crib round the clock. I'm really pissed off that he thought I was that dumb. It's not like I'm surprised he's such a huge scumbag, I'm just mad at myself for all the bullshit I fell for. It was easier than using my brain. Or the fuck knows. I walk along, taking even, comfortable steps, but meanwhile, I get myself more and more jacked up. I don't know when or how, but I'm gonna off them, 'cause there's no way I'm getting unwound until some medieval shit happens to them. I'm kinda sorry I missed my chance at the clarifier and didn't bash Buoy's face in then, but yeah, easier said than done, and plus I hadn't seen those pictures on Ducky's phone yet then.

I end up at the edge of town and keep going along the bypass. The traffic is crazy, sixteen-wheelers and shit, not like the night we plowed grampa. I've walked like, 5k already when a flashing squad car passes me and pulls over at the edge of the road. Two young cops get out. They want to stop me. I don't feel like explaining myself, so I jump over the ditch and make a break for the cornfields. I glance over my shoulder and see the two cops looking pretty stunned, but they're back to their senses in no time and one's already got his gun out, yelling at me to stop, but like hell I am. If I get locked up how am I supposed to off those two assholes? The cop yelps at me one last time to stop, but I blast off, my gears on high. The woods are right in front of me. Then I hear this huge bang. That dumbass shot into the air. For a second I think I'd better not dick around with them 'cause they might even end up popping me, but then I'm like, fuck it. These guys aren't badass enough to hold running target practice in broad daylight on the wheat fields. I keep sprinting. The two clowns start after me, but they've got no fucking endurance. I reach the first few trees, find a relatively clear trail, and continue bolting. Branches whack my face, drops of sweat run into my eyes, I've got zero idea where I wanna get to, but somehow the steady movement feels good. I'm like a robot, putting one foot in front of the other, but even the weariness and pain aren't the same. The burn in my lungs and the ache of my muscles feel good, like I'm breathing air with someone else's lungs, running with someone else's muscles. I don't stop, even when I feel like my heart's about to burst and there's battery acid flowing through my veins.

And when I finally think I've shaken those two loser cops, this huge fuckin' beast of a dude bursts out from among the trees and roars at me to stop, but before I can, I'm sprawled out, his knee on my back, my arm twisted, and by the time I know what's going on, he's already cuffed me. I guess he knows the woods better than I do. Or runs a lot faster. Or both.

100% COLOMBIAN

Nobody believed I would make it to the finals. I know this because all day everybody's been slapping my back and congratulating me, and every time I run into my mom, she hugs me and bursts into tears. Not like I'd have bet a bunch of money on myself either. After the hospital, there wasn't much time left for prep, plus I was sluggish as fuck from those damn sedatives too. For a while it didn't even seem likely that I could make the qualifiers, but then I was suddenly in the finals, and I even nabbed lane six. If I pound that cocksucking asshat from Dunaújváros, I can go to the Junior World Championships in Colombia. That'd be dope. Especially if what Ottó said is true and the blow really is cheaper than weed.

I thought a lot about stuff recently, while I was training, and at the poolside too, and every time I went through what happened in my mind, I always ended up at the same place, knowing that what I'd done was messed up, but it was the only legit thing to do. Zoli-boy would be avenged if those two motherfuckers died, but ending up in the slammer for it? No fucking way. It would've been okay to do it for Zoli-boy, but Ducky and Buoy aren't worth it.

After the cops caught me, they confiscated the phone and everything, and took me downtown. I didn't have any ID, so they called my mom in to identify me. I'd been stuck there for an hour already, my hands cuffed behind my back in the police-station corridor, when the two detectives who'd come to Ducky's place looking for his dad walked past me. I knew I had one minute max to convince them that I knew some things they'd wanna hear, and before I knew what I was doing, I called out to them. I was talking to the chick mostly. She seemed more chill. By the time I managed to blurt out that I had proof on the confiscated phone, a young busybody cop pushed me up against the wall full force, so I couldn't finish my sentence. Of course at first the two detectives didn't get who I was and what I wanted, so I stood there whimpering for five minutes, flattened against the freshly painted wall before they finally managed to check the pics. They just stared silently at the phone for a while. They must've really been shocked 'cause nobody said a fuckin' word for like, five minutes. All I saw from the corner of my eye was the grin fade from the dude's mug as he stared at the screen.

Buoy was still in the ICU unit. They had to amputate his leg, so they located him hella easy and then rounded up Ducky pretty fast too. After that, I wasn't as freaked out anymore that they wanted to off me, though I did jerk awake a couple of times at night, screaming too, or at least that's what my mom said. They questioned everybody. And I mean *everybody*. 'Cause they got it into their heads that they'd find out the truth or whatever. It was mostly the motives they obsessed over. They were wracking their brains for weeks. I was getting bored as fuck, but they didn't want to let it go, and then all the big geniuses finally realized what I'd been telling them for weeks already. That Zoli-boy had to die because he was annoying the shit out of Ducky and Buoy. I didn't say anything about the blackmailing, 'cause maybe Ducky was just bullshitting about that.

The newspaper said that Buoy *miraculously* survived the wild-boar attack and that he *obligingly cooperated with authorities over the course of the investigation.* His brother probably threatened him with some serious shit if he didn't get his lips moving. He also coughed up the truth during his *detailed and revealing confession,* admitting that they were the ones who forced Zoli-boy to leave the message on Ducky's voicemail.

The only thing that pissed me off was that Ducky finally got off in the end. In return for a hundred-and-fifty-an-hour, his old man's lawyers explained in court that the cocksucker was so spoiled by his parents that he couldn't understand the weight of his actions. Meaning that he's just like a psycho, which I hella agree with, but the glitch is that the only sentence he'll get is mandatory medical treatment. When I heard about it, I thought they were just fucking with me, but they said, nope, that's really what's going down, and then I started howling, *fucking motherfucker I'm gonna kill the goddamn bastard,* but I didn't end up killing anybody. I did lose it pretty hardcore though, so they sent me to rest up for a few weeks in the psych ward. I was in a room just like Brad Pitt in *12 Monkeys.* The first day I was there, they pumped me full of sedatives, 'cause I guess they were freaked out, thinking I'd off myself or something. There wasn't any point in telling the shrink that if I'd wanted to cash my chips in, I would've done it a long time ago. By the time night rolled around, I was a confused mess from the downers, with no idea how long I'd already been in the locked ward. But I do remember that I was flooded with this odd sense of serenity, as if I'd settled into somebody else's body and that nothing bad could possibly happen to this new body, even though sometimes I could barely open my eyes, and was drooling non-stop like the grampa on the bed next to me. Poor homie whimpered all day, and every time I looked up, he had his ball sack hanging out from under the blanket, but of course the nurses never fucking bothered to stuff his balls back into his drawers. One night gramps went to the john, no shits given that he already had a catheter, and he never came back. This observation facility was pretty bleak. I'd never seen so many crazies in my life. Okay, the world is full of idiots, but it's kinda creepy when you've got nut jobs milling around you all day. All I could obsess about was who I'd execute if they ever let me out of here. The nurses, though, they were hella fine. One of them looked just like Viki, except blonde, with bigger tits, and I thought I'd hit on her, but the sedatives knocked me out so hard that even though she pranced around all day in her see-through nurse's outfit, flashing her thong, and even though she pressed her tits up in my face when she messed around with the thermometer, and even though she smoothed my blanket really thoroughly over my crotch, I couldn't get a hard on, no matter what.

When they let me out of the hospital, everybody was nice as hell to me, at practice and in school, too. The teachers kept asking if I was all right and if they could help me in any way, which was fine for a while, but then they totally started getting on my nerves. The biggest letdown is that not even Coach Bandi fucks with me anymore, and that's sometimes even more disturbing than if he acted like he did before and screamed my ear off at every practice. And my mom. She's totally fucked up. I haven't seen her smile in two years since my father took off, and now I routinely wake up to her sitting by my bed staring at me with moist eyes in the dim room. When I catch her, I try and pretend to be asleep, but I think she knows I'm awake,

’cause after a few minutes she always gets up and leaves the room. My fits of rage have thinned out, though every time I think about Ducky, the purple haze takes over me and I really gotta keep focused so I don’t go slamming my fist into the first person who walks by. The shrink stuffed my head with the idea that I should try and learn to channel my aggression. I tried the method at practice: when Ducky’s grinning face flashes into my head, my nervous tension fuels my strokes. I deliberately imagined his cocky face in the prelims. I think maybe that’s why the heat went so well. I might’ve never made it into the finals without Ducky. But when Zoli-boy looks back at me from the bottom of the pool, I always freeze up.

As I mosey over to the starting block, I’m humming *Before I Forget* to myself. I put my stuff down, take off my warm-up suit, do a couple of arm circles, just like the stars on TV. I lean down, scoop up a bit of water, and wash my face. Meanwhile, they introduce the participants one by one. When it’s my turn, I look towards the stands. Everybody’s there. Viki and Niki, my homies, Coach Bandi, my mom, and even my old man. I wave, they clap, and urge me on, shouting. Camera’s flash, but by that time I’m already thinking about Ducky. The adrenaline always flares up in me anyway before the race, but I help it along. At those times, it’s like all my strength drains from my limbs, as if my thighs were about to collapse under my own weight. The only reason I’m not worried is because I know this feeling, and I know I’m in damn good shape. I didn’t even push to my limits in the prelims.

The judge gives the signal. I wait until everybody gets up on their starting blocks, adjust my goggles, and then follow them. I lean down, grab hold of the edge of the block, but don’t wait for the sound of the horn. I dive into the water alone. The cool water sucks the nerves out of me, then spits me out. As if it were playing with me. The others watch from outside as I swim to the edge of the pool, climb out nonchalantly, and walk back to lane six. I watch the faces from behind my tinted goggles. I surprised them. We get up on the blocks a second time. If I fuck up again, I'm disqualified. When the starting judge gives the signal, I lean down and firmly grab hold of the block. I fuse to it. When the horn sounds, everybody lunges and they hit the water almost simultaneously. Now it's only me left on the block. The stands explode in cheers. The others have already resurfaced and taken their first strokes when I finally jump after them. I try to extend the streamline as long as possible. I manage to find the proper angle where the boosting force and the kick work together most effectively. I pop up to the surface at ten metres, then start after the others with long, even strokes. It's like I'm hunting game. I work off the distance between us gradually. At two-hundred, I turn first, and then increase my advantage even more after every fifty. I'm not concerned with the others anymore. Maybe they're hoping my strength will run out, that I'll cramp up and won't be able to maintain this speed, but I up the tempo at half the distance. There's no fatigue, and I don't care that my muscles are slowly getting rigid and my lungs are burning. I extend the stroke even longer, grab hold of the water, and pull myself forward with it. I let my body carry me. I'm a shark. I imagine swimming together with Ducky. I keep up with him easily. I latch onto him. I don't want to lose sight of him. I don't want to get ahead of him or lag behind him. We turn together, kick off from the wall at the same time after the turn, and breathe together, too. We swim the same lap times. This makes him even more annoyed, but makes me calmer. Ducky's nearly choking. He starts to gurgle, tries to grab hold of the rope, nearly drowning before he finally gives up, doing the dead man's float, then slowly spilling down into the gutter. And I swim past him, grinning. They ring the cowbell at the last lap, and I'm coming up from underwater when my first chaser swims towards me in the fourth lane. I can't lose now. I pass the half-length mark. A few more strokes and the floats turn red. Now's the time to hit the finish, but when I see the display board, I turn onto the wall and push off again. I can't stop.

ABOUT THE TRANSLATOR

Born in 1975 in Vancouver, Ildikó Noémi Nagy grew up in the United States and studied in Budapest at the Franz Liszt Music Academy and Eötvös Loránd University. Her short-story collection *Eggyétörve* ("Broken in One"), written in Hungarian, appeared in German translation. Her translations from Hungarian into English include the novels *Lemur, Who Are You?* by László Garaczi and *Drug Diary* by Viktor Kubiszyn, as well as best-selling novels by Éva Fejős, including *Bangkok Transit.* Nagy has also created English subtitles for many Hungarian films.